Ramon Stared at Her Broodingly.

She was lovely, this American, and he was well aware that he'd looked at her too long and too closely, and that she'd reacted to his appraisal. But there was something so . . . different about her.

She would not stand out in a crowd, he decided. One would have to look closely at Penelope Baldwin to fully appreciate her, exactly as he'd just done. There was a piquancy to her face, with her high cheekbones and slightly pointed chin . . . and a mouth that curved beautifully—begging to be kissed.

MAGGI CHARLES
is a prolific author, who is also known to her romance fans as Meg Hudson. A native New Yorker, she is the mother of two sons and currently lives in Cape Cod, Massachusetts, with her husband. "People and places" fascinate her, and she and her husband travel many months during the year.

Dear Reader:

There is an electricity between two people in love that makes everything they do magic, larger than life. This is what we bring you in SILHOUETTE INTIMATE MOMENTS.

SILHOUETTE INTIMATE MOMENTS are longer, more sensuous romance novels filled with adventure, suspense, glamor or melodrama. These books have an element no one else has tapped: excitement.

We are proud to present the very best romance has to offer from the very best romance writers. In the coming months look for some of your favorite authors such as Elizabeth Lowell, Nora Roberts, Erin St. Claire and Brooke Hastings.

SILHOUETTE INTIMATE MOMENTS are for the woman who wants more than she has ever had before. These books are for you.

Karen Solem
Editor-in-Chief
Silhouette Books

Love's Other Language

Maggie Charles

Silhouette Intimate Moments
Published by Silhouette Books New York
America's Publisher of Contemporary Romance

Silhouette Books by Maggi Charles

Magic Crescendo (ROM #134)
Love's Golden Shadow (SE #23)
Love's Tender Trial (SE #45)
The Mirror Image (SE #158)
Love's Other Language (IM #90)

SILHOUETTE BOOKS
300 E. 42nd St., New York, N.Y. 10017

Copyright © 1985 by Margaret Hudson Koehler
Cover artwork copyright © 1985 by George Jones

Distributed by Pocket Books

ISBN: 0-373-07090-X

First Silhouette Books printing April, 1985

10 9 8 7 6 5 4 3 2 1

America's Publisher of Contemporary Romance

Printed in the U.S.A.

In memory of "my" Señora . . .
Doña Rosa Eugenia Dávila de Castillo Nájera

Chapter 1

THE EMBASSY'S FRONT DOOR WAS MASSIVE, MADE OF
intricately carved wood so dark it appeared almost black.
A large bronze knocker in the shape of a lion's head with a
gold ring in its teeth dominated the center of the door, but
the modern brass bell set into the frame on the right was
obviously more practical. Nevertheless, Penelope Baldwin hesitated for a long, agonizing moment before pressing it.

She was so immersed in her own thoughts that she was
barely conscious of the steady traffic streaming along
Massachusetts Avenue just behind her, or of the golden
sunshine that was caressing her gently. Spring, deep
spring, had come to Washington. Although the famous
cherry blossoms were gone until next year, the pink-and-
white dogwood and the rich lavender redbuds were in full
bloom, and the trees along the curbside were dressed in
bright chartreuse. This was the season of hope, promise,
anticipation, yet Penny Baldwin felt none of these, for she
was here upon an errand she dreaded.

She shuddered slightly, then finally pushed the bell and heard a paean resounding somewhere in the depths beyond. At this point, it was all she could do to repress the strong instinct to flee. She had the uncanny sense that nothing was ever again going to be the same for her if she walked through that huge, black door. Yet, were she to run away now, she would leave Mary de Villanueva waiting and worrying, and she owed her best friend's mother more than that.

Still, their meeting was going to be traumatic. Two deaths lay between them. It was a scant seven months since Dr. Villanueva, second only to the president in his country, had been brutally murdered by terrorists, his body later found stuffed into the trunk of a car that had been abandoned on a side street in the center of his nation's capital. It was less than three months since Marita Villanueva had died while on a skiing holiday in New Hampshire.

Mary de Villanueva had lost her husband and her daughter suddenly, violently, in the space between autumn and spring. Thinking of this, Penny wondered how Marita's mother could possibly want to see her. Their reunion could only bring back extremely painful memories.

She drew in a sharp breath as the embassy door slowly swung open, and then she had to stifle a scream. The man who stood before her was nearly as tall as she was, but he was so dreadfully misshapen that he seemed shorter, and the severe curve of his back was only emphasized by his tightly fitting livery. His dark hair was combed sleekly from a high forehead, and a scar, slashing an olive cheek, gave a final sinister touch.

Eyes that were as black as coal seemed to glow like embers as he peered at her, but the question he posed was polite enough. "Señorita?" he asked her.

He was waiting for her to state her business, Penny knew, but she couldn't bring herself to answer him. She glanced behind the butler into seemingly infinite shadows, glimpsing a great, gray stone staircase in the distance, and she felt as if she'd stumbled into a medieval fortress. Or was this, rather, a medieval prison?

The butler was watching her with a professional patience that was disconcerting. Finally she managed, "I'm Penelope Baldwin."

"*Si?*"

"I've come to see Señora Mary de Villanueva," Penny said.

The butler said swiftly, "Señora de Villanueva is not at home, señorita."

"Not at home" was clearly a figure of speech. It was Mary de Villanueva who had suggested three o'clock on this Wednesday afternoon for their meeting at the embassy, but evidently she had not told the butler she was expecting a guest. In fact, the great black door was already beginning to close slowly, right in Penny's face.

She protested, "Please! Wait!"

The man paused, the door halfway shut, but he made no move to invite her to enter. And there was a definite coolness in his voice as he said firmly, in heavily accented English, "Señora de Villanueva is not receiving, señorita."

"She will receive me," Penny told him with equal firmness. "I have an appointment with her which she made herself. If you do not permit me to enter, I am going to be late for it."

For a moment the door held steady. Then the man moved back and said reluctantly, "Come in, señorita."

He waited until she had stepped across the threshold and then closed the door, and there was an ominous quality to its dull thud. His face impassive, he said coldly, "You will stay here, please."

Penny nodded, apprehension mounting as she watched him walk, not toward the staircase as she'd expected he might, but through a door to the right. This, too, closed with a thud behind him, leaving her alone in the enormous entrance area, feeling as if there were a thousand eyes watching her. And, in a sense, there were. Intricate Indian masks, some wooden, some tin, some silver, lined the long wall to her right, broken only by the center door through which the butler had disappeared.

Interspersed among the masks were sconces that had probably once held candles but were now electrified. Either to conserve energy or to enhance the atmosphere, the candle-shaped bulbs in use were of the low-powered variety. The masks seemed to be leering at her in the dim light, and she shuddered.

The butler returned, and she had the impression that his initial coolness had intensified to actual hostility.

"You will come with me, señorita," he said stiffly. Although he spoke politely, the words had the effect of an order.

Penny followed him through the side doorway into a hall painted in a dull beige, with no embellishments. She could hear office machines clattering, and she realized that this hall must separate the residential part of the embassy from the business complex. This, Penny surmised, must be the chancery, where Marita had come to work after her father's death.

The first hall led into a second, and the butler paused in front of a door near the end of it. First he rapped on the door, then opened it and stood aside so that Penny could pass him. She hesitated, momentarily daunted by this alien setting. Then, before she could move a step, a man called out impatiently, "Come in. Come in, please!"

The office into which Penny stepped was plain, with a functional desk, a filing cabinet, and two or three occasional chairs. But there was nothing at all plain about the man who stood behind the desk. She stopped short at the sight of him, her eyes widening involuntarily.

He was tall—taller than she would have expected a

Latin to be, but he had definite Latin features. His thick hair was very dark, almost black, and there was a faintly olive cast to his skin. His features were cameo sharp and aquiline. But his clothes were as contemporary as Saville Row or Madison Avenue. His dark brown, single-breasted jacket had the subtle effect of drawing instant attention to the width of his shoulders and the slimness of his waist. His shirt was khaki-colored, his burgundy linen tie an effective contrast. Penny reversed her first opinion. Yes, he could be a matador. But he looked even more like a perfect young diplomat . . . outwardly. Nevertheless, his disturbingly correct exterior failed to conceal a primitive sensuality that Penny didn't doubt most women would find devastating, and she found herself resenting the tug of his "machismo," which she was too honest to deny.

He was shuffling through a stack of papers on his desk, his head down. And he said to the butler, *"Gracias, Juan."* Then, still without looking at Penny, he added, "Sit down, please, señorita."

Only then did he glance at her, and she felt a sharp and definite sense of shock, for his eyes were a clear, burning blue.

He indicated a small leather-covered chair to one side of his desk and she sat down, her knees suddenly shaky. The essential masculinity of this man was an assault on the senses. Just being near him had a dangerous quality.

Still holding the sheaf of papers, he said, "I am Ramon Martinez y Córdoba, señorita. I am an attaché here, and I am at your service."

His English was slightly accented, and this too had a provocative effect on Penny. She moistened her lips and said, "I am Penelope Baldwin, Mr. Martinez."

"Yes," he interrupted. "I understand that you claim to have an appointment with Señora Mary de Villanueva. Is that correct?"

His choice of words stung her. A dislike for him

surfacing despite his potent physical attractiveness, she said, "I do not 'claim' to have an appointment with Señora de Villanueva, Mr. Martinez. I have one."

"So," he said lightly, with an insolence that made her bristle.

Then he looked at her, really looked at her, and the arrogance of his gaze exceeded his verbal insolence, so that Penny felt herself beginning to burn from the top of her head to the bottom of her feet.

Ramon Martinez was undressing her! He was undressing her with those blazing blue eyes, carefully, meticulously. She wanted to clutch the jacket of her glen plaid suit, because she could feel him divesting her of it, first whipping the lacy handkerchief out of her breast pocket. His eyes lingered on her very narrow skirt and she wished it weren't quite so slimly fitted. She could feel the play of his hands on her hips as he tugged at the skirt. She could feel him unfastening the dramatic silver chains she used to accessorize this outfit, then concentrating on her white, front-wrapped blouse. She shivered, imagining those long, slender fingers deftly ridding her of her wispy satin-and-lace bra, then moving on to slide her matching bikini panties down over her gently rounded buttocks. Then his hands would be caressing her bare flesh, and next . . .

"Mr. Martinez!" Penny blurted, breaking off this much too erotic daydream and, afraid her cheeks were scarlet, wishing that there were a mirror she could glance into.

Ramon himself came to with a start at her use of his name, and he stared at her broodingly. She was lovely, this American girl, and he was well aware that he'd looked at her too long and too closely, and that she'd reacted to his appraisal. But there was something so . . . so fresh and different about her.

She would not stand out in a crowd, he decided. No,

one would have to look closely at Penelope Baldwin to fully appreciate her, exactly as he'd just done.

He estimated that the tip of her head would come just about to his shoulder. And he imagined that he could feel the enticing softness of her golden-brown hair against his chin. She wore her hair fairly long, and it was slightly waving, curving at the ends. Her eyes were large and a velvety brown. They reminded him of rich, well-aged sherry. And there was a piquancy to her face, with her high cheekbones and slightly pointed chin . . . and a mouth that curved beautifully and, in his opinion, begged to be kissed.

Even the scent of her was refreshing. It wafted across to him, and he identified it as a light, lavender fragrance. Old-fashioned. In fact there was a bewitchingly old-fashioned quality to this Penelope Baldwin, but Ramon was not about to let it deceive him. He had yet to meet an American woman who was not as contemporary as tomorrow, underneath whatever facade she might choose to present to the world. Too contemporary to suit his taste. He preferred his women unliberated!

She spoke his name again, even more sharply this time, and he forced himself to step back into his role. "Yes, señorita?" he queried politely.

"Look," Penny Baldwin said, "I'm sure there has been a misunderstanding. I've come all the way from Wareham, Massachusetts, to keep this appointment—"

"I regret that," Ramon interceded smoothly. "The fact of the matter, señorita, is that the señora is not at home."

Again, Penny was sure that "not at home" was a mere figure of speech, and she shook her head in denial as she opened her handbag and rummaged through its contents.

The letter that Mary de Villanueva had written her was almost at the bottom, the paper badly rumpled, but she produced it and held it up triumphantly. "Here," she said, thrusting it toward this man who seemed determined to make himself an adversary. "You may read this, if you like. You will find that in it Señora de Villanueva confirms our appointment for three o'clock this afternoon."

Ramon's blue eyes seemed to darken as they flickered over her. There was a coldness in his glance, almost a distaste, and Penny found this puzzling. Instant hostility was not a reaction to which she was accustomed, and she did not know how to meet it. Although there was no reason for Ramon Martinez to have welcomed her warmly, she could see no reason for his strange rejection, either.

She had no way of knowing that he was fighting some very strong impulses at this moment, warning himself, in fact, that he must not yield to this young woman simply because she seemed so sincere. Like all the others, he told himself dismally, she almost certainly was a fraud.

He shrugged in such a way that his indifference could hardly have been expressed more eloquently. And this shrug made him seem extremely foreign to Penny.

He said, "It is no matter, señorita. I do not wish to read your letter. I have seen other letters like it, I am sure. I regret that you have made a long trip to no avail, but I can only say to you that regardless of the letter Señora de Villanueva may have written to you, she is not receiving. I must insist that you accept that as final."

It had been a long day and an extremely tiring one. Penny had been nerving herself to endure the ordeal of confronting Mary de Villanueva. She'd been hoping only that she could remain sufficiently strong so that neither of them would shatter emotionally when it came time to speak of Marita.

Now the storm of protest that had been mounting within her swelled, and she faced the handsome, impassive man who stood across the desk from her with a defiance that made her brown eyes spark.

"I refuse to accept any decision of yours as final!" she

told him hotly. "Surely there must be someone in higher authority here. But regardless of that, or anything else, I can promise you I have absolutely no intention of leaving this embassy until I see Marita's mother!"

Marita's mother! For a moment, Ramon Martinez stood statue-still. Then he released his grip on the sheaf of papers he was holding, put them down on the desk, and sat down himself.

Penny stared at him helplessly. At the mention of Marita's name a visible change had come over him. An expression of intense pain had crossed his handsome face, but now he looked as wooden as one of the carved masks in the entrance hall.

He said slowly, "You make this very difficult, Miss Baldwin. Again I must tell you—in all honesty—Marita's mother cannot see guests at this time."

Shaken by this change in him, Penny asked, "Is she ill?"

"Ill?" His lips twisted. "What is illness?" he countered. "A condition of the body, the mind, or the heart? Señora de Villanueva has had two overwhelming shocks in a very brief time. This, I am sure, you already know."

"Yes, I do," Penny admitted.

"Then can you not see that she needs peace?" He flung the word at her, scorn blazing in his blue eyes, and Penny felt herself recoiling even though there was no reason to.

She said steadily, "I think you forget, Mr. Martinez, that I have been asked to come here. I shall be quite frank with you. I would have preferred to delay this visit until more time had passed, until there had been a chance for healing. As it is . . ."

"As it is?"

"As it is, Aunt Mary—Señora de Villanueva—has been imploring me to come. I teach school. This is our spring vacation period. I knew that if I didn't come now I couldn't make the trip until summer, and she begged me not to wait till then."

"I see."

"I don't think you do see," Penny contradicted him. "I think Aunt Mary has a need to talk to someone about her daughter, to talk to someone, that is, who really knew Marita. What has bothered me is that I don't know whether I'm up to talking about Marita or not. I was very fond of her. We were at college together; we roomed together. It is still very, very difficult for me to believe that she is dead."

He looked across at her, his eyes flat, dull. "I can appreciate that," he told her, his tone expressionless.

She was startled into a sudden realization. "Of course!" she exclaimed. "You must have known Marita. She'd been working here in the chancery since her father died."

He smiled faintly, in a way that made Penny certain his amusement was to her disadvantage. He said, "In most of the Latin American countries, señorita, people from certain families inevitably know each other. I have known Marita since she was a small child. So, if you knew her so well, why did she never speak to you of me . . . or to me of you?" His eyes darkened and his laugh was bitter as he continued. "We were to have been married shortly. Can you imagine why she would have failed to mention to her fiancé that she had such a good American friend?"

Penny stared at him, her cheeks flushed with color. She was embarrassed, having opened up such a wound where he was concerned. Yet she also resented his attitude. She said stiffly, "I'm sorry. I knew nothing about your relationship with Marita. You're right. She never did speak to me about you."

His face was impassive. "Nor, as I've said, did she speak to me of you. But it is of no matter, señorita."

"On the contrary, it matters a great deal," Penny protested. "Perhaps if I'd reached Franconia in time, if I had seen Marita, she would have told me about you!"

He frowned. "To what are you referring?" he asked abruptly.

Penny closed her eyes. The memory was still too vivid, too horrible. She said, "By the time I got to Franconia, Marita was dead."

"You were at Franconia?"

"Yes."

"How did that come about?"

"Marita telephoned me; she asked me to come."

"It would appear you are much in demand, señorita. First Marita requested your presence, now it is her mother who does so."

That was enough! Penny got to her feet, trembling with an anger she found very hard to suppress. She said tightly, "There is no point in trying to talk to you. For some reason I can't even begin to understand, you persist in twisting everything I say. Will you call the Ambassador, please? He will know who I am."

To her chagrin, his mouth—and God, what a beautiful mouth it was!—twitched with amusement. "That I cannot do," he said, with a singular lack of regret in his tone. "The Ambassador is in our capital for a conference with our President. So, I am afraid you will have to make do with me."

"Surely there must be someone here in higher authority?" she demanded, not caring whether or not he might consider this disparaging.

"Yes, certainly there is, but there is no one else who would be responsible in this particular matter. The Ambassador left me in charge of his family. I think that is the way one would put it. I am responsible in his absence for his family members. Señora de Villanueva is his sister-in-law, and thus a member of his family." Ramon shrugged again. "That is the way it is, señorita," he said with a definite air of finality.

"Very well, then," Penny said and picked up her

handbag. "I will go back to my motel and place a call to the Ambassador in your capital. You can't halt the entire intercontinental communications system, Mr. Martinez!"

"I would not wish to," he said, that glint of amusement surfacing once again. And, as he looked at her, it was difficult not to be amused by her, gently amused. There was a defiance in her stance that he found fascinating—a defiance that was far more provocative than she realized. It was difficult to repress the impulse to cross around the end of his desk and take her in his arms. He could imagine her initial outrage. But then, as he gained possession of her mouth, as he began to caress those beautifully rounded breasts, as he drew her close to his body so that she could feel his arousal, the outrage would fade, he was sure of it. Though their minds, their attitudes, were worlds apart, there was a current of something essentially primitive running between them, something that had little to do with reason. Ramon had been sharply aware of it since the moment she'd walked into the room. And Penelope Baldwin was aware of it too. He would have sworn to that!

But she was leaving. She was starting her defiant little march toward his office door, and suddenly Ramon couldn't let her go.

"Miss Baldwin," he said quickly, "wait, please!" He frowned, surprised because he was accustomed to being in command of himself. He seldom acted as impulsively as this. "Possibly I have . . . misjudged you," he said carefully. "You yourself would be the best one to convince me of that."

"I don't think I need to try to convince you about anything," she said coldly.

"Yes, I can understand why you would feel that way," Ramon agreed smoothly. "But I would also like to make you understand my position. As a beginning . . . would you do me the favor of telling me more about your friendship with Marita and about the trip you made to New Hampshire?"

He was every inch the diplomat as he said this—suave, charming, too charming, as far as Penny was concerned. She decided that she totally distrusted him. Nevertheless, if there was a bargain to be struck she was prepared to strike it.

"If I tell you what you want to know, will you take me to Señora de Villanueva?" she asked him.

He smiled, then shook his head slightly, as if he were dealing with a naughty child. "One thing at a time, please," he suggested.

"Very well," she conceded. "I've already told you that Marita and I were at college together. We were close friends. I think that Marita's mother presumes we remained close after we both graduated."

"And didn't you?"

"No."

Ramon raised quizzical eyebrows, and Penny added quickly, "We never had a disagreement; it wasn't that. It is simply that after we left school we went into two different worlds. That was nearly three years ago . . ."

He nodded. "Yes."

"We were both twenty-two when we graduated," she said. "I went into teaching. Marita . . . well, for the first couple of years she globe-trotted; I can't think of anything else to call it. I must have gotten two dozen postcards from her from two dozen different places. Just short messages. Marita always seemed to skim the surface quickly when she wrote, yet she had a surprising talent for getting a certain essence into what she said." Penny paused and then added slowly, "It always seemed to me that she was looking for something."

"For happiness, perhaps?" Ramon asked in a tone laced with bitterness.

"Perhaps. I don't know. Then there was the terrible matter of her father's assassination last fall . . ."

He winced, as if in protest at her words, but Penny was not about to change them. Whether or not it offended

Ramon Martinez's patriotic sensibilities, Marita's father had been assassinated. There was no prettier phrase for it.

She continued, "I understand that Marita came to Washington because her mother thought it might be good for her to work in the embassy for a time."

He nodded. "Yes, that is true."

"Well," Penny went on, "after she arrived here, Marita wrote to say that I must come down on my spring vacation, and I wrote back that I would love to do so. Then, in the middle of February, I had a call from her. She was staying at a ski resort up in Franconia. She sounded happy and excited, and she insisted that I take the next bus up there and join her. She said that she didn't want to wait till spring for our reunion. She knew we were having our winter vacation in school at the time. She said she'd rented a small chalet and had plenty of room for me and that the skiing was fabulous." Penny sighed. "I reminded her that I wasn't much on skis. I've never gotten beyond the novice slopes. But she assured me there were all sorts of devastating men around who'd be more than happy to help me."

"I can imagine," Ramon said, his tone caustic. "So, what did you do?"

"I told Marita it was out of the question. And then . . ."

"Yes?"

"She became very serious," Penny said. "She said, 'I need you, Penny. I'm involved in an affair of the heart, and I need the advice of someone I can trust.'"

"*Un asunto del corazón*," Ramon Martinez said absently.

"What?"

"A heart affair, as you said," he told her impatiently. "Go on."

"Marita could be very dramatic . . . and very persuasive," Penny said. "Finally, I agreed to make the trip. She had a timetable, we decided on the bus I'd take, and she said she'd meet me. But when I got to Franconia there was no one waiting for me. I finally found a taxi to take me out to the ski resort. Luckily, Marita had told me the name of the place. The Snow Palast. It's fairly new, one of those Swiss-style resorts with dark-timbered, white-washed buildings. The lodge is on the slopes of Crescent Mountain. There's a red gondola to carry skiers up to the top.

"It was gorgeous the day I arrived, and most of the guests were outdoors. The lobby was deserted, and when I went to the reception desk and pushed a bell for service a tall, blond young man came out of an inner office. I asked for Marita . . ."

"Yes?"

"Well, as soon as I spoke her name I knew there was something terribly wrong. Then this young man—his name was Eric Jenson—told me he'd been expecting me, but he hadn't known when I'd be arriving or he'd have met me. He seemed to find it difficult to go on after that, but finally he said Miss Villanueva's chalet was ready for me to use. Then he told me there'd been an accident."

She shuddered, the terrible memories overwhelming her. This was where she stepped back into the nightmare that had haunted her sleeping and waking hours since February. She'd kept the memories to herself, knowing that perhaps she should try to purge herself of their power by sharing them. But she'd found it impossible to let anyone into her private world to that extent.

Now, her voice shaking, she concluded, "Then Eric told me Marita was dead!"

Chapter 2

THE SILENCE THAT FILLED THE OFFICE WAS INTENSE, creating an invisible wall between Penny and Ramon Martinez. She saw that his lips were set in a tight, bitter line, and his fingers were taut as they toyed with a slender letter opener.

Finally, his voice pitched very low, he asked, "How did you react when they told you Marita was dead?"

"React?" She flung the word back at him. "How does anyone react to something like that? I was dazed; I was stunned. I couldn't believe Eric Jenson. He seemed to think I was about to faint. He offered me some brandy, but I didn't want it. So he took me over to a couch in the corner of the lobby and made me sit down. Then, after a time . . ."

"Yes?"

A chill swept over Penny. She felt cold to the core again, just as she had on that February afternoon in Franconia. She said, "Eric told me that the previous day the skiing conditions had not been good, but Marita had

gone up on the slopes anyway. She never came back . . .
though it was a long time before anyone realized that.
There is a kitchenette in the chalet she'd rented. She often
made her own supper there, instead of going back to the
lodge in the evening. So it wasn't until the next morning
that she was missed, and some time later the ski patrol
found her. It had started to snow that previous afternoon
and it kept snowing throughout the night. Eric inferred
that Marita could easily have been completely covered by
the snow, in which case they might not have found her for
weeks. As it happened, though, they did find her, and they
brought her back to the lodge and called a local doctor.
They were hoping against hope that it wasn't too late.''

Penny hesitated. Ramon's face was deathly pale. His
features could have been carved out of granite. Slowly she
went on, speaking quietly now. ''Marita was dead, of
course,'' she told him. ''The doctor felt that she must have
fallen while she was skiing and hit her head on a rocky
outcropping. The impact might not have caused her death,
but it probably rendered her unconscious, and the
exposure . . .'' She faltered briefly, then went on. ''She
had lain out there for hours, and Eric said it gets very cold
up on the mountain . . .''

Ramon Martinez was still holding the letter opener,
clutching it so tightly that the skin was stretched white
across his knuckles. Looking at him, Penny felt an odd,
twisting sensation. Pity? Compassion? She couldn't analyze it. She knew only that she wanted to go to him, to
throw her arms around him, to bring him close to her. So
she could console him? She suspected that she was
thinking more of herself than she was of him. She wanted
to feel the comfort of his embrace. Comfort? How could a
woman ever gain comfort from a man like Ramon
Martinez? Pain and passion, yes. But comfort?

He said impatiently, ''So this man told you it was cold
on the mountain. What else did he say?''

A new awareness was infiltrating Penny. This incredibly handsome, aloof man confronting her had been Marita's fiancé. He'd known Marita all her life; theirs had been an intimate relationship. Marita must have learned a long time ago what it was like to be embraced by him.

"Señorita," he persisted, "what else did he say?"

Penny flinched visibly from the memory of what had happened next, there at Franconia in February. And, thinking about it, she came to a sudden mental halt.

She said, almost dazedly, "I don't want to talk about it, Señor Martinez."

"You don't want to talk about it?" he said caustically. "You have said this much; you must finish. What else did Eric Jenson say to you?"

He was coming around the desk as he spoke, and Penny shrank away from him. The sudden, desperate notion of running away—regardless of Mary de Villanueva— swamped her, and she started for the door. But Ramon's hand clamped down on her arm with bruising firmness.

"You came here of your own volition," he snarled. "Now it is up to you to finish what you have begun. Do you understand that?"

His eyes were like blue ice, but it was an ice that burned instead of freezing. He looked like a man possessed by forces she couldn't even begin to comprehend, and she gasped, trying to free her arm. But his grip only tightened.

Tears filled her eyes, and she turned her head away from him, hating for him to see this display of weakness on her part. But he saw the tears, and the tenor of emotion that was crescendoing between them switched with a swiftness that astonished her.

"*Linda,*" he said, his voice soft, tender. "Forgive me. My behavior has been inexcusable, and I . . ."

His words broke off as their eyes met. Penny felt herself being drawn toward him by an irresistible force. She could not possibly have retreated. She was committed to raise her face to his, to let him kiss her eyelids, her tear-drenched cheeks, and then to let his mouth find hers as if this had been predestined, his lips moving over hers as if they'd been seeking for an elusive something and now, finally, had come to the end of that search.

The kiss deepened as Ramon's tongue probed, gently but firmly forcing her lips to part. And in the moment that followed, as she savored this first sweetness, desire spiraled within Penny.

She warned herself that she must not let herself get out of control. She'd never in her life let herself get out of control! She was about to push Ramon away when, to her astonishment, she felt him releasing her and then saw that he was reaching into a coat pocket and producing an immaculate white handkerchief.

He wiped away the rest of her tears with a gentleness that was almost more tormenting than his kiss had been. Then he said ruefully, "What a strange effect you have on me, *niña*." He seemed to be talking to himself, trying to explain something to himself. Then he said, "Please, may we resume?" His accent was a little more pronounced than it had been till now. And this, Penny suspected, was because he was as shaken as she was.

She sat down, glad of the chair's support. She watched Ramon resume his place behind the desk. He picked up the letter opener again but he merely held it between his fingers, his eyes intent upon her face.

"What did Eric Jenson tell you next?" he asked her, and she had to marvel at his composure. Diplomatic training, probably. How quickly he returned to the point, to the issue at hand!

She drew a long breath, trying to steady herself. She forced herself to plunge back into a memory she wished she could forget forever. She said slowly, "After Eric told me Marita was dead I . . . I asked if I could see her. You see, I couldn't believe she really was dead. So . . . Eric took me to the funeral home."

She saw that Ramon was clenching the letter opener again. But his voice was level as he asked, "Yes?"

"It was Marita," she told him.

He frowned. "You are telling me," he said, "that you identified Marita? Why was the embassy not informed of this?"

"There was nothing official about my seeing her," Penny said hastily, "and the embassy had already been notified. Eric Jenson told me that there would be a member of the staff flying up from Washington to . . . to claim the body."

"Yes," Ramon said tonelessly. "I did."

"Oh!" she said, expressing an entire range of emotion in that single exclamation. She swallowed hard. "I didn't know. I . . . I'm so very sorry. How . . . how terrible it must have been for you!"

"It was necessary," he said quietly. "And also my responsibility."

"But Eric Jenson could have identified Marita himself," Penny pointed out. "As it turned out, she'd been a fairly frequent visitor at the lodge for the past two winters."

It hurt her to make this statement, because it still seemed unbelievable to think that Marita could have visited New England time and time again without getting in touch with her. She tried to rationalize Marita's trips both to the man who was facing her and to herself. She said, "Marita kept pretty much to herself on most of her visits. Eric Jenson said she didn't make a point of being alone; she simply didn't mingle much. For instance, she seldom joined in the après-ski. That's why no one thought it odd when she didn't show up that last evening. Eric said she'd told him she liked to go to the Snow Palast to get away from the tiresome social life in Washington."

"I see." The words were like twin ice cubes.

"That's all I can tell you," Penny finished. "Eric found a room for me in the lodge, and I stayed overnight. I couldn't possibly have stayed in Marita's chalet, under the circumstances. The next morning Eric drove me into the village to get the bus. I went home and . . . frankly, I've tried to forget it, though that's been impossible. Then Señora de Villanueva wrote and asked me to come to see her. She said, 'Surely you will grant this request to talk to you about my beloved Marita.'" This time Penny met the attaché's eyes voluntarily. "I didn't want to talk to her about Marita," she said. "I still don't. But I could think of no decent way to refuse her."

Ramon Martinez said dryly, "I can appreciate your concern."

"Very well, then." Penny nodded. "Now that you know how I stand in all of this, will you be kind enough to direct me to Señora de Villanueva?"

She was surprised—and instantly resentful—when he shook his head. "I am sorry," he said, giving the phrase no real meaning. "I appreciate your telling me the details of your trip to Franconia, and I do not doubt that you were acquainted with Marita. Nevertheless, my answer must remain the same. It has become necessary for us to protect Señora de Villanueva for her own sake, as I think I have already indicated to you. What you have told me does not alter that fact."

Penny stared at him, appalled, and fury came to prompt her next words. She flung out the challenge. "You can't keep me from her!"

"Perhaps not forever," he conceded with a slight shrug. "But for the moment, I can indeed."

Penny said, biting the words, "Since you say the Ambassador is away, I must ask you to take me to his wife."

"She is not here, señorita," he told her.

"In other words," Penny said caustically, "she is not receiving either, is that it?"

Surprisingly he laughed, a genuine laugh. His teeth flashed in a smile that was so attractive Penny's heart did a strange flip-flop. She felt her pulse throb, and branded it as a traitor.

"Señora Phyliss de Villanueva is at a meeting, señorita," he said, the words underlaid with laughter. "As for the Ambassador, he will be returning to Washington by the weekend. I suggest you contact him then. Perhaps he can explain to you better than I why you may not see his sister-in-law. It was his decision."

"It was Ambassador Villanueva's decision?" Penny demanded.

"Yes."

"I don't believe that!"

"Then you have but to ask him yourself. However, I assure you it is so."

There was a ring of truth in his words that daunted her. She was not about to yield to defeat, but suddenly she felt herself in very hostile territory.

Striving not to let either desperation or discouragement color her voice, she said, "It is impossible for me to stay on in Washington for several days, just on the chance of speaking to the Ambassador on the phone."

"That is your concern, señorita, not mine," Ramon pointed out politely.

Even as he said this, there was something disarming about him, something dangerously provocative. Penny found herself focusing on his mouth as he spoke, this only evoking the memory of a kiss she'd never possibly be able to forget.

She could feel tears threatening again. Tears of frustration, anger, and another emotion she didn't even want to try to identify. She fought them back as she snapped, "If everyone in your country is like you, it's a marvel that we have such a thing as Pan-American relations! Oh, I know you undoubtedly have all sorts of diplomatic immunity, so there's no chance of my going to the police and bringing them back here with a search warrant, then insisting that you let me find Señora de Villanueva . . ."

"No, I do not think you could do that," he agreed coolly. "Though I would like to point out to you that the señora is not being held here against her will. Nor do I feel that this is a matter that involves diplomatic immunity."

"Well!" Penny stood and clutched her leather handbag defiantly. She met the coolly amused look in his blue eyes. "I can assure you," she told him, "that I will find some way of reaching Señora de Villanueva!"

"You surely will, my dear," a quiet voice told her, and she swung around to see Mary de Villanueva standing in the doorway.

Penny had first met Mary de Villanueva when she'd visited Marita in the college both girls had been attending. Later, the older woman had come to seem almost like a mother to her. Now she was shocked by "Aunt Mary's" appearance. She had aged terribly. Her hair, russet brown the last time Penny had seen her, had turned gray; she was appallingly wan, and deep shadows underlined her eyes. But she moved across the room swiftly, hugging Penny fervently then kissing her on both cheeks. Next she demanded, imperiously, "What is this about your having to find a way to reach me?"

"Mr. Martinez intercepted me," Penny said bluntly, painfully aware of those deep blue eyes watching her. "Then he refused either to call you or to take me to you."

"I wondered where you were," Mary de Villanueva admitted. "Juan finally told me that he'd taken you to the chancery, and so I came down directly." She turned to Ramon. "Did you tell Juan to bring Penny in here?" she demanded.

"*Si,*" Ramon replied quickly. "*Pero puedo explicar . . .*"

"We'll speak English," Mary de Villanueva said decisively, and Penny knew this was entirely for the benefit of their visitor. Although Marita's mother was an American, she spoke fluent Spanish.

"Please excuse me," Ramon said. "For a moment I

forgot the señorita does not speak Spanish. At least, I assume the señorita does not speak Spanish?''

"That's quite right," Penny told him frostily. "The señorita does not speak Spanish!"

He nodded. "Very well, then. This entire episode is my fault, Tía Mary. I assumed that the señorita was like all the others who have been contacting you. As you know, after the last young lady came here, the Ambassador issued definite orders to the effect that you were not to be bothered in this way again. When he left I promised him I would keep such visitors away from you."

Mary de Villanueva shook her head remonstratingly. "Penny is a very dear friend, Ramon," she chided. "She is entirely different from any of the others."

"May I ask how I was to know that?" he inquired reasonably.

"I should think you could have told it by looking at her," Mary de Villanueva said tartly. "I would say the other girls both looked and acted like what they were."

"Please!" Penny pleaded. "Would one of you tell me what you're talking about?"

It was Ramon who answered, after a brief hesitation. "Señora de Villanueva has been the recipient of some . . . unfortunate abuses," he said slowly. "Unhappily, this happens to people when they are well-known, when their names are in the news and there is a tragedy in their lives. When Marita was killed, there was a great deal written about her accident in the newspapers. Then, when Señora de Villanueva came here to visit her brother-in-law and his wife, it was reported in the society pages. Since then, the señora has received letters, phone calls, and personal visits from young women who claim to have been friends of Marita's. Inevitably they have sought favors, money . . ."

"How horrible!" Penny protested. Impulsively she turned toward Mary de Villanueva, who had moved away from them and now sat down slowly on a straight-backed chair, her face seeming even whiter than it had when she'd entered the room.

"Such a thing is not unusual," Ramon said. "Unfortunately, people are greedy."

"I have the feeling you'd like to say Americans tend to be greedy," Penny told him sharply.

"No," he denied quietly. "I do not feel that greed is a matter of nationality, señorita."

Their eyes met and clashed. Then they simply kept looking at each other, and Ramon clenched his fists as he forced his gaze away from hers.

He wanted to take her in his arms again, but this time he wanted to go beyond a kiss. He wanted to drown in the sweet scent of lavender that wafted about her. He wanted to bury his head in her beautiful hair and then take her to him. He wanted to touch her breasts until her nipples, hardening, would tell him that she was as aroused as he was. And, *Dios*, how she did arouse him . . . very much against his will! He had no wish at all to become involved with any American woman; he had too much else on his mind, too much that had to be done. And to become involved with an American who was also a friend of the Villanueva family would be unthinkable!

He forced himself not to look at her again but to concentrate, instead, on Mary de Villanueva, who seemed to have become absorbed in deep thought. Worried, he queried, "Señora?" and she managed to smile at him.

"It's all right, Ramon," she told him, then, turning her attention to Penny, said, "I think Phyliss is still at a charity affair they're having at the British Embassy this afternoon. She's English, you know," she added and went on, in response to Penny's puzzled look, "Phyliss de Villanueva. My brother-in-law's wife."

"Oh?"

"So," Señora de Villanueva continued, "you and I shall have tea in the family sitting room. Where is your luggage, dear?"

"My luggage?"

"Yes. Surely you brought your things here. You must have realized I'd expect you to stay at the embassy."

Stay at the embassy? Stay in the same building with Ramon Martinez? The thought was as head-spinning as it was impossible.

Penny said frankly, "No, Aunt Mary. I didn't think you intended to have me stay here, so I took a room at the Mayflower. It was the only hotel in Washington I could think of offhand."

"Well, then, we shall send someone over for your luggage. Will you arrange that, please, Ramon?"

Ramon's disapproval was obvious, but he said only, "If you wish."

"Then that's settled," Mary de Villanueva said placidly, ignoring the vibrations that were rocketing about her. "Come along, dear. We'll go upstairs."

She stood, plainly expecting Penny to follow her, but Penny drew back. She couldn't stay at the embassy! It was out of the question! For one thing, although she might not be an uninvited guest she would certainly—except where Mary de Villanueva was concerned—be an unwelcome one, if Ramon's present reaction was any indication.

He didn't want her here. This message came across loud and clear, and she had a strong suspicion that once the Ambassador had returned to Washington he would echo it. For that matter, his wife Phyliss might be expected to feel the same way. And any others who might be around. Penny faced the fact that this had been hostile territory for her ever since she'd walked through the embassy door.

Impulsively she said, "Aunt Mary, there's no need for me to stay here. I appreciate your invitation but, to be quite honest, I'd rather keep my room at the Mayflower."

She saw a flash of surprise cross Ramon's face, but Mary de Villanueva held her ground. "I should have made it clear when I asked you to come to Washington," she admitted. "I suppose I took it for granted that you'd know I'd want you with me. And I do, Penny, so very much. I not only *want* you with me for a few days, I *need* you. So please reconsider.''

All her life, Mary de Villanueva had been accustomed to wealth and position. She could be extremely autocratic. But right now there was a humility to her manner that was touching.

Penny felt tears sting her eyes, and she cast away caution. ''Very well, Aunt Mary,'' she said, not daring to look at Ramon. ''I'll stay if you want me to.''

Juan, the butler, was waiting for them in the vast entrance foyer. He led them past the staircase to a narrow corridor at the rear of the building, where there was a small elevator. The elevator was boxlike and airless, and although she wasn't usually bothered by such things Penny felt uncomfortable as they slowly wheezed and clanked their way upward through the building.

''I tell Tony all the time that this thing must be unsafe,'' Mary de Villanueva observed as they inched along. ''But, although there are only four stories in the embassy, the ceilings of the first three are so high that this is a much taller structure than an ordinary four-story building. The family quarters are on the top floor, so it would be exhausting to walk up and down the stairs all the time. At least, one of Tony's predecessors found it so and ordered this little horror installed.''

They had come to a groaning stop. The butler flung open the elevator door, stepped out, and stood aside to let them pass. When they had done so, Mary de Villanueva turned back to say, ''Juan, tell Elena to bring tea to the sitting room, please.''

He nodded, his face impassive.

Mary de Villanueva led the way down a narrow corridor that opened into a wide, square hall. The imposing staircase that started in the main entrance foyer below came to a flourishing end here, with a massive polished banister that curved into a guardrail. Rooms opened out on all sides, and Penny caught glimpses of spacious, sumptuously furnished chambers.

The room to which Mary de Villanueva took her was at the front of the building, overlooking Massachusetts Avenue. It was large and lined with windows, a charming room that was obviously well used. The couches and armchairs were big and comfortable, the upholstery a bit faded. Bright floral drapes splashed vivid shades of blue, green, and lemon yellow. A somewhat battered upright piano stood in one corner. There were books and magazines everywhere.

"This is where the family spends most of its free time," Mary de Villanueva said. "The fourth floor is the Ambassador's private residence. The rest of the building is rather official, as you shall see, although we do take all our meals in the dining room—which is a cavern."

She sat down on a long, low couch, surveying Penny, her smile wistful. "How lovely you are, child," she observed. "I've always said your hair is truly the color of honey. That raw, beautiful gold-brown honey. Nature does one of her best combinations in creating brown-eyed blondes. Now, tell me about yourself. Do you enjoy teaching school?"

"Yes." Penny nodded. "Yes, I do."

"And what of the romance in your life?" Mary de Villanueva persisted. "Certainly there must be a man . . . at least one man!"

Penny hesitated. There was indeed a man. Jeff Eldredge, in fact, was one of the reasons she'd decided to make this trip to Washington. She hadn't wanted to face spending the spring vacation with him.

She'd known Jeff for years, but it was only since they'd both come back to Wareham after college to teach in the same school that they'd had a real relationship. For the last year and a half especially, they'd spent a lot of time together. They were compatible in many ways, and she was deeply fond of Jeff. He wanted marriage, and maybe one day she'd discover that she did too. But that day hadn't come yet.

Usually, Jeff was not demanding; he let her set the pace. But although they enjoyed each other's company, Penny had always believed that there should be far deeper feelings in a relationship between a man and a woman than anything she'd yet encountered with Jeff. And Ramon Martinez's kiss this afternoon had only heightened that conviction! Admittedly, there was an inherent sexuality in Ramon that was lacking in Jeff, lacking, at least, in Jeff as she saw him. But to even think about Ramon in that light, she warned herself, was to venture into dangerous territory. She could not imagine life being anything but chaotic with a man like Ramon; each minute would present a challenge. Whereas with Jeff everything would be eternally sane.

There was certainly something to be said for saneness, for the familiar. Jeff and Penny had gone to high school together in the same building where they now both taught. They had been sophomores when Penny's parents had been killed in a car crash on their way back from a trip to Florida and she'd gone to live with her Uncle Fred in the big white-frame house on High Street.

Uncle Fred, a lawyer whose business frequently took him out of town, was a widower who'd never had a child of his own. His housekeeper, Mrs. Amelia Higgins, had long been accustomed to managing his bachelor household with a firm hand, and it had been an adjustment all the way around when Penny had moved in. Jeff, she remembered, had helped to make things easier for her then. Later, college had separated them temporarily. But now they were both back where they'd started from, in a sense, and it seemed logical to think that they'd be spending the rest of their lives together.

Penny became aware that Mary de Villanueva was watching her closely, and she said, "There is a man, Aunt

Mary, and he wants to marry me. But . . . I suppose I'm not sure, that's all.''

"Then he's not the one for you, Penny," Marita's mother said firmly. "You know when it is right. There is no substitute for real love." There was pain in her voice as she spoke, but then she brightened. "Ah, here's Elena," she said.

The maid who entered was short and stocky, with dark liquid eyes and a friendly smile. At least, Penny thought thankfully, all the members of the embassy staff were not as sinister as Juan or as hostile as Ramon Martinez!

"Penny, this is Elena," Mary de Villanueva was saying. "She will get you anything you require while you are here. This is Señorita Baldwin, Elena."

"Mucho gusto, señorita," the girl said.

"Doña Phyliss wishes the señorita to have the Rose Room," Mary continued, and Penny glanced at her sharply as she detected a rather odd note in her voice.

She also noticed that Elena looked startled, almost shaken. But the girl recovered quickly and smiled as she said in fluent but heavily accented English, "I will prepare it, señora."

When Elena had left them, Mary de Villanueva remarked, "She's a good girl. Very faithful."

Penny laughed a little shakily. "At least she's friendly," she observed. "Which is more than I can say of the butler."

"Juan? My dear, Juan has been with Tony for years. They've been all over the world together. I think Juan would die for Tony."

"And kill anyone else for him?"

Mary looked up sharply. "Why do you say that?"

"I suppose I'm being overly dramatic," Penny evaded as she accepted her tea and stirred a spoonful of sugar into it. "Probably it's just his looks that put me off, and that's wrong of me."

"Juan was in a dreadful accident several years ago,"

Mary told her. "The Villanuevas were in Madrid at the time. Tony was visiting an estate outside the city where they raise prize bulls for the *corrida*—the bullfight. Something happened, a bull charged him, and Juan intercepted it. He was badly gored but, almost worse, someone in the party shot the bull in the attempt to save him and the wounded animal fell on Juan. He was in the hospital for months thereafter, and he has been grotesquely misshapen ever since. Tony, of course, will be eternally grateful to him. He saved his life, after all. I imagine Tony will even take Juan into retirement with him."

"Does the Ambassador's wife feel the same way about Juan?"

"Phyliss? Oh, she takes him in stride, but then Phyliss takes most things in stride. She pities Juan, I'm sure. After all, his personal life came to an end that day outside Madrid. Since then, he has existed only for Tony."

Penny smiled ruefully. "You make me feel sorry for him."

"As I do myself," Mary de Villanueva admitted, "although that did not lessen my annoyance with him when I found he'd taken you to the chancery this afternoon." She reached for the silver pot, added tea to both of their cups, and then asked, "What did you think of Ramon?"

That was a loaded question! What, indeed, did she think of Ramon? To think of him at all was to make her pulse start pounding, to make her feel as if all the blood in her body was rushing to her head!

She said carefully, "He's very handsome, of course, but I found him quite hostile. He seems not only to dislike me but to actually disapprove of me!"

"I'm sorry that you made such unfortunate first impressions on each other," Mary de Villanueva admitted. "Ramon is like a son to me and there is certainly no reason why he should disapprove of you! Marita must have told him about you; she must have told him that she was going to stay with you when she went north, to go skiing.''

The remark was so unexpected that Penny did not have time to mask her surprise, and Mary de Villanueva read the expression on her face quickly and accurately.

"Didn't Marita stay with you?" she demanded urgently.

Chapter 3

THE QUESTION WAS CRUCIAL. PENNY SENSED THIS IMME-
diately but she knew she would be trapped if she tried to
lie.

"No," she said reluctantly, then started up in horror as
Mary de Villanueva seemed to ebb away before her eyes.
The color drained from the older woman's face and she
slumped back limply on the couch.

Penny was at her side in an instant, stroking her hair,
massaging her wrists, but there was no response. She'd
never before felt so helpless. But Mary de Villanueva was
breathing. Shallow, labored breaths, but at least she was
alive! After one last agonized glance at her, Penny ran out
into the great square hallway seeking the maid, but
although she called out Elena's name again and again her
voice merely echoed through the stairwell, tossing back a
ghostly challenge.

Frantically, Penny sought to find an intercom of some
sort, telling herself that in a place like this there must
surely be one. And there was. Just inside the sitting room

door, she discovered a brass bell set into the wall. She pressed it again and again.

Next she searched for a bathroom, where she dipped face cloths in cold water to make compresses. Then she went back and began to bathe Mary de Villanueva's waxen forehead, trying to still her shaking hands as she did so.

Elena came and moaned, *"Ay, Dios!"* Then she crossed herself and fled.

It seemed forever before a familiar voice demanded harshly, "What the hell are you doing to her?" Penny, thoroughly immersed in her own task, had been talking softly to the stricken woman, begging her to come back to them, and it took a moment for her to realize that it was Ramon Martinez standing at her side.

He was glaring at her, and she glared back. "What do you think I'm doing to her?" she countered angrily.

His glance was venomous, but there was an instant change in him when he dropped to his knees by the side of the unconscious woman and took her hand in his. His voice was astonishingly gentle as he said, "Tía Mary." Then, turning to Penny, he barked, "There should be a vial of pills in her purse. Get them!"

Penny found a square leather purse on a corner table and, opening it, saw a vial of small white pills inside it. She took them to Ramon, and he glanced at the label and said, "All right. Now, *agua, por favor.*" She merely stared at him, and he growled, "For God's sake! Get some water!"

Her cheeks stinging, Penny obeyed him, yet when she returned from the bathroom with a glass of water, he waved her aside.

"I have put a pill between her teeth," he said. "It will dissolve and start to work for her. But we do not dare try to make her drink yet. She is still unconscious."

He shook his head commiseratingly. *"Pobrecita,"* he said. "She has had too many troubles. She cannot take many more. That is why I did not wish her to see you, señorita. After you spoke to me, I was sure that you had been a friend of Marita's. But that, in my opinion, was all the more reason to keep you away from Tía Mary.''

"You thought that I came here to bring her more trouble?'' Penny asked, finding difficulty forming the words because the mere thought of this hurt.

Ramon shrugged. "It could hardly be otherwise,'' he told her flatly. He had put his finger across Mary de Villanueva's wrist and was taking her pulse with a competency that made Penny sure he knew what he was doing. He nodded and said, "Her heartbeat is stronger. That, at least, is good. Juan is bringing the doctor.''

Penny nodded, unable to speak, and walked over to the window, looking out at the broad expanse of tree-lined Massachusetts Avenue just beyond the strip of carefully tended lawn. This stretch was called "Embassy Row,'' famous, glamorous, known the world around. Yet there was nothing at all glamorous in the thought of the rich, lonely woman who now lay on the couch with her eyes closed, her face waxy.

As for Ramon Martinez, it seemed impossible to Penny to think that this hostile, arrogant man who was now pacing the floor behind her, impatiently awaiting the doctor's arrival, had ever kissed her! She felt as if she must have been dreaming that moment in his arms, when every nerve in her body had vibrated because of him. He had been a magnet, drawing her to him, making her acutely aware of a passion simmering beneath her surface that until that day had been foreign to her. As foreign as Ramon Martinez himself was.

And, right now, he was as alien as a man could be. There was no language between them, no communication at all. Penny only wished that she could hate him, that she could thrust off this insidious attraction he had for her. For the terrible part of it was that she knew if he should come to her at this very minute and put his arms around her, if he should draw her head against his shoulder and fondle her hair as he had earlier this afternoon, she would not be able to resist him! And she hated this weakness in herself almost as much as she wished she could hate him!

It was a character facet that was new to her. Penny had always been attractive to men and men had always been attractive to her . . . but on an entirely different level than this cataclysmic torrent of feeling that had surged with Ramon Martinez this afternoon. Otherwise, she thought wryly, God knows what would have happened to her by now! Her only serious involvement had been with Jeff. But now, after just one encounter with this handsome, arrogant Latin, she could see clearly that the love she felt for Jeff was like a mountain stream—crystal clear but very shallow. On the other hand, to love Ramon Martinez would mean plunging herself into a deep river, fraught with whirlpools . . .

Behind her, she heard Ramon say, "Ah, Dr. Farrington."

She turned to see a slight, gray-haired man carrying a doctor's leather bag. To her surprise, for she thought that he might have decided to ignore her presence entirely, Ramon said politely, "Miss Baldwin, may I present Dr. Farrington? He has attended Tía Mary since she has been here at the embassy, so we are fortunate that he is thoroughly familiar with her case. Miss Baldwin was with Señora de Villanueva when she had this attack, doctor."

The doctor nodded at the introduction, then turned his attention to his patient, and within a short time Mary de Villanueva was able to speak to him, but in a voice so soft Penny couldn't hear what she was saying. Shortly after that, the doctor suggested that Ramon carry Señora de Villanueva back to her own room, and when they'd gone he turned to Penny.

"This must have been quite a shock for you," he said sympathetically.

"It was indeed!"

"She'll be all right. She has been under a great emotional strain and her heart isn't what it was, but I'd say we have the situation pretty much under control," he continued encouragingly. "I'll stop back to see Mrs. Villanueva after I leave my office for the day. Meantime, let her rest . . . and I might advise some rest for you too, young lady. You look as if you could do with it."

Penny managed a faint smile. "I'll be all right," she told him.

He nodded. "I know youth has a way of recuperating quickly," he said, "but even so . . ." He turned to Ramon, who had just reentered the room. "Look after Miss Baldwin," he suggested. "This has been a nasty experience for her."

Penny could feel her cheeks growing hot, and she avoided meeting Ramon's gaze. Juan arrived to escort the doctor back downstairs, and Penny expected that Ramon would go with them. But, to her surprise, he lingered.

He crossed the room to a large sideboard and opened it, and she saw that it had been made into a bar, complete with a small refrigerator. As she watched, Ramon took out two glasses, put some ice in them, splashed in some Scotch without bothering to consult her about her preferences, then brought her drink over to her.

"Here," he said abruptly. Those disconcerting blue eyes were surveying her carefully. "The doctor is right," he conceded. "You are very pale."

The whiskey burned her throat, and despite herself she coughed. "Thanks a lot," she choked out then, not bothering to try to suppress her bitterness.

"For what?" he queried. "For causing you to nearly choke because you are unaccustomed to straight whiskey. . . or for telling you the doctor is right?"

She glanced up at him suspiciously, to see the trace of a smile playing around the corner of that wonderfully desirable mouth of his. But it quickly faded, and he looked down at her soberly.

"Perhaps this incident will convince you that it would be best if you do not stay here, señorita," he suggested.

Resentment flared, and she retorted hotly, "No. No, it definitely will not!"

"Surely you must see that Señora de Villanueva is in no condition to cope with anything more," he persisted. "I would think, señorita . . ."

"I wish you would stop calling me 'señorita,' " she interrupted irritably.

He shrugged, that slight, indifferent shrug that she found peculiarly irritating. "Very well," he said agreeably. "What then would you have me call you. Penny?" His pronunciation of the *e* in her name veered just slightly toward an *a* so that it became almost "Pay-ney" but not quite, and unexpectedly her heart gave a funny little lurch.

But two, she reminded herself, could play at the game of indifference. "Call me Penny if you like," she said carelessly.

"Very well, then. Penny," he said, and there it was again, that funny little lurch. "Perhaps we should get to the fundamentals. I no longer think that you wish to harm or upset Señora de Villanueva."

"No longer?"

"Well," he said, "when you first arrived I felt differently. Marita is . . . dead," he added, saying this with a peculiar flatness. "That cannot be altered. So to go through all the details with Tía Mary as you did with me would only be opening the wound all over again for her."

"I agree," Penny said levelly. "It's she who wished for a discussion, however, not me. I've already told you that."

"But now you surely realize that such a discussion would not be wise, do you not?" he asked her. "Evidently, the moment you began to speak to her about Marita she fainted. If, indeed, she did not suffer a slight heart attack.''

"She had asked me a question. It was the answer I gave that upset her.''

"Then what was the question?''

He posed his own question so imperiously that Penny retorted stiffly, "Señor Martinez, I would rather not discuss my conversation with Señora de Villanueva with you.''

"If I am to call you Penny," he said to her, "then I think you should call me by my first name. Ramon," he rolled the *r* softly, "or Ray, if you prefer. Americans often call me Ray.''

She could not possibly have called him Ray. She said, "I would prefer Ramon.''

She tried to imitate his *r* but didn't quite make it, and he smiled. But he only said, "To go back to you and Tía Mary. Officially, I am here as an attaché in this embassy, and so you could say that I am not entitled to so much 'rank.' But I have known the Villanuevas all my life, as I have already told you. I am close to the Ambassador, closer than I was to my own father. When he goes away, although the Minister Counselor of the embassy is in charge of the mission, I am entrusted with the care of the family, at least in the Ambassador's eyes. When you speak to him yourself you will perhaps understand this entire situation better, and you will be able to speak to him tomorrow. He will be returning then.''

"You told me he wouldn't be back till the weekend!'' she accused.

"Yes, I did. But I completely forgot, señorita—Penny, that is—that this Saturday evening we are to have a large reception here at the embassy. And the Ambassador would not wish to wait until the last minute to return for this.''

The explanation did not quite hold water. Either the conference that had taken the Ambassador back to his own capital had not been all that important, or what was happening right here in his embassy was even more so, Penny decided.

Could his decision to return early have had anything to do with her coming here? She smiled at the thought. The visit of a small-town schoolteacher to the bereaved mother of a former college roommate hardly came under the heading of a diplomatic priority!

She said carefully, "I am sure the Ambassador has every confidence in you. But I still . . ."

"But you still do not, is that it?" Ramon asked her.

"No," she said and, once again trying to escape from meeting his eyes, she turned toward the window, her glass of whiskey, barely touched, still in her hand.

In an instant he was behind her. She felt his hand on her shoulder, gentle yet so firm that she had no option but to turn and face him. He said softly, "I find you most enticing, Señorita Penny. I can think of nothing I would like more than to seduce you!" He laughed shortly. "Ah, the outrage I see in those beautiful, luminous brown eyes of yours. Is it a real outrage, *linda,* or are you merely a very good actress?"

Before she could answer, he went on, "As I've said, I would like to take you to bed with me, I would like to make love to you until I know every inch of your body . . . and you know every inch of mine. But that is a thing apart, *linda.* You tempt me, yes . . . but not so much that I am apt to forget my own obligations," he concluded with a loftiness that made Penny burn with anger. "No matter how desirable you may be, you cannot stand in the way here. You cannot stand in my way!"

It was a bruising moment. Penny was not only outraged, she felt as if she'd been thoroughly insulted, and there was a raw hurt to it, almost as if he'd actually violated her. She raised her hand, wanting to strike out at him, but he stepped back, an enigmatical smile on his face that only increased her ire toward him.

"So you also have a temper," he observed. *"Bueno.*
I've never liked my women to lack spirit."

She gasped at this. His women! She sought for a
suitable retort and, perhaps fortunately, was spared having to make it by the arrival of a tall, red-haired woman
who seemed to appear from nowhere, so swift was her
entrance into the room.

The woman smiled brilliantly at both of them, then
said, with a delightful British accent, "You must be
Penny." She came across the room, her hand out-
stretched. "I'm Phyliss de Villanueva, and I'm delighted
to have you here, my dear," she said warmly.

Years before, Phyliss de Villanueva had been a London
fashion model, and she still walked and dressed like one
despite the fact that she was now in her late forties. She
was not a pretty woman, but she was striking, with an
incredibly narrow waistline, a thin face dominated by
large, greenish eyes, and an air of complete self-assurance
that still managed to lack conceit. Penny liked her immediately. Here, she sensed, was an unexpected ally, and for
this she was grateful.

The Ambassador's wife kicked off slim, high-heeled
pumps in one graceful motion, then curled up in the
corner of a couch and said to Ramon, "Fix me a whiskey,
will you, Ray, love," making the "Ray" sound perfectly
appropriate. "And do sit down and be comfortable,
Penny, my dear. Now, where's Mary?"

Ramon, at the bar, said, "She's had another fainting
spell."

Phyliss de Villanueva frowned. "You called Dr. Farrington?"

"Yes. He's the closest physician and he always seems
able to come."

"Probably because he may not be the best and busiest
doctor in the world," Phyliss observed somewhat cynical-
ly. "Oh, he's an honest man, I'm sure. But I feel we
should insist that Mary see a cardiologist."

"I agree with you," Ramon said as he brought their drinks across the room on a small tray. A Scotch and water, sans ice, for the Ambassador's wife, and refills for Penny and himself—though this time, Penny saw, he'd added a liberal amount of club soda to her drink.

"What a sorry introduction to Washington this has been for you!" Phyliss said, turning to Penny. "When did you arrive here?"

"She came to the embassy at about three," Ramon answered for her, and Penny, glancing at her watch, saw that it was now nearly six. "I refused to let her see Tía Mary."

"I beg your pardon?" Phyliss queried.

"You heard me correctly, madame. It was not entirely my own idea, although I admit I did endorse it. Don Antonio suggested it, before he left."

"Come now," Phyliss scoffed, "are you trying to tell me Tony would keep someone Mary wanted to see away from her?"

"He felt he should."

"But why?"

"Because we both knew that Tía Mary thought Marita first went to Massachusetts last February to visit Penny, and that they then went on to New Hampshire together," Ramon said. "Don Antonio feels, as I do, that the tragedy of Marita's death has been enough for Tía Mary without revealing all the sordid details to her."

Penny looked up swiftly. "Sordid details?"

"Marita was not alone at the ski lodge, señorita. She had been having an affair with a married man. This was the *asunto del corazón* she was telling you about. We suspect that from time to time he joined her at the chalet she had rented. She told her mother she was visiting you first, and that you would be going skiing with her. This was a—what is it you call it?—a cover-up." This was the first time that Ramon's command of the English language had faltered since she'd first spoken to him, Penny reflected, and it was oddly endearing, perhaps because it was reassuring to know that Ramon Martinez was not entirely perfect!

"The Ambassador and I suspect that the man I speak of is someone known to us," Ramon continued, "and we are still trying to uncover his identity. There are a . . . number of things involved here," he added, hesitating slightly over this. "Anyway, we also suspect that he may have been with Marita at the time of her accident but did not wish to reveal himself."

Phyliss and Penny sat forward simultaneously, staring at Ramon as he said this, and Phyliss said, "Tony has mentioned nothing to me of any such suspicions."

"I realize that, madame" Ramon nodded, being strictly formal. "But then the Ambassador is not as sure about this as I am."

"And why are you so sure, may I ask?" Phyliss demanded.

"I knew Marita," he said simply. "She would never have gone off to ski alone if she had a man around." He did not try to disguise his bitterness. "When I went to Franconia to bring back Marita's body, they told me all the details too, you know," he said, and now he was speaking directly to Penny. "The weather was getting bad, Marita was on a ski trail that actually had been closed to the public that morning. Why was she there? I would say that it is because someone challenged her to ski there, and Marita could never resist a challenge! And, under the circumstances, I feel sure she must have had a rendezvous with someone—with her lover, I do not doubt. And then there was an accident that resulted in tragedy."

Penny could not repress the pang of pity she felt for Ramon as he said this and, again, she yearned to go to him, to try to console him. He, after all, had been engaged to Marita. He had loved her. Penny had to concede this, even though the mere idea evoked another new feeling in her. Jealousy?

My God . . . could she possibly be jealous of Marita? She'd loved Marita in her own way; they'd been the best of friends, even though Marita had acted strangely these past couple of years. But Ramon must have adored her, Penny thought, wincing as she did so. And now he was being forced to say that she had been unfaithful to him and that her infidelity had led to her death. Ramon, who in manner, appearance, and tradition was the epitome of a proud Latin—how galling, how degrading this must be for him!

He'd said he'd known the Villanuevas all his life. Had he and Marita been childhood sweethearts? It didn't seem likely, Penny admitted. Ramon must be in his early thirties, and so there was a disparity in age of probably seven or eight years. But by the time Marita went off to college there must have been an understanding between them, and it seemed odd, very odd, that Marita had never mentioned her handsome Latin fiancé, that she hadn't even had a picture of him in the room she and Penny had shared.

Now Phyliss asked, impatiently, "Is there really any truth to this wild idea of yours, Ray? If Marita was having an affair with a married man, do you have any idea at all as to his identity?"

Ramon shook his head. "No."

Phyliss raised her eyebrows, her expression cynical. "You tell me that Marita had a lover, yet you have no idea of who that lover might have been? I find that hard to believe, Ray."

"No valid idea."

Phyliss said sharply, "I hope you haven't said anything about this to Mary."

Ramon's shock was genuine. "Good God, of course I haven't!" he protested. "That was one of the reasons I tried to turn Señorita Baldwin away. I knew that once she and Tía Maria met it would not be long before Maria discovered that Marita had not visited the señorita at all. I did not know, then, that the señorita had gone to Franconia herself, after a call from Marita.''

"You went to Franconia?" Phyliss demanded of Penny.

"Yes," Penny admitted. "But by the time I arrived Marita was already dead.''

Phyliss said gently, "What a ghastly experience for you, child!''

"Yes, it was," Penny said, those terrible memories surging again. "After I . . . saw Marita, all I wanted was to get away from the place! The police said I could leave; they said the embassy was . . . sending someone. So I took the first bus out on Sunday. But ever since, I've felt I should have stayed till the person from the embassy got there." She looked across at Ramon. "You came alone?" she asked him.

He shook his head. "No," he said shortly. "Carlos Smith, our Legal Counselor, joined me. He was at a meeting in Boston at the time.''

"You should have gotten in touch with Mario," Phyliss said. "Mario is my son," she told Penny. "He's doing graduate work at Boston College.''

"I think Carlos did call Mario," Ramon said. "Mario was off skiing somewhere, if I remember correctly. He couldn't be reached.''

Phyliss held out her empty glass to Ramon, who obligingly went across to the sideboard bar and refilled it for her. "I take it," she said, "that now Mary has found out that Marita wasn't with you, Penny?''

"Yes," Penny admitted regretfully. "We were having tea; we'd only started talking, when this all came up. Before I could say anything further, Aunt Mary slumped down in her chair and fainted. I was . . . terrified," she admitted.

Phyliss rose. "I think I'd better go look in on Mary," she said.

"She is probably still asleep," Ramon said. "The doctor gave her a shot.''

"Nevertheless, I'd like to check." Phyliss turned to Penny. "You are staying here with us, aren't you?"

"Aunt Mary was rather insistent about it," Penny admitted uncomfortably.

"I shall be equally insistent," Phyliss declared. "I'm sure you'll be the first person Mary wants to see when she's back to herself again, and don't worry about it, my dear. I think the worst is behind you, as far as any revelations you may make to Mary is concerned. My personal feeling is that what you told her merely corroborated her own suspicions. But, anyway . . . did Mary mention what room you're to have?"

It was Ramon who spoke. "She is to be in the Rose Room," he said, and his voice was flat and cold as ice. "Tía Mary insisted on it, although she passed it off to Elena as your wish."

Penny saw Phyliss's start of surprise. Then the Ambassador's wife said, her voice oddly puzzled, "Marita's room?"

"Yes," Ramon Martinez said, "Marita's room."

Penny shivered. She'd never been superstitious, but now the thought of occupying Marita Villanueva's room gave her a feeling of real horror. She started to speak, to suggest that perhaps she could be placed elsewhere, but Phyliss was saying, "If that's what Mary wants, I suppose we should indulge her, although I admit to me it seems a bit . . . macabre. I hope you won't mind yielding to her wishes, Penny."

"No," Penny fibbed. "Of . . . course not."

Phyliss nodded. "Very well, then, I'll go along. Try to get some rest, Penny. I'll see you at dinner."

Phyliss left as smoothly and quickly as she had arrived, and only now did Penny dare to glance up and meet Ramon's eyes. It was like encountering blue fire, and she felt the intensity of an emotion that she knew could have nothing to do with her personally and yet was affecting her profoundly.

But then Ramon himself was affecting her profoundly. He had taken off his jacket while kneeling beside Mary de Villanueva, and the fabric of his khaki-colored shirt clung to the contours of his body in such a revealing way that Penny couldn't take her eyes off him. She'd already discovered that his arms were strong, muscular, his chest broad, his stomach flat, everything about him well toned, his litheness not concealing in the least a sense of latent power. For Ramon was powerful, she was sure of that. Powerful physically, powerful mentally . . . and over-whelming emotionally. He would be a very dangerous adversary . . . and an equally dangerous lover!

Now he asked mockingly, "Do you believe in ghosts, señorita? Penny, that is."

She was startled by the question. "What do you mean?" she evaded.

"Exactly what I said. When you learned that the Rose Room once belonged to Marita there was fear in your eyes, or so it seemed to me. Was I only imagining that? Or do you expect Marita's spirit to visit you, to challenge you as an interloper—"

"Stop!" Penny cried, the cry at the edge of a scream. Suddenly, she was so close to the end of her own emotional rope that she shuddered visibly, and the man standing in front of her was clearly taken aback. "How can you?" she choked. "How can you be so horrible?"

He bridged the distance between them in a single step, but this time when he put his arms around her she began to struggle, trying to escape an embrace she didn't want. She didn't want Ramon Martinez to so much as touch her! He was more of a monster than a man, she told herself.

Then, as his lips descended, all of that changed. His kiss was deep, penetrating, but even as it assaulted her sensually it also soothed her, and she felt a sense of safety, as though he were an oasis in danger's center.

Ramon molded the contours of her body with his hands as he kissed her. Then he muttered, "*Dios,* you have too much clothing on! Why must women wear suits like a man?''

There was nothing at all masculine about Penny's beautifully cut suit, yet she had to agree with him. She did have too many clothes on!

Ramon was encircling her ear with the tip of his tongue, and this sent pulsating, electrical waves coursing through her. Then he murmured impatient little words in Spanish into that same ear, and Penny found herself wishing that he actually would divest her of her clothes, as she'd imagined him doing earlier in his chancery office! When finally he released her she swayed back on her heels, so unsteady that Ramon caught her elbow to keep her from falling.

"Not here, *linda*," he said, his voice soft, warmly caressing. "Not here, not now. It isn't possible. But I can promise you, there will be a time . . ."

Chapter 4

THE EMBASSY WAS, IN EFFECT, A SMALL PALACE. ONLY the Ambassador's private quarters bore any resemblance to an average residence. The rest of the building was imposing, the rooms huge and ornate, decorated with an opulent dignity that was reminiscent of a much earlier age.

The Rose Room—even though on the "Ambassador's top floor"—was extremely formal, with high ceilings and long, narrow windows that went from ceiling to floor. The walls were papered in a rose, damasklike fabric; the furniture was gold and white. The rugs, draperies, and the rich satin bedspread were all in varying tones of pink and rose, ranging from the very palest to the deepest.

Penny could not imagine actually sleeping in such a room. She tested the bed tentatively, feeling certain it could not possibly be comfortable. But, surprisingly, it was.

Ramon had brought her as far as the door of the room, and now she wondered what she would have done if he'd

insisted on coming in with her. Not much, probably, she
conceded ruefully. She'd been beyond protest. It was as
well that discretion was evidently a basic part of a
diplomat's training!

Ramon had left her with the information that dinner
would be at eight and that Elena would come to show her
the way to the dining room. Dinner would be informal
tonight, he'd added. There was no need for her to change,
unless she wished to.

With this he'd bent forward, his arms at his side, and he
had kissed her. The kiss, with no embrace, had been
unexpectedly poignant. When he'd walked away down the
corridor toward the elevator, tears had brimmed in Penny's eyes and it had seemed as if she were viewing his tall,
receding figure through a mist.

Now she decided that she would change for dinner.
Maybe it was Ramon's reference to women wearing
clothes "like a man's" that made her want to put on
something very feminine tonight. Elena had unpacked for
her, a service to which Penny was unaccustomed. But the
girl had done a good job: everything had been put away as
neatly as if she'd done it herself.

She chose a white, Victorian-style blouse that had a
pin-tucked collar band, an embroidered bodice, and a
dropped drawstring waist with a pointed peplum. With it
she'd wear a slim-fitting navy skirt, and navy-and-white
spectator pumps.

This decision made, she looked longingly at the bed. It
was only now that she was beginning to realize how this
day had drained her, both physically and emotionally.
Even a fifteen-minute nap would help—but how could one
possibly fling oneself down on that magnificent satin
bedspread?

The need for sleep triumphed. Penny pulled the bedspread back and curled up atop the pale rose blanket
beneath. She closed her eyes, fighting off a feeling of

oppression. This was Marita's room she was occupying, Marita's bed she was sleeping in. Despite this, she soon fell asleep and was completely oblivious until she felt someone shaking her and heard Elena's voice calling "señorita! It is almost time to go down to dinner!"

Penny looked at her wristwatch and saw that it was nearly a quarter to eight! She virtually flew into her clothes, sponged off her face, applied a touch of eye shadow, blush, and lipstick, and quickly brushed her long, honey-colored hair so that it swirled around her neck. Then she followed Elena down the hall and into the creaky elevator, where the girl pressed the button for the second floor.

When they got out of the elevator, they walked down a narrow corridor then through a door that was like the entrance to another world. Beyond it, the hall widened. To the right, the massive stone staircase terminated temporarily with a wide, flourishing balustrade. The entire wall in back of the staircase—leading down to the main entrance foyer and the door that went to the chancery—was covered with magnificent murals depicting vivid Latin American scenes. Penny had been able to glimpse the murals only dimly in the semi-obscurity of the entrance foyer earlier in the afternoon.

The wide double doors at the end of the hall were closed, and this, Penny realized, would be the section of the building that overlooked Massachusetts Avenue. Midway along the corridor to the left, though, another set of wide doors had been flung open. It was toward this entry that Elena led her, and they stepped into a formal salon that could have been in Versailles.

Gold furniture that would have delighted a Louis of France was grouped around the room: chairs and couches upholstered in muted, striped satin. Ornate little end tables stood stiffly at carefully placed intervals, while magnificent crystal chandeliers dangled from the high

ceiling. The walls were done in white damask and there
was gold leaf trim everywhere. Rich oil paintings of the
French School, framed with wide, ornate gilt borders,
completed the totally luxurious decor.

Phyliss and Ramon Martinez were sitting at the far side
of the room where, to the left, more doors opened, these
revealing an enormous dining room. Ramon got to his feet
quickly when he saw Penny. He, too, had changed his
clothes and he was wearing a dark suit with a crisp white
shirt and a dark tie. He looked devastatingly handsome
. . . but disconcertingly proper. Phyliss, on the other
hand, had changed into a leopard-patterned caftan, and
with her feet thrust into flat gold sandals she looked
completely comfortable and very much at home. But then,
Phyliss would be at home anywhere, Penny suspected.

Ramon bowed slightly and said with frosty politeness,
"Good evening, señorita. What is your drinking pleasure?"

"A very dry martini, please," Penny said, determined
to show him that she too could be sophisticated.

"You will ask Juan to bring a martini for the señorita,
please, Elena," Ramon told the maid, and she nodded and
flashed him a wide smile before she turned away.

Phyliss said, "Sit down, darling, and make yourself
comfortable—if that's possible on these god-awful chairs.
We only come into this room for a before-dinner drink,
except on state occasions. Did you get any rest?"

Penny nodded. "Yes, I did," she confessed, still
surprised at herself for having been able to do so.

"Good. You looked frightfully tired this afternoon.
Incidentally, Mary is fully conscious again. She's a little
wobbly, but she's all right. She's having her supper in
bed, and the doctor's left her some sleeping pills so she'll
be able to drift off again. I'd suggest that you don't try to
see her until morning."

Penny had chosen a chair near the couch Phyliss was
occupying. Now she wriggled slightly. Phyliss was right.

This beautiful ornate furniture was dreadfully uncomfortable!

She said, "Frankly, I dread seeing Aunt Mary again. I mean . . . if something's going to happen every time we begin to talk about Marita . . ."

She could feel Ramon's eyes upon her, and she had the impression that he'd winced slightly when she'd spoken Marita's name. For the first time it occurred to her that she must be a constant reminder of Marita to him. And this wasn't a pleasant thought. Although he'd spoken almost unemotionally of his certainty that Marita had been involved with another man—a married man—her defection must have hurt him terribly. If nothing else, Marita's unfaithfulness must have seriously wounded his pride. And if he'd also loved her . . .

If? Why, Penny asked herself, was she questioning Ramon's love for her dead friend? Certainly he'd loved her. They'd been engaged; the wedding date had been set.

How could Marita even have looked at another man when she was engaged to Ramon? Penny posed this question to herself and could find no answer to it. She only knew that she couldn't imagine wanting another man, any man, if one could have Ramon Martinez!

She swallowed hard and was relieved when Phyliss said, "My dear, I don't think you need to worry about Mary having any further spells when you discuss Marita with her. The subject is out in the open; you've hurdled that initial obstacle. The shock is over. I'd say you should be on safe ground from now on."

"I am not so sure of that," Ramon observed darkly.

Phyliss frowned. "Why?"

"If this subject is pursued, Tía Mary is going to learn that Marita was not the innocent girl she believed her to be," he stated. "I do not think she is strong enough to handle such a revelation."

"Oh, pooh," Phyliss said airily. "Mary's stronger than you think. Ah, there you are, Juan," she added brightly.

Looking up, Penny saw the butler walking across the room with a tray. "Fetch me another Scotch, will you? Another for you, Ramon?"

"Thank you, I've not finished my drink," Ramon said.

The butler, more inscrutable than ever, handed Penny her martini. She sipped it appreciatively. It was ice cold, perfectly mixed. She suspected that Juan was the bartender and, if so, he was a good one.

For the next fifteen minutes Phyliss led the conversation into safe, noncontroversial channels. Then Juan appeared in the dining room entrance to summon them to dinner.

The dining room was a cavern, just as Mary de Villanueva had said. It was as Spanish in decor as the salon was French, with huge, dark, carved furniture, wrought iron sconces around the walls, and massive, dark oil paintings. The table itself, though large enough to serve twelve in comfort without expansion, was dwarfed by the size of the room.

Penny found Phyliss's amused eyes upon her. "Rather like eating in the middle of an airport, isn't it?" the Ambassador's wife observed.

Penny laughed. "Yes, it is," she admitted. "What an enormous room!"

"We need it when we have parties," Phyliss said, "but at other times we're lost in it. Incidentally, did Ramon tell you that we're having a reception Saturday night?"

Penny hesitated. Then she said, without looking at Ramon, "Yes, he did."

"You are invited, of course," Phyliss said, as Juan set the first course before them, a clear soup with cubes of avocado floating in it.

Dismayed, Penny said, "Thank you so much, but I couldn't possibly attend! I've brought nothing to wear that would be suitable for a diplomatic reception. Anyway, I'll have to get back to Wareham by Saturday. School resumes next Monday."

"It's difficult for me to fancy you as a schoolteacher,"

Phyliss said, attacking her soup with an obviously healthy appetite. "Don't worry about clothes, though. I'm sure we can arrange to find something for you. And I do think you'd enjoy the reception. Washington diplomatic parties are experiences, my dear."

"I'm sure they are," Penny said weakly.

Ramon laughed shortly. "They are experiences I could do without," he confessed.

Phyliss smiled. "Pay him no mind," she told Penny lightly. "Ray tends to be dreadfully antisocial, which is a rather terrible way for a rising young diplomat to be. One of these years you've got to mend your ways, Ray, and perhaps marry a rich American!"

Surprisingly, Ramon's eyes flashed at this. "Never!" he said fervently.

"Well, then," Phyliss went on, "a poor American, perhaps?"

"No American!" Ramon said firmly. Then, glancing at Penny, he had the grace to seem embarrassed. "I beg your pardon, señorita," he told her quickly.

"Why?" she asked him bluntly.

"Why?" Momentarily, he was taken aback. "Because, I suppose, my remark may have seemed disparaging to you, and that was not my intention."

Penny smiled. The martini, she decided, had given her a kind of Dutch courage. She said sweetly, "I don't consider your remark disparaging in the least. I'd feel the same way about marrying a Latin."

Ramon's eyebrows rose. "Oh?" he queried.

"Obviously," Penny said serenely, "our cultures do not mix."

"Now wait a minute," Phyliss teased. "I'm English, and I married a Latin."

"I'd say that you're a true international," Penny said quickly, and Phyliss's laugh rang out, free and clear. But Ramon did not smile. And he left the balance of the conversation to Phyliss and Penny as they progressed to an excellent roast veal, then on to a tossed green salad followed by a sinfully rich chocolate pastry.

Dinner finished, they went back to the gold salon for coffee and, again, Ramon was silent. Only when Phyliss directed a question at him did he speak, and then it was in monosyllables.

Finally he set down his coffee cup and rose, bowing to Phyliss as he said, *"Con su permiso,* madame."

"Of course, Ray, you're excused if you wish to be," Phyliss told him. "Though we shall miss your company. I suppose you're going out on the town, eh?"

Ramon shrugged. "Not exactly. However, I do have an engagement."

"Is she blond and beautiful?" Phyliss asked him.

He smiled. "As it happens, both," he said, and Penny had to bite her lip in order to retain any control at all over her composure.

"Well," Phyliss said, "just remember that Tony will be back tomorrow and he'll expect to find you clear eyed and ready for work."

"No fear," Ramon assured her, then turned to Penny again, bowing slightly as he said, "Good evening, señorita."

"Good evening," she returned almost absently, wondering what had happened to his calling her "Penny" with that heart-tugging little inflection.

Phyliss waited until they could hear his footsteps echoing down the great staircase and then said, "I wonder that every woman in Washington isn't in love with him! At least on the basis of his looks alone. If he were more encouraging, he'd have an entire harem just among the ladies of the Diplomatic Corps!"

Did this mean that Ramon wasn't encouraging to most of the women he met? Penny longed to pose this question to Phyliss, but she refrained from doing so. The last thing she wanted was for the Ambassador's wife to suspect that she had an interest in Ramon Martinez.

An interest? In a single day, the man had affected her as she'd never been affected before, and right now she was miserable at the thought of his going out into the night to meet any other woman, let alone someone who was blonde and beautiful!

"More coffee, my dear?" Phyliss suggested, interrupting this reverie. Penny nodded and watched the Ambassador's wife refilling the tiny cups with expert ease. She wondered how it was that a room could seem so empty simply because a man she'd never known until this afternoon had left it.

Penny awoke the next morning to the sound of rain. She got out of bed and went over to the long French windows and found that her room overlooked a small, walled garden at the rear of the embassy. It was a charming spot, with magnolias and azaleas in bloom around a stone bench set in one corner. A little oasis in the middle of the city.

Rain splashed into a birdbath over which a small, cherubic statue of Cupid presided. It was a steady rain, the kind that might last all day, and Penny's spirits flagged. She had hoped to get away from the embassy for at least a few hours, perhaps to do some sightseeing around Washington since she'd not been to the capital since she was a child. But this weather certainly was not conducive to sightseeing.

Perhaps, she decided, she might spend part of the day at the National Art Gallery, or in the Smithsonian. She'd been interested in seeing the great collection of paintings of the Italian School, which were housed in the National Gallery and the gowns worn by First Ladies at inaugural balls over the course of more than two centuries, which were kept at the Smithsonian. But, just now, neither prospect seemed appealing.

Penny dressed slowly and was wondering where one went to obtain breakfast in this palace when Elena opened the door and poked her head around its corner.

"Oh, señorita, a thousand pardons!" she exclaimed upon seeing Penny. "I only wished to know if still you were asleep."

"No," Penny said smiling, "but I am hungry!"

"You had but to ring, señorita," the girl protested. "I would then bring you whatever you wish."

"Perhaps another day I shall do that," Penny agreed. "But, right now where could I hope to find some coffee?"

Elena laughed. "In the dining room, señorita," she said. "Come, I will go down with you and see that you have what you wish."

As the elevator creaked slowly toward the second floor, Penny asked, "Isn't there a smaller room for breakfast and casual meals here in the embassy?"

"No," Elena said. "There is only that great chamber, señorita. I have often thought one must feel lost in it."

Remembering dinner last night, Penny said, "One does."

"Señora de Villanueva speaks sometimes of making one of the other rooms into a—what do you call it?—a breakfast room. But nothing has come to pass about it." Penny realized that the maid was referring to Señora Phyliss de Villanueva.

"I should think it might be a good idea."

"Yes, it would be," Elena agreed.

The elevator came to a stop, and Elena pushed open the heavy door and preceded Penny down the hall and into the dining room. They were over the threshold before Penny realized that the room was not empty. Ramon sat at the massive dining table with a man she'd never seen before.

She started to back off, but she was not quick enough. Ramon, rising to his feet, said with studied politeness, "Ah, good morning, señorita."

The other man swung around in his chair, then stood and viewed her with frank curiosity. He was heavily built, with a sallow complexion and graying hair, yet although he was not at all handsome in a conventional sense, there was something arresting about him. His rather small, closely set eyes were sharp and penetrating. He'd miss very little, Penny thought. His smile, on the other hand, was wide, expansive.

"So," he said, "you must be Penelope Baldwin! Welcome, *hija!* I am sorry I was not here to greet you yesterday, but welcome nevertheless. Here in our embassy you are technically in a small portion of my country, and so my welcome is doubly sincere and doubly significant."

This speech, presented by anyone else, would have seemed excessively flowery. But in his very slightly accented English this man made it sound as natural as saying hello.

Ramon, his face expressionless, interceded. "Señorita," he said, "may I present His Excellency Don Antonio Villanueva y López?"

The Ambassador! Penny glanced at her wristwatch surreptitiously. It was not quite nine o'clock. Don Antonio must have returned to Washington on a very early morning flight.

"Ramon," the Ambassador protested, "we do not need to be so formal. Penny is almost a member of our family, from what my sister-in-law has told me about her. Call me Tony, if you like, my dear. Or Uncle Tony, if you consider me that ancient."

Penny laughed. "Obviously, I shall have to call you Tony."

"Excellent," the Ambassador beamed. "Join us, will you please?"

"Really . . ." Penny began, but this time it was Elena who interrupted her.

"What would the señorita like to have with her coffee?" she asked. "Some eggs, perhaps?"

"No, thank you," Penny said. "Just toast, please."

"*Seguramente,* señorita." Elena headed for the kitchen as the Ambassador pulled out a chair for Penny. She slipped into it, marveling at the warmth of her reception from this man who, according to Ramon, had wished her to leave his embassy without ever going beyond the chancery!

Ramon seemed to be reading her mind. He said, "You might as well discuss now with Don Antonio the manner in which I received you yesterday."

The Ambassador had been stirring sugar into his coffee and he paused, his spoon raised. "Oh?" he inquired. "And how did you receive Señorita Baldwin, Ramon?"

Penny said quickly, "It really isn't necessary to go into it. Except that I do wonder . . ."

"Yes?"

"Well, I wonder why you left orders that I should not be admitted to the embassy, when you seem so genuinely pleased to see me here."

The Ambassador frowned, and Penny suspected that beneath his very smooth exterior manner this man was a fighter. Like Ramon, he could be a powerful adversary. He said tersely, "I left no such orders."

"I initiated the order," Ramon admitted quietly.

Penny's eyes blazed. "You told me if I were to await the Ambassador's return and come back to see him then, he would only uphold what you termed a joint decision," she reminded him.

"This is true, Ramon?" Antonio Villanueva asked.

"*Si*, Don Antonio. At least, it is partially true."

"Partial truth?" The Ambassador smiled wryly. "Perhaps you had better elaborate on that!"

Penny felt Ramon's glance sweep her face, but once again she forced herself not to look at him. She could only expect hostility in those blue eyes just now, and she didn't want to see it there. No, she wanted something else entirely from this handsome, enigmatic attaché . . . more's the pity! And she had to remind herself forcibly that he was basically a foe, not a friend, no matter how much he might seem to want her.

Ramon's voice was carefully controlled as he said, "Don Antonio, you will remember that you and I talked about Tía Mary the other day. We both expressed concern about her health. I am speaking of her mental health as well as her physical health."

The Ambassador nodded. "Yes. That's so."

"You told me that you felt she had been through enough, that she should be protected from further suffering. And that is what I was trying to do by preventing Señorita Baldwin from seeing her. I accepted the señorita's claim that she had been a classmate of Marita's in college, even though some of the others who had contacted Tía Maria earlier had made the same claim . . . and all of them wanted something."

Penny flushed. "Do you still feel I wanted something?" she demanded coldly.

"I think we have gone over that sufficiently, señorita," Ramon said evenly. "I have admitted I was mistaken in my original estimate of you. Nevertheless, you were a voice from the past, and I felt it best that Tía Maria should not hear that voice. I knew that you could not help but put a lie to what Marita herself had told her mother not long before she died." Ramon turned to the Ambassador. "As you know, sir, Marita had told her mother that she was going to visit the señorita and that they were then both going to Franconia to ski."

"Yes," Antonio Villanueva said, "and as we all know now, she did not do this. I can see why you acted yesterday in what at first seemed to be a very rude manner. Penny, my dear, you must forgive us if, in our concern for Mary, we've seemed less than hospitable to you."

"I do, of course," Penny said quickly, hoping desperately that this would put an end to the subject. To her relief, the Ambassador did not prolong it. He switched to other topics until they were speaking about Penny herself, about her job, and about her impressions of the embassy.

Then, to her horror, the Ambassador was suggesting that Ramon take her on a "grand tour" of the premises, and she quickly told him that his own wife had done this the night before. Essentially, this was true. After they'd finished their coffee, Phyliss had shown her over this floor. They'd peeked briefly into the huge kitchen, then Phyliss had taken her back toward the front of the building and on through the gold salon into the ballroom, which overlooked Massachusetts Avenue. It, too, was a study in gold and white, the dance floor smoothly waxed. There was a dais at one end for the musicians that doubled as a small stage. "We put on little plays and such on special occasions," Phyliss had told her. "Strictly for fun, of course."

Next Phyliss and Penny had walked up the great, winding staircase to the third floor, where the entire front of the building was given over to a huge library-lounge. Hundreds of books lined the walls, and Penny, hoping that they weren't all written in Spanish, had managed to get close enough to some of the titles to verify that they weren't. Although this room was as large as the vast dining room, the comfortable couches, armchairs, and shaded lamps gave it a club atmosphere that was inviting.

"We use this for informal gatherings, primarily," Phyliss had said. "I have my bridge club here, our hospital aid society meets here, things like that. Actually it's a friendly room, large though it is."

The formal guest rooms, reserved for distinguished visitors, were also on the third floor, and Penny was glad that she did not belong in that category. It would have been much too lonely to occupy the vast third floor of the embassy all by herself, and there was no one else in residence there at the moment. Also, when she'd awakened that morning it had been with a new feeling about occupying the Rose Room that had once been Marita's. Marita, after all, had been her friend. At one time in their lives, they'd been very close to each other. That morning she'd had the persistent feeling that Marita would want her in the Rose Room; she would want her doing exactly what she was doing.

Now, at least, she could tell the Ambassador that she had seen the embassy, courtesy of his wife, and that she had found it magnificent, although a bit awesome.

He laughed. "I agree," he said. "This dining room," he went on, waving a hand at their surroundings, "is oversized, outrageous, not at all suited for family living. Yet when we have a function, the space is filled. Embassies, for the most part, are scaled for diplomatic entertaining—at least this one certainly is. But for the moment"—he was pushing back his chair and rising as he spoke—"I must get down to the chancery and find out what has been going on in my absence."

Ramon rose too, but the Ambassador said, "Enjoy a second cup of coffee with the señorita, Ramon," and the attaché reluctantly resumed his place.

The room seemed darker without Antonio Villanueva's vital presence. Juan came in with a huge silver coffee pot and refilled the coffee cups. Penny had not really wanted a second cup of coffee but now she meticulously added cream and sugar, making quite a production out of blending the brew because she didn't want to look at Ramon.

Finally she had to, though, when he said, "Why did you not tell Don Antonio that I actually asked you to leave here yesterday?"

He saw her cheeks flush slightly, but she said only, steadily, "I had no special reason, except that I'd just met the man and it didn't seem a very auspicious moment to go into something like that."

"I see," he told her gravely, but she shook her head at this.

"No, you don't see!" she contradicted him. "My not telling him had nothing to do with any desire to protect you, if that's what you're getting at."

"It would not have occurred to me that you might have a desire to protect me," he said gravely, and this was true. The more he thought about yesterday, the more he was disturbed not only by his reception of Penelope Baldwin, but by everything that had subsequently passed between them. And, as he remembered the softness of her mouth beneath his, and the feel of her lovely body in his arms, he had to force himself to be formal and reserved, because otherwise there was no way in the world that he'd be able to prevent their prior encounter from being repeated!

When Elena appeared, to say that Señora Mary de Villanueva was awake and had asked that the señorita come to see her as soon as she was free, Ramon felt as if he'd been reprieved.

Penny stood up without finishing her coffee and said, "Excuse me, please."

Ramon nodded, forcing himself to be every inch the diplomat as he said, "Of course." But now it was he who avoided her eyes, because he didn't want her to see the flame of desire that he was certain must be burning in his.

Chapter 5

MARY DE VILLANUEVA'S ROOM WAS A COUNTERPART OF the Rose Room, except that it was decorated in soft tones of blue. Mary lay in the center of a large bed, propped up by pillows. She was still very pale and there was a frailty about her that was frightening. She looked so vulnerable.

Penny tried to get a grip on her shaky emotions as she bent to kiss the older woman lightly on the cheek. It wouldn't do for both of them to dissolve into tears, and she feared this was much too likely to happen.

Mary's blue eyes were appealing. "Penny," she said softly, "I'm so sorry!"

"Sorry?" Penny was honestly puzzled. "For what?"

"For fainting as I did. It must have frightened you."

"Of course it frightened me," Penny agreed. "But that's surely nothing for you to be sorry about! It must have been a scary experience for you too."

"It wasn't the first time something like that has happened," Mary admitted wryly. "I've had a heart problem for quite a while. It's nothing that can't be managed if I do what I'm supposed to do, but that's something I don't even want to talk about just now. Are you comfortable, dear? Why don't you draw up a chair? You and I have a lot of ground to cover.''

This was the last thing Penny wanted to hear! She wasn't prepared to ''cover a lot of ground'' with Mary de Villanueva. She knew it could only be terrain that would concern Marita, and she wasn't sure she could handle any further recollections of that terrible time at Franconia.

Perhaps Ramon was right, she found herself thinking. Perhaps I shouldn't have come here. Not now, anyway. It would have been easier if we'd let a little more time pass.

Masking her reluctance, she chose a small armchair upholstered in sapphire velvet and pulled it over to the bedside. Watching her, Mary de Villanueva observed, ''You look tired, dear. Didn't you sleep well?''

''Yes, as a matter of fact, I did,'' Penny said. ''I do feel rather tired though. Perhaps it's the change in climate. It's considerably warmer here than it is in New England.''

''True,'' Mary said. Then she closed her eyes, and Penny felt a stab of alarm, fearful that the fainting episode might be about to be repeated. But after a second Mary opened her eyes wide again, and she said, her voice surprisingly firm and strong, ''Penny, let's start exactly where we were when I so ungraciously fainted. You were telling me that Marita didn't visit you last February. Is that right?''

Penny clenched her hands together, literally wringing them. ''Please, Aunt Mary,'' she pleaded. ''Must we go into the past? I admit I'm beginning to agree with Ramon Martinez. I don't think it's good for you to look back just now. It's painful enough for me . . . so I can imagine what it must be like for you!''

''It's painful, yes,'' Mary admitted. ''But the intensity of the pain has dulled somewhat. Maybe it would be more accurate to say that it's been replaced, to an extent, by resentment. More than resentment. Hatred. And that's a strange emotion to me. I've never hated before.''

Mary de Villanueva had been a beauty in her younger days. Now, sorrow and poor health had taken their toll, but there was still a faded loveliness about her that was very appealing. Penny thought, with a wrench of her heart, that Mary didn't look like a person who could ever hate anyone. And she remembered that Ramon had reminded the Ambassador that they were concerned about both Mary's mental and physical health. Was it possible that this lovely, lonely woman was slipping over the edge of whatever abyss it is that divides reason from madness, because of her grief over her husband's and her daughter's deaths?

She asked cautiously, ''Aunt Mary . . . why should you hate anyone?''

Mary de Villanueva did not flinch. She said steadily, ''Because I am not at all sure that Marita's death was an accident, Penny.''

Penny sagged back in her chair, thoroughly shocked by this. ''What are you saying?'' she demanded.

''I think there is a strong possibility that Marita was . . . murdered!''

''You can't mean that!''

''Ah, but I do mean it,'' Mary de Villanueva said firmly. ''I've thought of nothing but this since last February. I've gone over the whole thing again and again and again. And I feel certain that there was someone with Marita at Franconia. A man. A man who, for selfish reasons, was taking advantage of her. Maybe he didn't actually kill her himself, but I am certain he caused her death. So, can you wonder that I hate him?''

Mary de Villanueva sat up a bit higher on her pillows, and there was tenderness in her expression as she surveyed Penny. ''I don't blame you for being shocked, dear,'' she said. "But certainly you can understand that I'll never be able to rest until I find out who the man in Marita's life was . . . and what he did to her!"

Penny said carefully, "Aunt Mary, I don't know anything about any man in Marita's life." And, despite what Ramon had told her, this was true. "Marita didn't come to visit me in February," she went on, "but she did telephone me and she asked me to join her in Franconia. I . . . I took the bus up there but she was . . . she was dead by the time I arrived." Penny swallowed hard, unable to meet the older woman's eyes. She said, "I spoke to both the management at the Snow Palast, where Marita was staying, and to the local police. They definitely considered it an accident. Marita had gone skiing by herself, despite the fact that the weather was not good. While she was up on the slopes, it started snowing. They surmised that she must have fallen and struck her head . . ."

Penny paused, looking across at Mary de Villanueva anxiously, more than half afraid that she might faint again.

But Mary de Villanueva was made of sterner stuff than that. She said emphatically, "I will never believe that Marita went skiing alone on a day like that."

Well—on that Ramon and Marita's mother were agreed!

"Marita was an experienced skier, and she did have a degree of common sense," Mary continued. She paused, then asked, "Did the people at the lodge say she'd been staying there alone?"

"They didn't say she hadn't been," Penny said. "Marita had rented a small chalet on the grounds, and I imagine she must have been staying in it by herself or she wouldn't have invited me to come up and join her. Most of my conversations at the Snow Palast were with the manager. He's a young man named Eric Jenson . . ."

"I believe Carlos spoke to him," Mary said. "Carlos Smith is our Legal Counselor. He went to the lodge with

Ramon. Carlos and I have talked about this. He had the impression that Marita was alone, just as you did. But I understand that those chalets are spaced well apart on the lodge grounds. It would have been easy enough for Marita to have anyone she wanted join her in the place she rented, with the people in the main lodge being none the wiser.''

"I suppose so," Penny admitted. Then she ventured, "Do you have a definite person in mind, Aunt Mary? Have you any idea of who might have gone up there to see Marita?''

"No," Mary said. "But Ramon shared my suspicion that there was someone; he even went up to Franconia to try to find out for himself. That was just before Marita died. He refuses to talk about anything that went on between them, and it is my feeling that they quarreled. Ramon came back to Washington a short time before the alleged accident.''

Mary sighed. "As I told you before," she said, "Ramon is like a son to me. His mother was my closest friend for many years. She was a lovely person. Half Irish—that's where he gets those blue eyes. She died of tuberculosis, which is still more prevalent in my late husband's country than it should be. Ramon was about twelve at the time. His father was desolate; he never recovered from Patricia's death. There were just two children, Ramon and a brother who was four years younger, Roberto.

"The Villanuevas and the Martinezes were close family friends. Mario, whom you will be meeting shortly, is Phyliss and Tony's only child, between Ramon and Roberto in age. Ramon is thirty-two. Roberto would have been twenty-eight.''

Would have been. So, Ramon's only brother was dead!

"Mario and Ramon and Roberto and Marita were all together a great deal growing up," Mary de Villanueva continued. "Both families assumed that Roberto and Marita would marry. Things are still done that way.

sometimes in Latin America, although not as often as they used to be. Still, some of the wealthy, prominent families like the Villanuevas and the Martinezes do tend to make plans for their children.

"Ramon went off to college and then entered his country's diplomatic service. His work is . . . rather specialized," Mary said vaguely. "When Marita finished school here in the States, she and Roberto became engaged . . ."

"She never mentioned anything about it," Penny put in.

"The engagement was a short one. Roberto met with . . . an unfortunate accident," Mary de Villanueva said, and then, sitting up a little straighter, reached for a vial of pills on her bedside table. "Get me a glass of water, will you, my dear?" she requested.

"Of course." In the adjoining bathroom, Penny ran water until it was cool and filled a glass. Then she watched anxiously as Mary swallowed her pills.

"Are you sure you're all right?" she asked, worried because Mary seemed so pale.

"Perfectly," Mary assured her. "I'm just trying to do what the doctor ordered." She settled herself against the pillows again and said, "You may remember that Marita did a lot of traveling for that first year or so after school?"

"Yes, indeed I do remember it!"

"To my mind, she was trying to escape. Roberto's death had been a terrible shock to her. Finally she came home again . . . and then last fall she faced another shock—when my husband was killed. It was then that I decided it would be a good idea for her to come to Washington and work in the chancery. She needed to occupy her mind. Also, Ramon was here. He's always been like an older brother to her.

"I spent the winter in Taos. I have a place there and the climate suits me. At New Year's, Ramon and Marita became engaged. Because it was such a short time after my husband's death, we announced the engagement very quietly. At first I was delighted. But then I began to wonder about it," Mary admitted.

"Why, Aunt Mary?"

"Because . . . there was something wrong, from the very beginning. I've tried to analyze it, and I suppose that what it comes down to is that there was no joy between Ramon and Marita, no joy at all. I felt that there was something seriously lacking in their relationship. I was distressed when they set a date for the wedding. They would have been married later this month, had Marita lived. I tried to talk to Marita; I even tried to convey the thought to her that if she decided not to marry Ramon none of us would hold it against her. But she evaded me, and then she went to Franconia.

"Now I find it almost impossible to discuss any of this with Ramon. He avoids being alone with me. He pretends to assume that this is because talking about Marita—and her death—is painful for me, as indeed it is. But I know these are subjects that must be discussed. I think the truth is that Ramon is afraid I will find him out if we get into any real dialogue."

Penny frowned. "Find him out?"

"Yes," Mary nodded. "He is burning himself out, in my opinion. He is consumed with hatred and self-reproach. One can't go on living with negatives forever, Penny. There has to come a time when . . ."

She broke off, her eyes widening slightly, and then she smiled. "I might say 'speak of the devil,' Ramon," she observed lightly. "Penny and I were just talking about you."

Ramon Martinez advanced slowly into the room, and Penny felt that he was walking straight into her heart with every step he took. He was wearing a gray flannel pin-striped suit, and he looked like an especially virile fashion plate. His blue-and-white shirt had a small white collar, and his tie was striped with maroon and navy. He was impeccable, right down to his Bally, black-tasseled loafers.

But he was simmering beneath that smooth facade. Penny sensed it, and she flinched because this aura of anger was so tangible. Why? Why did Ramon appear to be angry so much of the time?

He approached Mary's bed then bent to kiss her lightly. Straightening, he said, "Elena told me the señorita was with you, Tía Mary. There have been three phone calls for you thus far this morning, señorita, from a man who seems to think we are holding you captive here in the embassy. He was alarmed because you did not return to your hotel last night. His name is Jeff Eldredge," Ramon added, holding out a sheet of white notepaper to Penny as he said this, "and I have written here the telephone number where you may reach him. I think the entire staff would appreciate it if you would return his call.

Penny accepted the sheet of paper with a cool "Thank you," but her composure faltered when her fingers brushed Ramon's hand.

"You are looking better this morning, Tía Mary," Ramon observed, and Penny decided that he was also an accomplished liar. In her opinion, Mary de Villanueva looked terrible.

"I'm feeling better, thank you," Mary told him. Then she glanced toward a golden shaft of sunlight that was slanting through the bedroom windows. "The rain seems to have stopped," she observed. "Why don't you take this child out and show her some of Washington's famous sights, Ramon?"

Before Penny could even utter a protest, Ramon said smoothly, "It would be a pleasure to do so, but one that must be deferred, I am afraid. I have an important appointment in the chancery in half an hour and a full schedule for the balance of the day. Perhaps another time, señorita?"

"It really won't be necessary," Penny told him stiffly.

"I've been to Washington before." She didn't add that she'd been all of eight years old on her last trip to the capital, which had been a short one.

"My loss," Ramon said with a suavity that was irritating. Then, "Don't you think you should be resting, Tía Mary?"

He could not have made it clearer that he wanted Penny to leave the room, and she glared at him resentfully. Even Mary de Villanueva frowned as she said, "I've been resting enough, thank you. Having Penny here is doing me a great deal of good."

"Then I am delighted," Ramon said with a smile that came nowhere near reaching his eyes. "If you will excuse me . . ."

He kissed Mary de Villanueva again in farewell, nodded briefly to Penny, and sauntered out of the room with that easy and arrogant grace that Penny found extremely annoying.

Once he'd gone, Mary sighed. "He is an enigma," she confessed. "But . . . enough about Ramon. Tell me about this man who's been calling you all morning, Penny. Should you go return his call now?"

"No. It can wait a bit longer," Penny said.

"Is he important to you?" Mary asked.

"Yes. Jeff and I teach in the same school, and we've been . . . quite close, this past year or so."

"And I suppose he wants you to marry him?"

Penny laughed. "Yes, as a matter of fact, he does."

"But you're not in love with him, are you, darling?" Mary ventured perceptively, picking up the threads of the conversation that they'd begun yesterday. And, until yesterday, Penny might have been able to say without hesitation that she cared a great deal for Jeff Eldredge. She did care for him. But in the course of twenty-four hours she'd learned that there were emotional dimensions she'd not even been aware of when she'd left Wareham. In all the time she'd known Jeff Eldredge, he'd never even begun to teach her the meaning of passion as Ramon Martinez had managed to do in just one easy lesson! In fact, she couldn't relate passion to Jeff at all. Not now.

But love and passion, she tried to tell herself, were not the same thing at all. These . . . these impulses that she felt for Ramon had to be transitory, whereas the solid affection she and Jeff shared . . .

The rationalization didn't wash. So, in answer to Mary de Villanueva's question, she said uncertainly, "I'm not sure."

"If you're not sure, you don't love him," Mary stated, much as she had the day before, and this led into the subject of her own romance with her late husband. She had met him when he'd gone to make a speech in San Francisco, where she'd lived as a young girl, and there had been something between them from the very first instant. An awareness, a spark . . .

There had been an awareness, a spark, between Ramon and herself from the very first instant yesterday, Penny remembered uncomfortably. And she tried to steer the conversation into other channels, to talk about the Ambassador, and Phyliss, and Washington. Anything but Ramon!

Doctor Farrington stopped by to see his patient shortly before noon. Penny left them alone and walked back down the corridor to the Rose Room. That shaft of sunlight in Mary's room had been temporary. The rain had returned, and now it splashed against the windows as Penny looked down into the little garden to see the small Cupid, which seemed sodden even though it was fashioned out of stone. There was a desolation to the secluded corner, too, that touched something deep within her, evoking a peculiarly personal response.

She knew that she should telephone Jeff, but she kept putting off sitting down and placing the call through the embassy switchboard. One problem was that thinking of Jeff was disturbing, because when she tried to conjure up an image of his familiar face she found it difficult to do so. She asked herself how she possibly could have forgotten him so totally in only a couple of days. And she knew that the answer was that in stepping through the massive doors of this Massachusetts Avenue embassy she'd literally stepped into another world. A world that fascinated and intrigued her, even as it frightened her.

It would be folly to let herself become too enmeshed in it, because it wasn't her world and, she told herself, it never could be. It would be folly to become too involved with Ramon Martinez. But something deep inside her told her that—despite his aloofness—this was precisely what was going to happen if she stayed in Washington much longer. Common sense warned her that her best course of action would be to go back to Wareham as soon as possible, now that she'd talked to Mary de Villanueva. She'd told Mary all she could tell her about Marita. There was nothing more to say.

Ramon. She found herself thinking that he must have been a very somber little boy after his mother died. Twelve was such an impressionable age—at the threshold of adolescence, yet still in childhood. And she suspected that he must have been a lonely child, even though he'd had a brother who had died only within the past three years. Even now, for all of his surface poise and that almost studied air of indifference, Ramon seemed to her a lonely person. Essentially reserved, there was a dignity about him that would be hard to penetrate, almost as hard to penetrate as his pride. And she suspected he'd take refuge in that Spanish pride of his . . . no matter what!

But the dignity, the pride, and the aloofness were all cloaks for loneliness. Mary de Villanueva was right. Ramon had been hurt badly, and it showed. Though she didn't know the reasons why this should be so, Ramon was burning himself out . . .

Penny turned away from the window, looking for a temporary escape as she searched for a book to read, or even a magazine to thumb through. But the room was devoid of any such material, and she remembered that even back in college Marita had never been much of a reader.

Marita's room. Although she was comfortable in it now, she did wonder why Mary de Villanueva had wanted her to stay in this particular room when there were so many other guest rooms available in the embassy that would have been without painful associations.

There were two closets in the room, one on either side of a large, ornate chest of drawers. Elena had hung Penny's clothes in the closet to the right, which had been empty. Now, mildly curious, she moved to the closet to the left, opened the door, and froze.

It was as if the clothes hanging there bore a signature. Colors, patterns, fabrics that most people wouldn't dare wear were juxtaposed in a rainbow array that spelled out the name Marita as surely as if Marita herself had penned it, with that scrawling, open signature that always ended with an upward loop at the end of the final *a*.

Shoes—slim, bright shoes, echoing the clothes—were neatly arranged on racks, while sweaters and blouses were layered in plastic cases on the shelves. Marita had been dead for over two months, but her clothes were still there, as if awaiting her return.

Shaken, Penny went to the chest of drawers, realizing now that Elena had put all of her own smaller things in the dressing table. She slid open a center drawer and the echo of the spicy, tantalizing scent Marita had always worn assailed her nostrils. One drawer held Marita's night-gowns, another drawer her slips and bras, and yet another held gossamer stockings in an array of shades. There was also jewelry, a snapshot album, purses made of exquisite leather in all sorts of shapes and sizes, perfume and cosmetics, and handkerchiefs with intricately embroidered *M*'s in their corners. A framed picture of Ramon, which once had evidently adorned the dresser top, had been placed in a top drawer face up. Yes, come to think of it, there was nothing reminiscent of Marita on the surface of the room. But the chest and the closet—in their way, they reminded Penny of Pandora's box.

She slowly sank down onto the bed, surprised to find that her knees were wobbly. She had come here to bring solace to a bereaved mother—but not to resurrect a ghost, she told herself shakily. She had left Marita, the physical Marita, in that funeral home in New Hampshire. Marita had been dead! That Penny had seen for herself. Yet in this room, with her scent still wafting through the air now that the drawers had been opened, she seemed tantalizingly, provocatively alive.

Someone knocked at the door and, briefly, Penny was too stunned to answer. Then she summoned all the voice she could muster and called, "Come in."

It was Phyliss, dressed in outrageous fuchsia lounging pajamas that shouted at her red hair yet were not all that incompatible.

"Just wanted to tell you, luv, that we have *comida* at one o'clock," the Ambassador's wife informed her. "Don't dress up; you're fine as you are. It's strictly *entre nous*. Occasionally some of the staff join us, if Tony's been discussing something or other with them. I gather you've met Tony?"

"Yes. I interrupted his breakfast. He's charming."

Phyliss came closer, narrowed her eyes, and peered slightly. Penny realized that the Ambassador's wife probably needed glasses. She tended to be a bit nearsighted herself—for the past couple of years she'd been wearing glasses when driving—and so she recognized the symptoms and smiled inwardly. Vanity, vanity! But somehow this little foible made Phyliss all the more endearing.

Phyliss asked, "Has something upset you? You rather look as if you've been seeing shadows where there should be sunshine."

Penny was tempted to hedge, but then thought better of

it. "I *have* been seeing shadows, to tell you the truth," she admitted. "I didn't realize until just now, when I opened the door to the second closet, that all of Marita's things are here."

"I know." Phyliss nodded. "That's why I was startled when I learned that Mary wanted you to use this room. She's been keeping it as if it were—well, as if it were a shrine to Marita. True, it's been less than three months since Marita died, but even so, this is rather ghoulish. I've asked Mary if she wouldn't consider donating the clothes to our hospital-aid thrift shop, but she flatly refuses. She spends hours in here, usually when I'm out because she knows I don't approve. Elena keeps an eye on her for me; she tells me about it."

"But it's all so inward, so morbid," Penny protested. "I suppose what I'm trying to say is that there's no outward trace of Marita. All her bric-a-brac has been cleared off and stashed away, there are no pictures of her anywhere . . ."

"I know," Phyliss agreed. "And, God knows, I sympathize with Mary. In fact, there have been moments when I've felt as if my heart were going to break for her. But even so, there's something frightfully gruesome about this. As I've said, I was surprised that she'd want you to stay in here. I should add that it surely indicates she thinks very highly of you, my dear. Incidentally, I haven't seen her this morning. How is she?"

"Better . . . but so awfully frail. I stayed with her till the doctor came." Penny hesitated, then plunged. "Phyliss," she asked, "does Ramon Martinez live in the embassy?"

"At the moment, yes," Phyliss said. "He had an apartment not far from here, but it was in an old building. They've sold the place and they're going to tear it down. Tony suggested that Ray move in until he can find something he really wants. Do you know, sometimes I think Ray is more like a son to Tony than Mario is. But then, of course, Mario wouldn't be a diplomat if you made him an instant ambassador.''

"What does Mario want to do?''

"Just now, he plans to be a great sculptor,'' Phyliss said, smiling. "In the past, he's been a poet, a violinist, a geologist. He tried ranching one summer and found that it definitely was not for him. He does rather go from one thing to another, but he's good at a number of them, including sculpturing. He'll have to show you some of the things he's done. In fact, he'll undoubtedly want to do a bust of you.''

"I'm afraid I won't be here that long,'' Penny said quickly. "I haven't told Aunt Mary yet, I didn't want to chance upsetting her again, but I really should leave tomorrow, Phyliss.''

"And miss the reception?'' Phyliss asked, dismayed.

"I'd love to stay for it. But I do have to get back to school the first thing Monday morning, and there are quite a few things to attend to before then,'' Penny said. "Also, as I've already told you, I've nothing to wear to an affair like that.''

Phyliss hesitated. Then she said, "Darling, I rather hate to bring this up. As I've already told you, clothes for the reception will present no problem. I'm sure you could borrow something of mine. It wouldn't be too difficult to take a tuck hither and yon. Or, for that matter, we could go shopping tomorrow and find something for you. But the fact of the matter is that Mary told me even before you got here that she planned to make a very special request of you. She wants, very much, for you to attend the reception, and to wear a dress of Marita's!''

Chapter 6

Phyliss and the Ambassador were in the Gold Room when Penny arrived there prior to the time for lunch. They were talking to a pretty, dark-haired girl whom the Ambassador introduced as his cousin, Conchita Lopez. Conchita, he explained, was working as a secretary in the chancery so that she might have the opportunity to improve her English. But Conchita, Penny soon found, had had some of her schooling in the States, and though she had a charming accent, her English was almost as fluent as Penny's own.

Ramon arrived with a tall, white-haired man who was introduced as *Licenciado* Smith. He bowed over Penny's hand with a dazzling smile. The white hair, she decided, was premature. He was surely not more than forty, and he was tall, deeply tanned, and extremely handsome. Carlos Smith. Penny remembered that it was he who had been at a meeting in Boston when he'd been summoned to Franconia to meet Ramon and bring Marita's body back to Washington.

Marita. If memories created ghosts, then hers was everywhere here in the embassy. It seemed to Penny that this was the worst possible place for Mary de Villanueva to be staying. She decided that she was going to speak to Phyliss about it and suggest that Mary go back to Taos, or possibly take a trip to Europe for a change of scene.

Penny was given the chair of honor to the Ambassador's right at the long dining table, and Carlos Smith sat next to her. Ramon and Conchita were on the opposite side of the table, with Phyliss at the end, next to Ramon.

Carlos Smith proved to be a delightful luncheon companion. He and the Ambassador kept up an easy banter, flattering Penny outrageously and delighting her as they did so. *Licenciado*, they explained, was the title Latin Americans bestowed upon a lawyer. "It means he is licensed," said the Ambassador with a knowing glance at Señor Smith. "That can cover any number of things, and Carlos is indeed a man of many talents! He was a civil engineer, a bridge builder, before he became a lawyer. He is also a terrible flirt!" The Ambassador wagged his finger, and the handsome lawyer laughed. "Watch yourself, Penny!" she was warned.

And she did indeed need to watch herself; this she knew—but not with *Licenciado* Carlos Smith! The source of her personal danger was speaking in rapid Spanish to Conchita, and Conchita was answering him with equal intentness. Penny wished, wryly, that she could understand what they were saying to each other.

Once or twice the Ambassador and Señor Smith spoke briefly of business, and Penny became aware that the attractive, white-haired diplomat, despite his carefree manner, was extremely astute. As Legal Counselor he was, according to protocol, next to the Minister Counselor of the Embassy in rank. The Minister Counselor, in turn, was next to the Ambassador himself and stepped in as a temporary Chief of Mission when the Ambassador was away. As it happened, the Ambassador explained to

Penny, their Minister Counselor was away himself just
now on a long leave of absence due to illness. Thus Carlos
Smith was, in effect, second in command.

"It is he to whom you must complain if you do not find
everything as you wish it, and I am not here," the
Ambassador said teasingly.

Inadvertently, she glanced across the table at Ramon
and found that he was looking at her with a darkly intent
gaze. His blue eyes seemed indigo just now. Conchita had
turned to Phyliss and was talking to her in low tones and,
overhearing scraps of their conversation, Penny gathered
that they were finalizing plans for the Saturday night
reception. Ramon fell into a stony silence, and once they
had finished dessert—before the coffee had even been
poured—he pushed back his chair and said to Phyliss,
formally, *"Con su permiso,* madame."

Antonio Villanueva raised his eyebrows. "You must
leave us?" he asked his attaché.

"Yes, if you will excuse me, sir. I have an appointment
at the State Department at three o'clock," Ramon said,
speaking in English. For her benefit? Penny wondered.

"Then of course you must go," the Ambassador
agreed.

Once again, Ramon made his exit. This seemed to be
becoming a habit when he was in the same room with her,
Penny brooded ruefully.

After a moment, Carlos Smith laughed. "That young
man," he said, "he takes life so seriously! With two
beautiful girls to talk to, he spends most of his time
scowling at his plate."

Antonio Villanueva nodded thoughtfully. "Ramon has
been increasingly preoccupied of late," he admitted.
"Sometimes I have the impression that he is carrying a
burden around with him."

"Perhaps he is," Conchita said unexpectedly.
"Marita's death was a terrible shock to him, Don Antonio. Don't you think he still grieves for her?"

"Did he ever?" Carlos Smith asked lightly.

The Ambassador frowned and said something swiftly in Spanish, then, with a glance of apology at Penny, said, "I asked the *Licenciado* why he felt impelled to make such a remark. I think we all realize that Ramon must still grieve for Marita."

"Then I can only say that I think he's found a way of consoling himself," Carlos Smith persisted. "There is a new woman in his life, you know."

"Carlos!" Phyliss protested.

"All right, all right," Carlos said mildly, waving a deprecating hand. "Though I do not see why the thought upsets you, Phyliss. To me it is natural that Ramon should have found someone; it is the way it should be. Ramon is a young man, a very handsome young man. If he has come upon a young woman who will give him solace, what is so wrong about it?"

"Nothing," Phyliss said, a slight edge to her voice. "Depending, perhaps, upon who she is. Do you know her?"

"I have seen her," the Legal Counselor admitted. "A couple of weeks ago she was in the cocktail lounge at the Shoreham with Ramon. She looked familiar to me. I think she works at one of the Scandinavian embassies. She is a very Nordic type, blond, very cool. The proverbial ice maiden. But if Ramon finds warmth in her . . ."

"You're impossible, Carlos," Phyliss said, but she said it lightly.

Carlos Smith smiled. "I notice women," he admitted. "When they are beautiful, I look at least twice at them."

"We all notice women," the Ambassador said smoothly. "Now, shall we go back to work? Conchita?" He circled the table and gently kissed Phyliss's cheek. "Till later, *querida*," he told her.

Phyliss reached for his hand and pressed it lightly. Obviously, Phyliss and Antonio Villanueva were devoted to each other, and Penny found herself slightly surprised by this. Phyliss was so totally English, the Ambassador so thoroughly Latin, despite his American education. They were a strange pair and yet a right one, and the certainty of this made her feel good. Perfect marriages were rare.

When the others had left them, Phyliss turned to Penny to ask, "More coffee, my dear?"

"No, thank you."

"Then," Phyliss said reluctantly, "I think we'd better get on with it, luv. I saw Mary just before I came down for lunch. She asked that we select one of Marita's dresses and bring it to her room. She'd like to have you try it on."

Phyliss said, "This lilac one would be lovely with your coloring. So would the turquoise, for that matter. Or the white."

The Ambassador's wife had flung the closet door open and was surveying the formal dresses that hung on the left side, lifting out one after another then returning them to their places after a brief inspection. Although she acted with her accustomed casualness, Penny suspected that Phyliss disliked this task as much as she herself did, and she asked suddenly, "Why, do you think?"

Phyliss turned to her. "Why?" she echoed.

"Why do you think Aunt Mary wants me to wear one of Marita's dresses? I was very fond of Marita. I suppose there's no reason why I should feel strange about this, but I do. It's . . . distasteful. I'd much prefer to go buy something of my own. Though, as I've told you, I shouldn't even be here for the reception!"

Phyliss nodded, and then said seriously, "I know we've no right to try to keep you here, Penny. You have a job to go back to, and I understand your concern about it. But I think there's a way to accomplish both things. If you'll permit me to do so, I'd like very much to make you a present of an airplane ticket to Boston. I know you came down here by bus, which is a long jaunt. But if you fly you can be back home in no time at all. Suppose I tell Mary that you really do have to leave Sunday morning. I'm afraid it's going to be difficult enough for her to accept that, but I think she'll be crushed if you don't attend the reception.''

Penny thought of her own "reception" at the embassy, and of the way Ramon had tried to turn her away entirely. Since then, their relationship had wavered between very hot and very cold, and right now Ramon seemed to be determined to keep things on the cool side.

She said slowly, ''I appreciate your offer, Phyliss, but it's really not necessary for you to buy me a plane ticket.''

''I know it's not necessary,'' Phyliss assured her, ''but it's something I'd like to do, and I hope you'll let me do it. We can drive you to the airport Sunday, and you'll be in Boston in an hour or so. Then you can take a local bus back to your hometown. But please, my dear, give us your time in the interim and plan to attend the reception Saturday night. And to please Mary, for whatever foolish reason, wear one of these dresses . . . even though I can well understand that it must make your skin crawl to even think of doing so.''

''It does,'' Penny admitted. ''I don't know why it should, but it does. Perhaps if I knew why Aunt Mary wanted me to do this, I wouldn't feel quite so squeamish about it.''

Phyliss said thoughtfully, ''To be honest with you, I don't think it would do a bit of good to ask her. I doubt very much that Mary would give you a straight answer. I've a feeling she thinks this is going to prove something, and I can't imagine what. But you and Marita are quite alike in build. You're about the same height, the same size. Marita's hair was much darker than yours, but even so . . .'' She paused, then after a moment said, ''You know . . . I think that's it! I think Mary wants to remind someone of Marita! I think she wants to make it seem as if Marita will be there haunting us at the reception!''

Phyliss shivered, momentarily shaken by her own

theorizing. But she quickly regained her composure and asked briskly, "Which is it to be? The turquoise, the lilac, or the white?"

"They're all lovely," Penny said unhappily. "I think I'd like the lilac one best, though."

It was a stunning dress, full-length, fashioned of chiffon that draped from the left shoulder in three tiers. The gathers were held by a beautiful gold-and-amethyst brooch, and the right shoulder was bare.

"It should be gorgeous on you," Phyliss conceded, "and I'm sure that Marita must have had earrings that will match that brooch. I'd say you should go for gold strappy sandals with it. At least we can go shopping for those tomorrow! Now, shall we get along to Mary's room?"

It was raining again as Phyliss and Penny went down the corridor to Mary de Villanueva's room. A dismal day, and Penny's spirits were as gray as the weather. But she obligingly slipped out of her skirt and blouse and donned the beautiful lilac dress, feeling her skin grow clammy as she did so. Still, she managed to camouflage her feelings and even to twirl around like a model in front of the two older women. Mary, lying back against her pillows, said, "It's perfect, my dear. It looks as if it were made especially for you."

This was true. The dress was stunning, and its beautiful flowing lines molded Penny's figure more perfectly than any garment she'd ever owned herself. But then, she'd never owned anything half this expensive.

The modeling over, she and Phyliss lingered to have tea with Mary. Then Penny admitted that she was tired and went back to the Rose Room to take a prescribed *siesta*. The rain was still beating down and there was a chill to the room, which seemed to her to be full of shadows. But even so, she fell asleep as soon as her head touched the pillow and awakened only when Elena came to tell her it was time to dress for dinner.

Conchita joined them at dinner that night, as did

Ramon, but it was the Ambassador who did most of the talking at the dining table. Even Phyliss seemed preoccupied.

Once again, Ramon left before the dessert was served, and as he left the room Conchita said in an undertone, "I wonder if Ray really has gotten involved with some Swedish or Norwegian girl!"

"Conchita," Phyliss reproved, "you're sounding as bad as Carlos Smith!"

"Well, he does seem to be especially busy," Conchita pointed out, and no one denied this.

They went upstairs to the library after dinner, and the Ambassador challenged Phyliss to a game of cribbage. Conchita, remembering that there was a good movie on at a neighborhood theater, suggested to Penny that they might go see it, and Penny was more than glad to accompany her. She badly needed to get out of the embassy, if only for a couple of hours.

Although Phyliss warned them that there were purse-snatchers operating in the vicinity of all the embassies, the two young women opted to walk to the theater, and their sortie was without incident. The movie was a comedy, light and entertaining. By the time they started back toward Massachusetts Avenue, Penny felt as if she'd been revitalized.

Conchita was a refreshing person to be with, too. She'd confessed that she was actually a very distant cousin of the Ambassador, "but Don Antonio shelters everyone with his family tree," she'd added laughingly. She had a bubbling personality, and she chatted freely about the Ambassador and Phyliss and members of the embassy staff in general. But although she'd brought up the subject of Ramon and a possible Scandinavian girl friend at the dinner table, she stayed away from it now. She also avoided discussing Marita or Mary de Villanueva, so although Penny had wanted to ask her if she'd known Marita well she decided to save this, and other questions, for a future time. She suspected that although Conchita was frank and fun loving, she could quickly be put on her guard.

Once again the rain had stopped, and the night air was cool and refreshing on their walk back to the embassy, although not completely free of the humidity that so often affects Washington. Conchita was also living at the embassy, but this, she said, was a temporary arrangement, for she'd decided to take an apartment with a couple of other girls.

"Uncle Tony is not too wild about the idea," she confessed. "Even though he is quite liberal, he still has some of the old-fashioned ideas about women. But I want to be on my own while I am here in Washington. Later, when I go back to my own country, I know it's going to be different. We're 'modernized' and all that, but not at all as emancipated as the general publicity about today's Latin women would have you think. Latin men are—Latin men!" Conchita concluded, just as they reached the embassy building.

Conchita had a key to the front door, and as they walked into the vast entrance foyer, she said, "It's spooky in here, isn't it? It gives me gooseflesh to come in here by myself late at night. There's something almost medieval about it. You half expect to see a ghost in old Spanish armor come clanking out of the shadows."

This was so exactly how she felt herself that Penny smiled appreciatively. "One of these nights, I expect I will!" she admitted.

"Believe me, you're not alone!"

They took the creaking elevator up to the top floor, said good night, and Penny reluctantly returned to the Rose Room.

Elena had switched on the bedside lamp for her and turned down the bedcovers. The lovely pink and rose colors blended warmly, invitingly, but Penny could not shake a sudden feeling of depression. Depression . . . and apprehension as well. A bad combination, she decided.

She undressed and slipped on a pale pink nightgown that had a matching robe. Now she wished that she'd thought to pick up a couple of books when she was in the library earlier that night so she'd have something to read. Briefly she gave thought to venturing down to the lower floor, but the idea wasn't at all attractive. Too many shadows to be dealt with on the way!

She tried to focus on the next day, when she and Phyliss had agreed to go shopping together for gold sandals. Chances were that Marita probably had at least one pair of sandals in the closet that would go well with the lilac dress, but Penny already knew from experience that they wouldn't fit her. Once, in college, Marita had wanted to borrow a pair of white shoes Penny had just bought, and they'd proved to be at least two sizes too big for her.

Thinking about the sandals, though, made her decide to take another look at the dress she'd be wearing to the reception. She knew now that there was no graceful way of getting out of attending the affair, even though she dreaded the whole thing.

She opened the closet door, completely unprepared for the sight that met her eyes. The lilac dress lay in a crumpled heap on the floor. Even before she lifted it, Penny could see that it had been horribly damaged. It had been slashed to shreds, deliberately and viciously slashed.

Shocked, she sank back onto the bed, holding the strips of ruined material between shaking fingers. The amethyst pin was still tucked into what had been one of the shoulder folds. Obviously, whoever had done this hadn't been interested in stealing a lovely piece of jewelry. No, this had plainly been an act of vengeance.

After a long time, Penny rolled the remains of the dress into a tight wad and thrust it into the farthest recesses of one of the closet shelves. But though she was able to put the dress out of sight, it proved impossible to put it out of mind. Nor could she stand to stay here, in that room, any longer.

On their tour of the embassy, Phyliss had shown her a small kitchen at the end of that floor and had told her to feel free to make use of it at any time. "It's perfect for midnight snacks," the Ambassador's wife had said with her usual blitheness. "It saves one from making a safari down to the nether regions or summoning help when all that is wanted is, perhaps, a cup of hot milk."

As she remembered this, the thought of a cup of hot milk began to seem infinitely appealing to Penny. She slipped on her robe, tying the matching sash around her waist, slid her feet into terry scuffs, and then started out on her trek, hoping that she'd be able to find the right corridor and the right door.

She was successful in both attempts, and she was smiling with satisfaction as she found herself confronting gleaming cabinets, a refrigerator, and a white enameled stove. But her pleasure was short-lived. She was no sooner over the threshold than she realized she was not alone.

Ramon was in the act of opening a box of crackers. On another occasion it might have amused her to see that he had set out a jar of peanut butter on the kitchen table—for such fare seemed so out of type for him—but right now it wasn't in the least funny.

She started to retreat hastily, then saw his hands appear to freeze in mid-air. He said, with grave politeness, "Señorita! Please don't leave!"

"No, that's all right," she said quickly, nearly tripping over her own feet in her haste to retreat.

He smiled disarmingly, then shook his head. "Penny," he said, and despite herself her heart lurched when she heard him pronounce her name, "you must have come here with a reason, no?"

He surprised her, because it seemed to her that his

accent was more marked than usual, and he seldom mixed up his English as he had just done.

"Do not let me . . . hamper you," he said, hesitating midway through the sentence to search for a word that might do. This, too, was unlike him. Then he added, *"Por Dios! La leche!"* And he went to rescue a pot of milk under which the burner had grown dangerously bright. "You see," he said wryly, "you surprised me even as I evidently surprised you. I was making *chocolate*." He gave the word a Spanish emphasis, pronouncing each syllable. "Will you join me?"

She was about to refuse, because the last thing in the world she could envision was sitting down at the small kitchen table to drink chocolate and eat peanut butter and crackers at midnight with Ramon Martinez. Then she realized to her astonishment that he actually seemed to want her to stay.

"Do you have enough for both of us?" she asked feebly.

Ramon shrugged. "One can always make more. Sit down, won't you?"

Penny sat down, but she felt that she should pinch herself to be sure that this was really happening. She watched as Ramon blended what appeared to be a mixture of finely grated chocolate and sugar into the hot milk, using a small wire whisk. Then he added a couple of fairly lavish dashes of cinnamon to the mixture, whipping it once again until it frothed.

"It is our way," he said as he passed her a cup brimful of hot liquid. "I hope you like it."

She tasted it and said honestly, "It's delicious."

"Gracias," he said with a smile. Then he added, "So, did you and Conchita enjoy the movie?"

"It was amusing," she admitted.

"Not X-rated?" he teased.

"No, it wasn't X-rated," Penny informed him rather tightly. "Look . . . does everyone around here know what everyone else is doing? How could you possibly have found out that I went to the movies with Conchita tonight?''

He laughed, and as she watched him Penny wished that she could encapsulate this moment and keep it with her forever. It was wonderful to see Ramon laugh, wonderful to see his eyes sparkle in a way that made them an even deeper sapphire in tone. He said, ''No, to answer your first question first. Everyone around here does not know what everyone else is doing. As for finding out about the movies, I came back here early and asked where you were.''

This surprised her so much that she was unable to comment on it.

''Among other things,'' he added, the smile faded and he was looking as serious as he usually did, ''I wanted to tell you that I am glad you have decided to stay here and attend the reception Saturday. Phyliss is right. It would be too bad for you to leave Washington without seeing this aspect of the diplomatic life.''

''Even though you don't like such things yourself?'' she ventured.

''Yes, even though I do not like such things,'' he agreed. ''I am . . . how would you say it? I am a hermit . . .''

She chuckled. ''I find that hard to believe.''

''And why would you find it hard to believe, Penny?''

There. She felt that lurch again.

''Because you . . .'' she began, and then she floundered, knowing that she couldn't possibly continue with what she'd been about to say to him. How could she tell him that it would be beyond anyone's belief to think that a handsome, plainly virile man like himself would choose to lead a life of isolation? She had no doubt that he must be viewed as a tremendously good catch in Washington; she could imagine the invitations he must receive to balls, debutante coming-out parties, all sorts of social events.

Ramon had gotten up to refill their cups with hot chocolate, and he put the empty pot in the sink as he surveyed her carefully. Then, with that same care, he crossed to the table and put down the two cups he was carrying. But he did not again sit down himself. Rather, he reached out to Penny, clasped one of her hands in his, and slowly, inexorably, drew her to her feet. Her chair slid back as she rose.

"Perhaps you should not tell me why you think I could not be a hermit," he suggested. "Perhaps I might be flattered to the point of conceit if I heard your reasons. Perhaps, again, I might not be flattered at all. As it is . . ."

He released her hand, but then his arms encircled her, and she felt his lips touch her forehead with a stirring gentleness. They moved on to linger on her mouth, and when her own lips parted his kiss became a claiming thing, sending a spiraling ribbon of desire twisting through Penny. It was impossible not to respond to him.

He said huskily, "*Querida,* I want you! I have wanted you since the moment you walked into my office. How can that only have been yesterday? *Vida,* I am dying of a hunger that only you can satisfy! Penny . . ."

She moistened her lips. "Come with me," she whispered, as if there were suddenly ears to hear them.

She sensed a brief instant of withdrawal, of indecision on his part, but then the man triumphed over the diplomat. He held her closely to his side as they made their way down the empty corridor, and it was not until they were in the Rose Room and had closed the door behind them that it occurred to Penny how awkward it would have been if they'd encountered someone on their way.

But even that didn't matter to her just now. Only Ramon mattered. Only Ramon and his sudden and wonderful nearness.

He untied the sash at her waist and slid the robe off her shoulders, tossing it lightly onto a nearby chair. Then he

stared at her as if mesmerized, and she knew that the
rose-shaded lamp at her back was revealing every outline
of her body beneath the sheer fabric of her nightgown.

He said, his voice even huskier than it had been before,
"You are so lovely, *querida*. So beautiful. I am not sure
that I deserve you, *vida de mi vida*."

She could barely manage a whisper. "You deserve
me," she told him, and she implicitly believed that this
was so.

He'd left his suit coat in the kitchen, and she watched
him fumble at the buttons on his shirt. Then, in a swift
moment, she went to help him, approaching him in a way
she'd never approached a man before, kissing him as she
unfastened each button until she'd come to his waist.

His belt was fastened with a wide, silver buckle, and
she found it impossible to undo it, she was trembling so.
Ramon took over and with one swift movement dispensed
with the rest of his clothing until he stood before her,
naked and proud. And he had reason for pride. He was an
Adonis of a man, perfectly formed; she had never seen
anything more beautiful.

He said gently, "You still have your nightdress on,
querida." But before she could touch the sheer fabric his
fingers had found it. He lifted the nightgown over her head
and then, as she stood revealed to him, said simply, "*Ay,
Dios!*"

They merged into each other's arms, kissing and
caressing, exploring until they knew every facet of what
had been unknown between them until now. They touched
the most secret places, restraint gone in the face of desire,
until they were intimately acquainted with each other's
body, ecstasy flooding them in waves as symbolic veil
after veil was removed to be cast aside. Finally they fell
onto the bed by mutual accord, Penny in such a state of
rapture, of anticipation, that she longed for him to take
possession of her. She positioned her body, ready to
receive him, her invitation so enticing that he gasped and

then, in that last instant, asked urgently, "*Querida*, you are sure? You are sure?"

Penny had never been more sure of anything. As Ramon filled her with his maleness, all the nuances of emotion and color and love and understanding that had escaped her until now blended with her frantic desire for him, and she moved with him toward a culmination that matched the sun, the moon, and the stars in glory.

In the aftermath of love she lay within the circle of his arms, suffused with a sense of being protected, of being beloved. He nestled his face against her hair, murmuring things to her in Spanish that she didn't understand but which she didn't need to understand. Then she closed her eyes and fell asleep, and there came a terrible moment when she awoke to find herself alone in the bed.

But he couldn't have stayed here. She accepted that, her logic prevailing. He had taken a tremendous chance in coming into her room in the first place.

Nevertheless, it was bleak without him. For a long time she lay peering through the darkness, and when she did drift back into sleep it was a restless sleep. In time it deepened and so, to her dismay, she finally overslept. It was ten o'clock when she awakened, and she quickly pushed the bell to summon Elena. The girl appeared so quickly that it seemed certain she must have been waiting right outside the door.

The maid laughed at her discomfiture and told her that she would bring coffee and toast. "Madame de Villanueva," she said, meaning Phyliss, "said that you were not to be disturbed. She felt that you needed to rest."

Remembering the predawn hours she'd shared with Ramon, Penny felt a pang of guilt, but it was short-lived. It was impossible to feel guilty for very long about an experience between Ramon and herself that would forever be golden in her memory . . . no matter what happened.

After she'd finished her coffee and toast, Penny went to the library and found it deserted. She discovered any

number of books that she'd like to read, settling finally for
an old copy of Daphne du Maurier's *Rebecca,* in which
she was soon engrossed. Despite its size, the library was a
comfortable room. Time passed quickly in it.

At noon, she stopped in briefly to see Mary de
Villanueva, who was sitting up in an armchair by the
window. To Penny's relief, Mary was willing to chat
casually. Marita was not mentioned.

As Penny was about to leave to go downstairs for lunch,
Mary said, "Phyliss has told me that you have to get back
to Wareham on Sunday, my dear. I'll accept that, but I
hope you'll consider coming to me for a long visit once
school is out. Not here," she added hastily. "Nor in Taos,
for that matter. I prefer a cooler summer climate, and I'm
thinking of renting a place in Carmel."

"That sounds terrific," Penny replied, which was true
enough. But despite the fact that a summer in Carmel with
Mary would indeed be something to look forward to, she
felt wary about committing herself to it. She was relieved
when, once again, Dr. Farrington arrived for what had
evidently become a daily visit, and so she could escape.

Chapter 7

PENNY WAITED UNTIL THE LAST POSSIBLE MINUTE TO GO down to the Gold Room for a glass of wine before the midday meal. She found the Ambassador and Phyliss there with Conchita and Ramon. Also present were two middle-aged doctors who were in Washington to visit the facilities at the National Institutes of Health in Bethesda, with the thought of augmenting various health programs in their own country.

The doctors spoke very little English, and so the Ambassador and Phyliss were obliged to converse with them in Spanish. Penny was placed between Conchita and Ramon at the dining table. And, although Conchita was her usual bubbly self, Ramon was distressingly silent, a virtual stranger. It would have been easy for Penny to have imagined their midnight rendezvous in her room . . . except that his kisses, his caresses, and their final glorious culmination had affected her so deeply that she was still very much shaken by them.

How could Ramon be so unmoved? She asked herself

this dolefully. Was he regretting last night? It hurt her to think that he might be. Maybe he really was a hermit at heart! Could a man be both a hermit and a wonderful lover?

For Penny, the tension mounted with each course, and it was a relief when a tall, red-haired young man burst into the dining room just as the dessert was about to be served. He grabbed Phyliss and kissed her soundly, and then bestowed a full measure of unabashed admiration on Penny as they were introduced.

This was Mario!

He was not handsome, but he was very attractive. His color was much like his mother's, and he had a sprinkling of freckles across the bridge of his nose, but he had his father's dark, eloquent eyes. He pulled an extra chair up to the table, placing it between Conchita and Penny. This, in turn, forced Ramon to move down the table a space, which he did rather dourly.

"Sorry, Ray, old man," Mario said affably, with more than a trace of his mother's British accent.

"Quite all right," Ramon rejoined stiffly.

Mario refused any lunch, but he did accept the huge helping of chocolate torte that Elena brought him. "Still trying to make me gain weight, eh?" he teased her as she set it before him.

She giggled and protested, "Oh, señor!"

Except for Ramon's definitely cold presence, the balance of the meal would have been pleasant, for Mario chatted easily with the two girls.

When lunch was over, Conchita and the men—except Mario—went back to the chancery, Conchita promising Phyliss that she would come upstairs later in the afternoon for a final check on the many details relevant to tomorrow's reception.

Then Phyliss asked, "Do you have any plans for the afternoon, Penny?"

Before she could answer, Mario interrupted to say,

"Yes, she does. Penny and I are going to play that game called 'Tourist.' I'm going to take her sightseeing."

"Really," Penny protested, "that's not necessary. You just got home, after all."

"I don't do things because they are necessary," Mario rejoined promptly, and his mother laughed.

"You can believe that!" she advised Penny.

"Very well, then," Penny said. "If you're sure you really want to go."

"I'm sure." Mario surveyed her feet. "Are your shoes comfortable?"

"Yes."

"Well, then, if you'll excuse me while I go change mine, we'll be off."

Penny was smiling as Mario left the room. But then she sobered, remembering that there was something she had to tell Phyliss. Something unpleasant.

Hesitantly, she broached the subject of the slashed dress and Phyliss's quick gasp betrayed her shock. "Who would do such a thing?" she demanded incredulously.

"I wish I knew!" Penny admitted.

"You must have been terrified when you found it," the older woman said. "I shudder to think of you alone in that room. You should have come and wakened me, Penny."

Penny had visions of pattering down the hall to the Ambassador's private bedroom and rousing Antonio Villanueva and his wife and she said, "The deed was done by then, Phyliss. There was nothing you or I could do about it. There isn't anything you and I can do about it. But . . ."

"Yes?"

"It seems to me," Penny said slowly, "that someone hates either Marita's memory . . . or me."

Phyliss considered this, her lips tightening. Then she said, "Why should anyone hate either you or Marita's memory? Good God, here in the embassy we've always been like a big family. And, for that matter, you, Ramon,

Conchita, Tony, and I are the only ones living here at the moment. Mario will be, of course, now that he's back.''

"What about Elena?" Penny asked, hating to pose the question.

"Elena has a room at the back of the third floor," Phyliss said. "She shares it with another maid, Dolores, whom you may have noticed around. Dolores works mainly on the second floor. Juan has a small apartment on the third floor, too. Our other help live outside the embassy."

Then Phyliss said abruptly, "It was ridiculous to put you in the Rose Room in the first place. I shouldn't have gone along with Mary's idea about that. Why don't we move your things to another room right now?"

Penny shook her head. "It would upset Aunt Mary," she said. "And that would be needless. After all, I'll only be here two more nights."

Mario, entering on this sentence, paused in the middle of the room and stared at her in consternation. "Did I hear you correctly?" he demanded.

"Yes. I have to go home on Sunday."

"Dios!" He clapped his hand to his forehead. "You might have told me, Mother. I thought she was going to be her all spring."

"Penny teaches school," Phyliss informed her son.

"Kids were never so lucky in my day," Mario said. He crooked an inviting arm. "We're wasting time," he told Penny. "My chariot awaits. Is the señorita ready?"

"Yes," she answered and took his arm, but hearing him say "señorita" reminded her of Ramon, and it was as if a shadow had suddenly fallen across the room.

Nevertheless, the afternoon with Mario was a delight. They did all the tourist things like going to the top of the Washington Monument, pausing in sudden awe before the massive statue of Lincoln in his Memorial, and then going on to pay tribute to Jefferson, too. They whirled through the Smithsonian, then rented a paddle boat with dual controls and paddled it furiously around the Tidal Basin.

On the way back to the embassy they stopped at a Hot Shoppe for frosted root beers, and Mario said, for the hundredth time, "To think all the while I've been in Boston you were only forty or so miles away, and I didn't even know it!"

He was outrageous. He made Penny feel totally desirable. She let herself bask in the light of his admiration, thoroughly enjoying it.

Mario drove a red Alfa Romeo, which suited him perfectly, and he weaved it expertly through the Massachusetts Avenue traffic. He swung into the circular driveway that flanked the embassy entrance, parked beneath the porte cochere, and then sat for a moment looking across at Penny, unexpectedly serious.

"Speaking of Boston," he said, "I'll be going back there myself before too long. This is just a respite for me. I'm more or less floundering around at the moment, taking some graduate courses at Boston College."

Penny smiled impishly. "Your mother says you're multi-talented."

"Is that the way she put it to you? She was a bit kinder than usual, if so. Penny . . . when I do get back to Boston I hope you and I can see a fair bit of each other. I enjoy being with you. In fact, I'd say we go well together, if this first experiment is any indication. Of course, in the old days I'd have latched onto a guitar and come serenading you beneath your bedroom window. But that's not quite my style."

"Mario!" she protested.

He grinned. "I'm a fast worker," he warned her.

"Obviously!" she agreed, unable to resist smiling at him in return. But then she said, more seriously, "It's not that I wouldn't like to see you, once we're both back in Massachusetts. But . . . ."

As if on cue the embassy door swung open and Ramon emerged through it.

He started visibly when he saw Mario and Penny, but then masked his surprise so competently that Penny wondered if she'd really seen the quick expression that crossed his face. An expression of displeasure, she'd say, mingled with . . . with what? A flash of jealousy?

Mario said affably, "Ray! Where are you heading?"

"I have a dinner engagement," Ramon said, his handsome face expressionless.

"You mean you won't be joining us around the family board tonight," Mario teased. "Okay, then there'll be all the more for me!"

It was a statement with a double meaning and, as if to underline this, Mario's eyes lingered on Penny. And she could feel herself flushing as Ramon merely surveyed her coldly.

"Can I offer you a ride?" Mario suggested to Ramon.

"Thank you, but my car is parked right around the corner."

"Very well, then. I've got to garage this one. I'll see you at dinner, Penny."

"Yes." She nodded and got out of the car, painfully aware of Ramon's eyes still upon her. Just now they looked as icy as the North Atlantic in winter. However, he said courteously, "I have a key. I will open the door for you."

"Thank you," she said, trying to be as formal about this as he was. Then, as he bent to insert the key in the lock, she noticed that his fingers were shaking ever so slightly.

The door swung open, the cavernous entrance foyer looming behind it. Penny started to pass Ramon with another perfunctory "Thank you," but his voice stopped her.

"Penny," he said.

She swallowed hard, wishing that there were a way to melt this man for once and all, so that she'd no longer have to face these unpredictable swings in his mood.

"I cannot help but wonder about you," he confessed. "Do you forget so quickly?"

"Forget?" she queried, managing to make the question a calm one even as a needle-sharp twinge of triumph shot through her. She knew very well what it was Ramon was referring to. He was as acutely aware of what had happened between them last night as she was!

"I know that Mario has a lot of charm and also that he is highly susceptible to lovely women. But even so . . ."

There was something about his tone that grated, and Penny's voice grew cold as she asked, "Yes?"

"Is it just instinct with American women to—what is the expression you use for this?—to play . . ."

"To play the field?" she finished for him.

"Yes, that is exactly it." He nodded. Once again his accent seemed more marked than usual, and Penny was beginning to recognize that this was something that happened when Ramon was ruffled emotionally.

She forced a smile. "You're suggesting that I'm playing the field?" she asked him coolly.

"I do not know what to suggest about you, Penny," he said, and then regardless of the fact that they were standing at the very entrance to the embassy he took her in his arms so suddenly that she could not move away from him quickly enough to avoid his embrace. His kiss was searing, demanding, and when he lifted his head again her lips felt bruised. She saw that his blue eyes had darkened, the ice gone. But his tone was steady as he murmured. "No, I do not know what to suggest about you. I do not know what to think of you. But I intend to find out!"

At dinner that evening Mario sat in Ramon's usual place. But even Mario seemed somewhat subdued, and it was a quiet gathering. Phyliss and Conchita were primarily concerned with details for the upcoming reception. The Ambassador was, as always, courteous and smiling, but tonight even he seemed remote. Dessert over, they went their separate ways, the Ambassador setting off to attend a meeting, while Phyliss and Conchita went upstairs to pore over the guest lists one more time.

Penny was left with Mario, who promptly suggested that they go and explore Washington's nightlife, but Penny shook her head.

"I promised Aunt Mary I'd look in on her," she said, "and I didn't sleep very well last night. If I'm going to be up to tomorrow night's festivities, I'd better get to bed early."

Walking down the corridor to Mary de Villanueva's room, Penny frowned, remembering the termination of her encounter that afternoon with Ramon. They had been interrupted by Juan; the butler had emerged noiselessly from the shadows as if he were a part of them, or they of him.

She wondered if he had seen Ramon kiss her and knew that he must have. This was disturbing. She was trying not to cast Juan as a sinister figure, but it was difficult. On the other hand, it would be far too easy to fasten suspicion on him, and she could not think why he should have gone into the closet in her room and slashed Marita's lilac ball gown.

This reminded her that she was going to have to tell Mary de Villanueva that she would not be wearing the lilac dress, and that was something she didn't look forward to doing. But she soon found that Phyliss had paved her way for her.

Mary was sitting in her armchair again, her eyes bright, her color definitely improved. "Penny," she said, "Phyliss tells me there was a spot on the lilac dress that none of us noticed."

Bless you, Phyliss, Penny thought, as she said aloud,

"Yes, that's so. I've tried on the white one, though, and I like it even better."

"Good. Did you find some sandals you like?"

Penny had forgotten all about shopping for shoes, and so, apparently, had Phyliss. She grinned wryly as she said, "No, I didn't. But then, I didn't try to. That's something I'll have to attend to in the morning. Mario wanted to take me sightseeing, and we spent hours doing all sorts of things . . ."

"An excursion that seems to have agreed with you," Mary de Villanueva said approvingly. "Nor do I blame you." She laughed. "Mario's outrageous," she said frankly, "but he's also delightful. As long as you don't take him too seriously, you'll be fine with him."

"My thoughts exactly," Penny agreed.

Mary sobered. "Penny, my dear," she said quietly, "I have another favor to ask of you. Especially since you're going to wear the white dress to the reception, will you also wear the rubies? They would go so beautifully with it."

"The rubies?" Penny queried.

"Marita's rubies," Mary de Villanueva said. "She inherited them when she was twenty-one. Didn't she ever mention them to you?"

"No, she didn't." It was beginning to appear that there were a number of things Marita had never mentioned to her, Penny thought.

"That was just like Marita," her mother said fondly. "She never really cared for material things. It used to worry me, to tell you the truth. She was such a champion of the underdog, and sad though it is, in a country like my husband's there are so many underdogs! Over the centuries, there have primarily been two classes, the very rich and the very poor. It is only recently that a middle class has begun to emerge. The extremes always bothered Marita."

Penny said slowly, "Marita used to speak, occasionally, of going on to medical school or of taking some special training so that she could go back to her own country and work with people who really needed help.''

Mary smiled. ''She talked to you about that, did she, and yet she didn't mention the rubies! That was typical of her. Well, my dear, the rubies are in the embassy safe, and I shall have Ramon get them out first thing in the morning.''

Penny hesitated. ''I wish you wouldn't ask me to wear them.'' She almost added, ''Or Marita's dress, either,'' but this was a favor to which she was already committed, and it seemed a small thing to do for Marita's mother. Wearing the rubies was something else again. ''They must be terribly valuable,'' she went on. ''To be honest, Aunt Mary, I don't want the responsibility of wearing them.''

''What responsibility?'' Mary asked impatiently.

''If I were to lose them, or if they were stolen, I could never replace them.''

''Surely you don't think I'd expect such a thing of you?''

Penny smiled. ''No, of course, I'm sure you wouldn't. But even so, I would feel terrible about it.''

''I appreciate that,'' Mary said equably. ''But, in any event, the loss would be your own.'' And, as Penny looked at her questioningly, she continued, ''Marita left her rubies to you. Apart from a formal will, she left a note asking that her executor—and I am her executor—make a few bequests. So you see, Penny, I have merely been keeping the rubies in trust for you. Now they will be yours.''

Penny was at a loss for words. But Mary de Villanueva, seemingly unaware of her discomfiture, went on talking. She was speaking about tomorrow's reception and how sure she was that Penny would enjoy it. Penny tried to focus on her words, but she found her thoughts straying.

It wasn't that she didn't appreciate Marita's gesture, she told herself. In fact, the gesture was so completely like

Marita that it would be impossible not to be touched by it. But to accept the rubies as a bequest would, in a quite literal sense, be playing into Ramon's hands in a way she didn't want to do. In the very beginning, he had cast her in the role of a fortune hunter, she thought despondently. Now this legacy from his dead fiancée only seemed to confirm his suspicions.

By dusk Saturday evening the embassy had been completely transformed. It was a true palace now, rich and glittering, the vast entrance foyer ablaze with lights from great overhead chandeliers that brought out the crimson in the rich carpeting that covered the reception area and extended on up the sweeping staircase.

The caterers had taken over and had draped the long tables that flanked the far wall of the dining room with snowy damask. Now they were bringing forth all sorts of magnificent molds and canapés and delicate pastries. Florists had converted the Gold Room and the ballroom into pastoral wonderlands. And, finally, the musicians arrived. As Penny went down the corridor toward Mary de Villanueva's room she could hear them tuning up, far below her.

Mary, taking Dr. Farrington's advice, had decided against attending the reception herself. She met Penny at the door wearing a vivid-blue caftan, and though she still looked fragile she was also lovely and appealing.

Penny had dreaded this particular encounter, even though she'd never before in her life looked as she did right now. Her mirror had told her that she was beautiful, garbed in Marita's white gown.

The full-length dress was made of heavy satin, with a gold-beaded edging. The bodice was tuxedo-style, and a gold sequined belt encircled Penny's slim waist. She and Phyliss had dashed out that morning, using one of the embassy limousines, and had found the perfect pair of high-heeled gold sandals to complement the dress. And though ordinarily Penny would have liked large, pearl jewelry to go with her costume, she knew that Mary de Villanueva had other plans for her.

Mary stood back, surveying Penny, and tears started to her eyes. "You look so beautiful, my dear," she whispered. "Except for the color of your hair, you could be Marita!"

A strange chill swept over Penny as she heard this. She felt as if she'd stumbled into a masquerade—and she had no concept of the role she was going to be expected to play. But she had the sudden conviction that this was a dangerous game . . . with life-and-death stakes!

She forced a smile, but it was unnecessary because Mary had already turned away and was taking a pale-blue leather case out of a dressing-table drawer. She approached Penny again, her eyes shining. "Here, my dear," she said. "Now these are yours!"

Penny opened the case with trembling fingers. Another Pandora's box! The thought came unbidden. But once she had raised the lid, she could not suppress a gasp. The rubies were beautiful! There was a pendant, a single, fiery stone surrounded by diamonds, and matching earrings. The jewels were dazzling, and Penny knew they must be very expensive. Yet, despite their beauty, she felt herself recoiling from them.

She cried, almost desperately, "Aunt Mary—you can't give these to me!"

Mary said serenely, "It is Marita who gave them to you, Penny. Here, try on the necklace."

She let Mary guide her to a mirror, and with icy fingers she fastened on the pendant and the earrings and then stared at her own reflection.

She looked nothing at all like Marita, she told herself impatiently. Yet she had the uncanny feeling that right now she was Marita, and that she was staring at Marita instead of herself! The necklace emphasized both the whiteness of her skin and the beautiful cut of the exquisite dress she was wearing. She'd never looked lovelier, that was certain, yet there was no satisfaction at all to be derived from this. When, finally, Conchita burst into the room—stunning, herself, in a yellow gown that perfectly suited her dark coloring—Penny felt as if she'd become rooted to the spot before the mirror, and she was convinced that it would be beyond her to go downstairs and face up to the evening that lay ahead.

But, after a long and tense moment, Conchita prodded her along. In that moment, Penny caught the expression on the Latin girl's face and knew that she'd been thoroughly shocked by this vision that was Marita yet not Marita.

Conchita spent a few minutes talking volubly to Mary de Villanueva. But then she said firmly, "We must go now. *Hasta luego,* Tía Mary," and she gripped Penny's arm with a firm hand, almost pulling her out of the room.

Once in the elevator, she turned to Penny and said, "This is incredible! I had not thought you were at all like Marita, but in that dress, wearing the rubies . . ." Conchita broke off and shook her head, then after a moment asked directly, "Why are you doing this, Penny?"

"Because Aunt Mary asked me to," Penny admitted. "She was so insistent about it I was afraid she might have a relapse if I refused her. Now I almost wish I'd taken that chance. I feel . . . miserable."

Conchita patted her arm consolingly. "Do not worry," she advised. "This is for one evening only, and so if it pleases Señora de Villanueva for you to do this, that must be for the good."

"Let's hope so," Penny muttered under her breath.

The receiving line had already formed at the top of the staircase. Beyond, the crystal chandeliers were dazzling in the Gold Room, and candles flickered throughout the great dining hall. In the ballroom the orchestra had begun to play a slow, romantic waltz that was perfectly in keeping with the mood that had been set.

Phyliss, gracious and lovely in gray chiffon, was smiling as she received her guests, shaking hand after hand as she said all the proper things an Ambassador's wife was supposed to say. Tony, at her side, was urbane and charming in his dinner jacket. Next to him, *Licenciado* Smith was standing with a woman who Penny presumed must be his wife, though she seemed an unlikely candidate. She was a dumpy little woman, wearing a floral-print dress that, unfortunately, was not at all becoming. But the *Licenciado* was especially handsome, his white hair gleaming like snowy satin.

Other members of the embassy staff, most of whom Penny had never met, filled out the line. Conchita nudged her toward it, and she whispered in protest, "Oh, no!" But there was no escape.

She shook Phyliss's hand as if they were being introduced for the first time, and Phyliss said, "You look smashing, luv," but Penny could see the shock, the look of real dismay, that flashed into Phyliss's eyes. Even Tony de Villanueva was shaken momentarily. He said, *"Dios!"* and closed his eyes, but then he opened them and smiled at her, giving her a hug and a fatherly kiss on the cheek. Then, with his face close to hers, he said so softly that no one else could hear him, "Take care, child." And, again, Penny felt that unpleasant little chill sweep over her.

Carlos Smith was unperturbed. He complimented Penny with his eyes, then introduced her to his wife, and Señora Smith said, stiffly, *"Mucho gusto."*

Penny went on to other handshakes and when, finally, she got to the end of the line, Mario was waiting for her.

He grinned down at her. "I thought you'd never make it," he told her, then added, "Didn't anyone ever tell you that it's a sin to be as beautiful as you are tonight?"

He didn't wait for an answer, whisking her first to the dining hall for a glass of champagne and then on to the ballroom. As they danced, Penny began to feel as if she were not at a masquerade, but as if she'd become immersed in a Cinderella world.

A Cinderella world. That would mean, wouldn't it, that eventually midnight would come, and that then this whole charade would be over? She could find no satisfactory answer to her question, and so she let the glamour of the moment possess her. Mario was an expert dancer and, although he'd been indulging in the champagne, neither his sense of balance nor his timing was affected. He swept her into the tempo of the music, and after a time she felt almost giddy. Then suddenly someone was standing beside them and Ramon was tapping Mario's shoulder and saying, formally, *"Con permiso."*

Mario released her with a reluctant smile. In the moment before they began to dance together she had the chance to really look at Ramon, and she was not at all prepared for the sight of him in formal clothes. Black suited him perfectly, for one thing, and so did the white shirt with its pleated front and small-winged collar and the narrow black bow tie, which had been fixed at exactly the right angle.

It was, indeed, a sin for any man to be as handsome as Ramon, she found herself thinking dizzily just as the music switched to a slow, sensuous, Latin beat.

Ramon started to dance with her, and she was mesmerized. Mario had been a very good dancer, but Ramon was superb. He danced with the dignity and the gravity that was so much a part of him, but there was also a sway to his hips, a provocative grace. As he led her through a series of intricate steps his movements were very, very sexy.

Penny responded to him like a moth being lured to a flame. And my wings will be singed, if I keep on letting him affect me like this, she warned herself. But even as she filed away this warning, she knew that she had very little choice in the matter. She'd never believed that a woman could be swept off her feet by a man, but that's what had happened to her.

She knew that he was watching her closely; she was sure that he could see the pulse throbbing at the base of her throat, just above the point where the ruby necklace encircled it. Reading her would be like reading an open book for him. And at that precise moment, she realized fully what he'd done to her. He'd not only possessed her, he'd devastated her! She had fallen totally in love with him!

This knowledge was so overwhelming that she looked directly into his eyes and then shrank back as if a wasp had stung her—because there was no love in their blue depths, not even a hint of desire. Right now, Ramon was looking at her as if he despised her!

With a short but savage gesture he pulled her closer to him and then snarled in her ear, "Why in hell are you wearing that dress? To say nothing of the rubies?"

Penny recoiled. She tried to pull herself away from him, but he held her so tightly that she couldn't move. And she hissed between her teeth, "I'm doing this because Aunt Mary wanted me to. If you don't believe me, ask her!"

His grip relaxed, but he didn't answer her. And when, finally, she glanced up at him she saw an expression of such sadness on his face that it made her catch her breath. His expression, as nothing else could have, brought home to her the fact that he had been about to marry Marita. Seeing her like this, in his dead fiancée's dress, must not only have been a shock but must have stirred up terrible memories for him, only adding to his pain. Momentarily, this made him seem very vulnerable to her. Ramon, she thought, had suffered too much. He'd lost his mother when he was very young, then his brother, then Marita. It was no wonder that there was a kind of permanent shadow that never quite lifted from the deep blue eyes that contrasted so startlingly with his handsome, Latin face.

Blue eyes. As she looked at Ramon, Penny became

aware that the orchestra was playing "Spanish Eyes," a song she'd always loved. If she remembered correctly, the lyrics began with something about blue Spanish eyes.

As she watched him, Ramon seemed literally to shake himself, as if he were trying to cast away memories, and Penny said gently, "I'm sorry. I'm so very sorry."

"Why?" he asked, seeming honestly perplexed.

"My wearing this dress and these jewels must bring back sad memories for you.

"No, no," he said impatiently, "you misunderstand me. It is not that you make me sad, Penny. It is rather that . . ." He shrugged. "This is not the time to go into it."

The orchestra switched to another tempo. Penny saw Mario approaching and was surprised when Ramon waved him off. But the silence between them became acute, and Penny had to break it. Finally she said the first silly thing that came to mind. "Are all of you Latins just naturally good dancers?" she asked him lightly.

He didn't even try to conceal the flash of anger, which, though brief, was surprisingly intense.

"All we Latins, eh?" he asked bitterly. "Do you always generalize?"

"You tend to generalize about American women," she reminded him.

"There, again, you are wrong," he said flatly.

The music ended. Mario came to claim her, and this time Ramon let her go. After that, a number of other men on the embassy staff asked her to dance, but Ramon did not approach her again. Occasionally she glimpsed him. But even when he was just across the room from her, he seemed to be miles away.

Chapter 8

IT WAS WELL AFTER MIDNIGHT BEFORE THE ORCHESTRA stopped playing and the reception came to an end. Penny, really feeling like Cinderella, wondered if she could ever again completely resume her own identity after that evening—an evening that would have been a magic one if only she and Ramon had not argued. He'd ignored her so completely after that single dance that she felt he might as well have slapped her in the face. The effect upon her had been very much the same. The pain of his rejection actually stung her.

After tonight, she told herself firmly, she must put Marita and Marita's gowns and Marita's rubies behind her. Tomorrow she'd be going back to Wareham. Monday she'd be back in school, teaching teenagers who weren't always eager to learn the basics of the English language. The time in the embassy would soon seem a fantasy. It had to, for the sake of her future peace of mind!

Penny also tried to tell herself that at least one good thing had come out of the evening. She'd done what Mary de Villanueva had asked her to do, and if that made Mary any happier the effort was worth it. She only wished she could understand why Mary had been so insistent about what had turned out to be an impersonation. More than one member of the embassy staff had been shocked when they'd seen her, though they had tried to camouflage their feelings. But Marita's ghost definitely had been present at the reception. And Penny was responsible for having brought it there.

Conchita had come back upstairs with her, as the last of the guests were saying their farewells to the Ambassador and Phyliss, and she'd lingered to ask, ''Did you enjoy yourself tonight?''

''Yes, it was fantastic,'' Penny had answered, which was true enough. And Conchita had seemed satisfied with her reply.

They chatted for a few minutes and then, yawning, Conchita left her. Once by herself, Penny immediately took off the ruby earrings and the necklace, then remembered that the blue case in which they were kept was still in Mary de Villanueva's room, and it was much too late to go and get it.

She was tempted to seek out Ramon and ask him to return the jewels to the embassy safe. But she was sure that he would consider such a request a very obvious ploy, and after his behavior tonight she was damned if she was going to give him the satisfaction of thinking she was seeking him out—much as she yearned to do exactly that!

She stood with the jewels in her hands, looking around the room helplessly. There really were no good hiding places. Finally she put the rubies in a zippered compartment in her own handbag. Probably the first place a thief would look, she thought ruefully, but she couldn't think of a better one.

She slipped out of the beautiful white dress and put it back on its hanger, then returned it to the closet. And then she really did feel like Cinderella. The coach had been

turned back into a pumpkin, and there was no Prince
Charming who'd come searching for her with a glass
slipper.

Once in bed, Penny found it impossible to get to sleep.
Moonlight splashed through the tall windows, and the
shadows were a study in contrasts, ranging from pale
silver to ebony. There seemed a hush in the air, an aura of
expectancy, and Penny's ears became so attuned to the
silence that she heard the footsteps in the corridor outside
her room even before the knock came—a single, sharp
knock.

Ramon! She told herself that it must be Ramon, and all
the resolutions she'd been making dissolved, leaving not
even a mote of dust behind them. For a moment, she
couldn't move, thinking about him standing out in the
corridor, probably still dressed in those formal clothes that
made him even more devastatingly handsome than usual.
She told herself, a catch in her throat, that she'd been
wrong about Prince Charming. Her Prince Charming was
waiting for her, right outside this room!

She didn't bother to put on her robe. Barefoot, she
pattered across to the door, then cautiously drew it open,
ready to admit him and to close it quickly, so that he
would not be apt to be seen. But Ramon wasn't there.

There was a night-light in the corridor, a dim light, but
it still gave enough illumination so that Penny immediately saw the piece of white notepaper, folded in half, that lay
just outside the door.

She picked it up, curious. Was Ramon playing some
sort of Latin game with her? Was this a modern counterpart of the serenade? Was he, perhaps, going to suggest
that this time she come to his room?

Penny took the piece of paper back into her room,
closed the door behind her, and switched on the bedlamp.
Unfolding the paper, she saw that a few words had been
printed across its surface. They looked as if they'd been

done with a marking pencil. *"Querida,"* she read, "come down to the garden."

Querida. Ramon had called her this Spanish term of endearment not once but many times. Yet even so, the note was simply not Ramon's style. She sat down on the edge of the bed, puzzling over this, wondering next if this were the sort of caper that might appeal to Mario. Would he be apt to suggest a predawn rendezvous in the little garden in back of the embassy?

Penny doubted it. Mario was too forthright. If he'd wanted to take her down into the garden he would have come to her room and gotten her, without resorting to this sort of subterfuge. And, concluding this, a smile twisted her lips. Maybe all the things she'd heard about Latins were true! Maybe one of the men she'd danced with that night had thought up this little intrigue. Everyone she'd danced with had said outrageously flattering things to her. There was a chance that one of her dance partners had decided to take matters a step further!

Penny switched out the bedlamp, then stood up and slowly moved across to the window. And there below her, in the little garden, she saw a man. His features were shadowed as he stood near the bordering edge of cedars, so that she could not see him clearly. Then a fleeting ray of moonlight brushed his dark hair with silver, and all at once she was sure that it really was Ramon after all!

As she stood in the window, her figure was also revealed by a shaft of moonlight. This she realized as her visitor raised an arm and beckoned. And Penny, before she realized what she was doing, nodded back a vigorous affirmative.

She quickly donned a pair of jeans and a cotton knit top, thrust her feet into her terry scuffs, and let herself out into the corridor, quietly closing the door behind her.

She'd not ventured into the elevator alone before, and she didn't relish doing so now. Since the first time she'd ridden up with Mary de Villanueva she'd disliked it, perhaps because Mary had so plainly mistrusted it herself. She thought of using the staircase, but she would have to walk down three long, curving flights, and they were very dimly lighted at that hour. Penny had no desire to risk a fall, nor could she imagine navigating them soundlessly. This left the elevator as her better choice, and so she opened the door to it, stepped in, and pressed the button marked one.

The elevator started to descend slowly, creaking and grinding every inch of the way. Penny tried to convince herself she was imagining that it was vibrating more than usual. Then suddenly it lurched and, to her horror, began to gain momentum. She frantically pushed buttons and heard a bell ringing as the car plunged downward, and she knew she was going to crash.

A distant voice seemed to be coming closer. "She's a very fortunate young lady," the voice said. "Twisted her ankle, and I'd say she's bruised her ribs. But I doubt she's broken any of them."

Penny opened her eyes to see Dr. Farrington bending over her. Then, slowly, she focused on the faces that made a montage in back of him. The Ambassador, Phyliss, Conchita . . . and Ramon.

She saw flowered curtains at the window and put things together enough to know that she was lying on the couch in the Ambassador's sitting room. Rallying what strength she could summon, she tried to sit up, only to be pushed back against the pillows gently but firmly by Dr. Farrington.

"Not so fast, young lady," he cautioned her. "We may have a slight concussion to deal with. We don't want you moving around just yet."

Weakly, Penny obeyed him, primarily because she had no alternative. Her head throbbed, and the mere act of trying to sit up had made her feel nauseous. Then, as she leaned back, her eyes swept directly to Ramon's face as if they'd been directed there, and she was startled by his expression. He was pale, and his blue eyes were almost unfocused with a pain that made her wince, and this only made her the more aware of some of her own aches and pains. But she wondered why Ramon should be so . . . so distraught. This was one incident he'd had nothing to do with.

By way of explanation, she said very slowly, "It was the elevator. There's something wrong with it." And then she shuddered, the horror of that moment when the elevator had begun to careen downward returning with a clarity that was sickening.

Phyliss said gently, "We know, luv. I've always hated that damned elevator. I've said it was a death trap. Tony, I told you . . ."

The Ambassador, looking more than a little distraught himself, said, "Yes, *querida,* you did, and you were right. Juan should have warned me further about it, of course. It is his function to take care of such things. Yet, principally, I have myself to blame. As you know, I seldom use the elevator myself. I prefer the exercise the stairs give me. But even so . . ."

The doctor was packing his instruments into his worn black-leather bag. He said, "I suggest that one of you men carry our patient back to her own room. I'd prefer she doesn't do much walking for the next few hours. I'll be back to check on you around noon, Miss Baldwin, when I come to see Mrs. Villanueva. You're bound to feel some aches and pains, but I'm sure there's nothing too serious for us to worry about. Just a few precautions . . ."

Penny managed a feeble, "Thank you, doctor."

"I will see you out, doctor," Antonio de Villanueva said, but the physician shook his head.

"That's quite all right," he told the Ambassador. "I know my way."

"You will have to take the stairs, of course."

Dr. Farrington smiled rather grimly. "I can use the exercise," he conceded.

"Conchita," Phyliss said, once the doctor had departed, "why don't you go on back to bed? You won't be fit for anything tomorrow. It's a good thing it's Sunday."

"Are you sure I can't do something to help Penny?" Conchita asked.

"No," Phyliss said. "Not now. Penny will probably want your company tomorrow, but right now she needs to rest."

The Ambassador had elected to walk as far as the staircase with the doctor. Conchita left, and so there were only the three of them still in the room—Phyliss, Ramon, and Penny.

Phyliss said, "Trust Mario to sleep through this whole thing! He'll be furious when we tell him about it. Ray, you might as well run along too. Tony can carry Penny back to her room."

Penny saw Ramon swallow hard, his handsome face twisting with an emotion she couldn't define. Then he said, politely but firmly, "No. I will take Penny myself, madame."

As he spoke, he moved toward the couch, walking awkwardly, for Ramon. He was so visibly upset, in fact, that again she was puzzled. True, it was Ramon who had lured her to go downstairs, she reasoned. But even so, he had no reason to blame himself because the elevator had been faulty.

Phyliss said, "I shall get back to bed myself, then. This has been a long night! Be gentle with her, Ramon." To Penny she said, "I'll see you in the morning, luv."

Ramon nodded to the Ambassador's wife, but he didn't speak. His arms were infinitely gentle as he lifted Penny into them and carried her down the hall toward the Rose Room. Despite her growing fatigue—the deep fatigue that follows in the wake of trauma—she wished that this were a journey that could continue forever. As she rested her head against Ramon's strong, muscular shoulder she was—incredibly—totally happy, for the moment. But even in her present state, she was only too well aware that it was a happiness that couldn't last.

Still, it was exciting, provocative, to fantasize about how marvelous it would be if she could simply stay within the circle of Ramon's arms forever. When he lowered her carefully onto her bed and then asked, abruptly, "Where is your nightdress?" she was startled, taken aback, not by his words but by the oddly irate way in which he'd posed the question. And now he added angrily, "Don't be needlessly modest with me, Penny. Where do you keep your nightdress?"

She'd had no intention of being "needlessly modest." He knew what she looked like, after all . . . he knew what every inch of her looked like! As the memory of his pleasure in her during that midnight time they'd shared came back to her, her cheeks flamed.

She said meekly, "My nightgown's hanging just inside the door of the closet to the right. But before you get it, will you look in my handbag, please, and be sure the rubies are still there? It's on the closet shelf."

He frowned. "To hell with the rubies!" he said roughly. "Before I look at anything else, I want to get you into bed."

He found her nightgown, a lovely silken thing that fused varying shadows of green together, from emerald to pale lime. Then he gently eased her cotton top over her head and slipped off her jeans and her panties, and she marveled at the feathery lightness of his touch. She stole a glance at him and saw that his face was expressionless. He was intent on the task at hand as he helped her into the nightgown, raising her slightly until he'd smoothed it out below her hips. Then he lifted her, still with that exquisitely gentle touch, so that he could pull the bedclothes down to a point where she could slide beneath them.

Dr. Farrington was right. The aches and pains were

beginning, and they were far more intense and assorted than anything Penny had ever experienced before. Nevertheless, the comfortable bed felt very good to her, and having Ramon so near felt even better. Suddenly she knew that above all else she didn't want him to leave her tonight, even though, she conceded ruefully, she was in no shape for a night of passion.

He switched on the pink-shaded table lamp, and there was a rosy glow to its light that, touching his face, made his eyes seem like embers. Slowly, carefully, he sat down on the side of the bed, then asked, "I am not hurting you, am I?"

She started to shake her head, only to find quickly that it was not a wise move. So she said, "No. Not at all." Even if he were hurting her, she wouldn't want him to get up again.

Then she looked at him more closely and saw that his face was taut and his manner so intent that she felt a pang of alarm. Ramon was wound tight as a watch spring right now, and she sensed that he was exercising tremendous control over himself, over his own emotions.

"Penny," he said, "the doctor left some sleeping pills for you and I will give them to you in just a minute. But there is something I must ask you first. Why were you leaving the embassy at such an hour?"

"But I wasn't leaving the embassy," Penny protested. "I was going down to the garden."

"The garden?" She shrank back as he posed the question, for his face had become a mask of fury. "Why, in God's name, were you going down to the garden?" he demanded. "What sort of a rendezvous had you arranged?"

She couldn't believe this. She said, "You know very well that I was going down there to meet you. That's what you asked me to do in your note."

"My note?" He looked totally perplexed. "What note? What in hell are you talking about?"

"You brought a note to my door asking me to come meet you in the garden," she told him.

He stared down at her scornfully and said, "I do not play silly little games, Penny. *Dios,* why would I send you a stupid note to try and arrange—what would you call it?—a tryst with you?"

And this was true. "You're right," she agreed, "I should have realized that you never play little games. You're much too deadly to indulge in such frivolities as a midnight meeting by Cupid's statue, aren't you?" She spoke bitterly because she was feeling that she'd made a fool of herself by her actions tonight. Thus, she was completely unprepared for Ramon's reaction.

He glared at her. "So, they've told you about me, is that it? Is that why you are cringing from me? Have you grown afraid of me, Penny? Is that it?"

She drew back from him, hurting physically and confused mentally as she stared at him. "I don't even know what you're talking about," she mumbled.

"No?" he demanded. And then he said bleakly, "Don't lie to me, Penny. I am sure that by now either Tía Mary or Phyliss or Mario or Conchita, or even the Ambassador himself, has told you that I bring catastrophe to those close to me. I am sure that they have told you I was responsible for my own brother's death!"

"No," she said in little more than a whisper. "No. No one has told me that!"

"How kind of them!" he said bitterly. "How discreet!"

Looking at him, Penny forgot her own physical pain in the face of the terrible hurt she saw in his eyes. She yearned to reach out to him, to draw his dark head close to her, and to run her fingers through that wonderfully thick, raven hair as she tried to console him.

Could she console him? She had to admit that she was not at all sure, and this was an agonizing confession to make to herself, because she wanted so desperately to help him. It took very little intuition to know that just now Ramon Martinez was struggling through some very deep waters. Deep and dark waters, with, she suspected, little if anything at all to light his way.

Seldom had she felt so helpless. She could not even be a consolation to Ramon physically tonight, she thought sadly, and she would have given a great deal to be able to offer herself to him at that moment, to open herself to him like a flower.

Finally she compromised by reaching out a hand that was more imploring than she realized, and she touched Ramon's knee. He started as if she'd struck him, fighting to mask the torment on his face as he turned to her.

"What is it, Penny?" he demanded wearily.

"Aunt Mary told me that your brother had died," she confessed. "She said that he'd been engaged to Marita. But that's all she said, Ramon. That's all anyone's said."

"Yes, Roberto was engaged to Marita," Ramon said wearily. "I still wonder why you never knew about this . . . about a lot of things that involved Marita. She was more secretive than I realized."

"I think she led two lives," Penny ventured.

"And what is that supposed to mean?"

"I think that when she was here in the States, in college, she acted like an American girl. When she was in her own country she was different, she did tell me that. I gathered that she was required to be much more circumspect."

He laughed shortly. "Circumspect? Is that the word for it? What you are saying is that when Marita was in college with you she ran wild, *verdad?*"

"Not wild, exactly . . ."

"Penny, you do not need to dissemble with me. It does not become you," he said. "Regardless, you are correct to a point. When Marita was at home, she was expected to maintain a certain standard of conduct, that is true. But she was very young when she and Roberto became compromised to each other.'' He broke off and shook his head. ''I am sorry,'' he said then. ''That was a bad translation. In Spanish, *comprometido* means to be engaged. In English, it is of course something entirely different.''

He paused, and Penny wished that she could read his mind, translate his thoughts so that she could understand them. Then he said, ''Roberto was four years younger than I, so only three years older than Marita. Although their engagement had long been an understood thing between our families, it was not formally announced until Marita came home after graduating from college. At that time, my father had died, and I was entrusted with the management of his estate. It took up a great deal of my time, and so I did not keep an eye on Roberto as I know now that I should have. He was twenty-five; I suppose I felt he was old enough to have some sense. But you see . . . in many ways he was like Marita. He, too, wanted to run wild. And he did.

''When I found out about some of the things he was doing, I confronted him. This was late one evening, in the library of our hacienda. He had come to see me, as it happened. He wanted money. Roberto usually did want money. I realized too late that not only had he been drinking but that very possibly he was high on drugs as well, or I would not have argued with him as I did. I would not have said the things to him I did. I would have postponed a showdown between us until the next day.

''As it was, I told him that he could get the hell out of our house. I told him that as far as I was concerned he was disinherited and that, for a variety of reasons, he had no right to marry Marita. He accused me of loving her myself; he said I'd always been jealous of him. I finally became so furious with him that I knew if I stayed with him I would do something I would regret, so I left him with the parting statement that I was going to the police about him . . . something I would never have done. Even now I feel he should have known that.

"If I had gone to the police, there would have been a scandal that would have rocked our country, because Roberto and some of his colleagues had become involved in a very dangerous game. An international game. I had suspected this, and that night, after talking to him, I was sure of it. But I did not realize that he would . . . die for his cause. I was walking out into the inner patio beyond the library when I heard a shot. I ran back, and he was already on the floor, the gun beside him. He'd fallen with it still clutched in his hand. I went to him, I knelt beside him, and I knew at once that he was dead. I must have cried out for help, though I don't remember doing so. The servants came, and they found me kneeling there, holding the gun by then . . .''

Stark misery contorted Ramon's face, but he managed to say caustically, "This does not surprise you, I suppose. After all, we Latins are noted for our violence, are we not?"

Weak though she was, torn though she was by this terrible story he'd just told her, Penny rallied, and her voice rang out with surprising authority. "Don't talk to me like that!" she commanded.

He had the grace to look ashamed. And, after a moment, he said quietly, "Forgive me. I should not have burdened you at a time like this with the story of my past."

"I think you know you haven't burdened me," she said levelly. "And . . . I want to hear the rest of it. What happened, Ramon?"

"What happened?"

"Yes. What happened when you were found with the gun in your hand?"

He said, his voice very tight, "At first some thought that I had shot Roberto. Even when it was proven that his wound had been self-inflicted, the rumor did not die, not. for a long while. Even today, I am sure there are those who consider me a murderer.''

"Ramon!"

"You asked me, Penny. Even Marita, for a time, suspected me. But Marita was having her own problems. Finally I convinced her that the sane thing would be for us to marry. Then . . .''

Abruptly, he stood up. "I have inflicted too much on you," he said. "You should have taken the sleeping pills long before now.''

"Ramon!"

"No, Penny, do not protest. I am going to get you a glass of water, and then you can take the pills and . . .''

"Ramon," she interrupted softly, "it was you out there in the garden, wasn't it?''

"That again?" he demanded caustically.

Penny forced herself to stay calm. "There's a note in the top drawer of the dresser," she told him. "Get it and read it, will you please?''

He glanced at her curiously and then shrugged, as if this could not possibly be a matter of any importance. But once he'd taken the note out of the drawer, once he'd read it, his attitude changed.

"Where did you get this?" he demanded.

"Someone knocked at my door after I'd gone to bed," she told him. "I found this note lying on the floor outside. After I'd read it, I went over to the window. I could see a man standing in the shadows, down there in the garden, and I was sure it was you.''

"Why?"

"I recognized your hair.''

"My hair?"

"He had very dark hair.''

He shook his head. "Dark hair, so it must be me, eh?" he asked. "You are incredible! You generalize about Latins when you should be specific. But when you come

upon something you could logically generalize about, you
become specific instead. Good God! Most of the men on
the embassy staff have dark hair!''

''Not the ones I know,'' she persisted. ''Mario has red
hair. The Ambassador is getting rather bald. *Licenciado*
Smith has the whitest hair I've ever seen. I don't know
any of the others on the staff that well. Of course, there's
Juan—he has black hair, but I'd say this man was taller
than Juan. And he was not . . . misshapen.''

''So,'' Ramon finished for her, ''it had to be me!''

''I didn't say it had to be. I said I thought it was.
Otherwise, I certainly would not have considered going
down there . . .''

Unexpectedly he grinned and, although his face was
still darkly etched with the shadows of worry and fatigue,
the smile lightened it, and Penny gasped at the impact of
his charm. He said almost lightly, ''You flatter me,
señorita.'' Then, instantly, he sobered. ''I intend to find
out who was responsible for this note,'' he told her,
waving the piece of paper that he still held in his hand. ''I
have a suspicion that it was one of the susceptible young
men on our staff. We have two or three bachelors here at
the moment who tend to behave like lovesick calves if
given the slightest opportunity. Possibly someone you
danced with tonight . . .''

He broke off abruptly. ''We have disobeyed the doctor's orders long enough,'' he told her. ''Now you must
take the pills, so that you will rest well.'' He held the
water for her, treating her gently, carefully . . . as if she
were a child. But although she loved his ministrations,
Penny did not want to be treated like a child by him.

Then he said, ''My room is second to the right. You
should not walk unless it is absolutely necessary. But if it
becomes absolutely necessary, if you need me, come to
my door and knock.''

She wanted to tell him that she already needed him, that
she was going to need him forever, but she knew that he

was in no mood to pay serious attention to such a statement from her. Not tonight. He leaned over her, and she held her face up to him like a child waiting to be rewarded.

His kiss was tender, gentle, and exquisitely sweet. Long after he'd left her Penny could feel it on her lips, where it lingered to become part of a night of dreams in which Ramon was sometimes the hero but at other times—to her subconscious distress—the villain.

Chapter 9

PENNY WAS STIFF AND SORE WHEN SHE AWAKENED Sunday morning. Her ankle throbbed painfully, her ribs hurt, and her head ached. She struggled out of bed and made it as far as the bathroom and back, but that was more than enough of an excursion. As she slid back into bed, gratefully propping her foot up on an extra pillow, she knew there was no way she could possibly make the trip to Wareham that day.

For one thing, it would be impossible for her to navigate three long flight of stairs, and that was the only exit route from the embassy. Even if by some miracle she was able to manage this, even if a couple of the embassy staff could be persuaded to carry her down the stairs and she could then arrange to be whisked to the airport in a diplomatic limousine, there would be the matter of coping with transportation once she was in Boston, and she knew she'd never be able to handle getting into the city itself from Logan airport and then taking a bus to Wareham.

The thought of staying on in the embassy gave her

mixed feelings. Common sense told her she shouldn't linger in a world where she didn't belong. On the other hand, there was so much still unexplained, especially after last night.

Who was the man who had tried to lure her down into the garden, and why had he wanted her to meet him there in the moonlight? She discounted Ramon's theory that one of the embassy staff may have taken a sudden fancy to her to the extent of trying for a post-midnight rendezvous. It didn't make sense. The diplomats in the embassy were sophisticated men of the world, experienced. Despite what Ramon had suggested, she could not envision any of the men she'd met at the ball last night playing the sudden role of a lovesick swain.

Also, it had taken effort to get up to the fourth floor, sneak down the corridor, leave the note outside her door, and escape without being seen. Considerable effort, and risk as well, she decided as she thought about it. Why would someone want to make such an effort?

There had to be a strong motivation, and the more she thought about it the more she concluded that this motivation, whatever it was, had very little to do with romance. No, someone had wanted her to go back downstairs last night for something else. Someone had wanted her to take the elevator and . . .

She sat up in bed, wincing from the pain that attacked her as she did so. Because the elevator had seemed so unreliable ever since she'd been in the embassy, it had not occurred to her until now that what had happened to her in it could have been anything other than an accident. But now she wondered if someone—the man with dark hair who'd been waving to her there in the garden?—had deliberately tampered with the elevator's mechanism. It was a chilling thought.

Penny shrank back against the bed pillows, conscious that her heart was beating violently, thumping against her chest. Who would want to do such a thing to her? Even more important, *why* would anyone want to arrange an "accident" in which she could have been killed? Or, at the least, injured far more seriously than she had been. She'd gotten into a jazz aerobic dancing class recently, and because of that training, she'd automatically relaxed instead of tensing as most people might have done, when she'd known the elevator was going to crash. Had her body been tensed at that moment of impact, she could have been hurt—severely. As it was, she'd been lucky. Very, very lucky.

Shaken, she pushed the bell that would summon Elena, and once again the girl appeared so promptly that it seemed she'd been waiting right outside.

"I am so sorry about what happened to you, señorita," she said immediately. "What a terrible thing! *Dios!* You could have been . . ."

Elena had been about to say "killed," Penny knew, but she bit back the word at the last instant and, with a wonderful lack of self-consciousness, crossed herself solemnly. "We are most glad that you will soon be all right," she said. "Señor Martinez says that you are not to get out of bed this morning, and he also told me that I must bring you a nourishing breakfast," Elena told her. Penny wondered how it had happened that Ramon had taken it upon himself to assume authority in this particular department. "You would like an omelet, yes? And perhaps a croissant with some jam?"

"Not too much, please, Elena," Penny pleaded. "I really don't have much appetite. What I want more than anything else is a cup of coffee."

"And you will have that in an instant," Elena promised.

It took a bit more than an instant, but very shortly Penny was sipping her coffee, and the brew had never seemed more delicious to her. She felt as if her senses had been sharpened. She was conscious of the warm golden quality of the sunlight streaming through her windows, and of the lovely shades of pink to deep rose in which the room was decorated. She was aware of the softness of the blanket covering her legs and of the downy comfort of the pillows under her head. It was a sybaritic feeling, all of this, and she found herself luxuriating in it, glad, very glad, that she was alive. Was this the reaction of everyone who'd had a brush with death? She wondered about that and was convinced that last night, that was exactly what she'd had. A brush with death.

She became desperately anxious to talk to someone about last night, about the note, about the elevator, about the man in the garden. But her choice of confidantes was limited. Though she could not have said why, these were subjects she didn't want to get into with either Phyliss or Conchita, and certainly not with Mary de Villanueva. That left the Ambassador, Mario, and Ramon. She ruled out Mario immediately. She could talk to the Ambassador, she supposed; she could voice her suspicions to him. But the person she really wanted to talk to was Ramon. Yet she knew that, even if the chance came for her to be alone with him, she'd hesitate when it came to being frank with him about these particular subjects.

Why? This Penny asked herself and was almost afraid to answer her own question. She didn't want to believe that the man in the garden might have been Ramon after all, despite his denials.

Elena came back to get her breakfast tray, and she was holding a beautiful arrangement of pink roses in a milk-glass bowl. Beaming, she said, "These have just come from the florist for you, señorita."

Penny reached eagerly for the small white envelope attached to the bouquet, certain that the flowers must be from Ramon. But she was wrong. The card read, "At least now you'll have to stay with us for a while longer, and that will give me a chance to get to know you much, much better." And, in a flourishing hand, it was signed, "Mario."

She fought back a sharp sense of disappointment as she enthused about the flowers for Elena's benefit and agreed to have them placed in the center of the dressing table, where they'd be plainly visible from the bed.

"Señor Mario wants to come and see you as soon as you wish to receive visitors," Elena told her, making Penny suspect that the maid had known all along who'd sent her the flowers. "Also Señorita Conchita, Don Antonio, and Doña Phyliss. And Doña Mary as well. They have entrusted me to inform them when you wish to see them. They do not want to disturb your rest."

Elena had not mentioned Ramon, Penny realized dismally. Evidently he'd not added his name to her list of future visitors, and she found this hard to understand. Last night he'd been so gentle with her. So tender, so loving . . .

"I think I will try to go back to sleep for a while," she told Elena, principally because she didn't want to see any of the others right now, much as she liked all of them.

The maid nodded approval. "I will draw the window-shades so it will not be too bright in here," she told Penny. And she promptly proceeded to do so.

Left alone, Penny lay back against the pillows and stared into space. She felt tired. Tired and dispirited. She knew that this was because it was after ten o'clock in the morning and she had heard nothing from Ramon. She managed to turn onto her side and to ease herself into a comfortable position, and after a time she dozed. It was a light sleep, but it was dream filled. In her dreams, a dark-haired man was standing in a moonlit garden, and he was serenading her with his guitar. He was playing "Spanish Eyes." When he looked up at her, she saw that he had Spanish eyes himself. Blue Spanish eyes.

At noon, Dr. Farrington stopped by. He'd bound Penny's ankle with an elastic bandage the night before, which he now removed. After a careful survey, however, he rebound the ankle, then said cheerily, "You're doing fine. I want you to stay off that foot as much as possible for the next few days, though. When you do walk, I'd advise that you use a cane and keep your weight off the ankle as much as possible." He stood. "Well, now," he said, "I'll be on my way to see Mrs. Villanueva." He seemed to enjoy having two patients in the embassy.

Elena brought Penny a delicious lunch of chicken salad, hot rolls, and a delicate caramel custard. Despite her lagging appetite, she managed to eat most of it. She knew that she couldn't stave off her would-be visitors much longer after that, and with Elena's help she brushed her hair and touched her lips with gloss, and then announced to the maid that she was ready to receive anyone who wanted to see her.

During the balance of the afternoon, they all came to see her: Phyliss, Mary, Mario, Conchita, and the Ambassador himself. Ramon remained conspicuously absent.

Phyliss had brought her a cane, unearthed from a closet somewhere within the recesses of the embassy. "If you look hard enough and far enough, you can find just about anything right on the premises," Phyliss had said airily.

Late in the afternoon, Penny decided to try walking around the room with the aid of the cane. Although she moved slowly, and although it did hurt, she'd had more than enough of being in bed. This gave her the opportunity to check her handbag to be sure that the rubies were still there, something Ramon had overlooked the night before. They were, which was a relief. And she'd decided she'd have to return them to Mary de Villanueva at the first opportunity.

She sat up in an armchair to eat her evening meal, and she'd just finished when Elena came to say, "Madame de Villanueva has suggested that perhaps you might like to try to come as far as the Ambassador's sitting room, so that you can watch television."

With the invitation, Phyliss had given Elena a beautiful caftan, patterned in tones of jade, pale gold, and rose.

"Madame says it will be easy for you to wear this," Elena said. "There is no fitting, no fastening to be accomplished."

Penny smiled. "I think I'll give it a whirl," she decided.

"Then I must buzz Madame," Elena said. "She wishes to come and help you."

There was a telephone on the bedside table, but Penny had not yet used it. She realized, guiltily, that she'd not yet returned Jeff's call. She'd been more out of it today than she'd thought she was, she conceded, for she should have called him if only to tell him that it would be impossible for her to be back at school in the morning. They'd have to get a substitute. She should probably have phoned the School Superintendent's office for that matter, though it was doubtful that there would be anyone around on a Sunday. And she should have called her Uncle Fred as well. He'd be expecting her any time now.

She watched Elena dial, evidently using an in-house intercom system, and the girl spoke in Spanish to whoever answered the phone at the other end of the wire. But when she'd hung up, she said, "Madame will be here directly. Now, let me help you with this garment."

When Penny had donned the caftan, Elena said, "It is very becoming to you, señorita. Just a little bit more lipstick, perhaps?"

Penny nodded and added the lipstick when Elena brought it to her along with a hand mirror. She glanced toward the telephone and knew again that she should make her calls. Yet she couldn't bring herself to do so. Later, she promised herself.

Phyliss arrived and said, "Well, luv, I'm glad you feel up to joining us. Now, let me take one arm. You stay at her other side, Elena, in case she falters."

Although Penny made slow progress, she did not falter. With Phyliss helping her, and Elena ready to catch her if she made the slightest misstep, she inched her way down

the hall. She'd just reached the head of the staircase when
Ramon, coming up, got to the top step and came face to
face with her.

He looked at Penny, looked at her cane, and once again
he seemed suffused by an emotion she couldn't define.
But he recouped almost instantly and said politely, "I'm
glad to see you up and about again, Penny."

"I'm glad to be up and about," she managed to answer
him.

In the distance a telephone rang, and Elena sped to
answer it. She came back to the door of the Ambassador's
sitting room to say to Phyliss, "It's for you, madame."

Phyliss said, "Help Penny, will you, Ray? She's so
wobbly I'm afraid she'll fall down if she tries to go it
entirely alone. How about joining us for a gin and tonic,
incidentally?"

"I would like that," Ramon agreed easily.

What an enigma he was! He'd been avoiding her all
day—at least it certainly seemed so—yet now he took
hold of her arm as if he were thoroughly enjoying making
this gesture. He moved his body a shade closer to hers
than he really needed to as they started off again toward
the sitting room.

Then, as he noted Penny's shaky progress, he said
impatiently, "But this is ridiculous!" And before she
realized what he was about to do, he'd swooped her up in
his arms, cane and all, and was carrying her with an ease
that gave a good idea of his latent strength.

"Perhaps you had better go and get ice, Elena," he
suggested to the maid, who was watching them with a rapt
expression on her face. Elena nodded and started off
toward the kitchen, which was at the rear of the floor.

Ramon moved on easily toward the sitting room. Once
inside it, they could hear Phyliss talking on the phone in
the adjoining bedroom. But for the moment they were
alone, and Ramon, his eyes darkening, bent his head so
that his mouth met Penny's lips in a kiss that was totally

devastating, so overpowering that had he not been holding her in his arms she would never have been able to rely on the cane alone for support! As it was, she clung to him, and their kiss deepened until she felt as if she'd been fused to Ramon. He relinquished his claim upon her mouth and nuzzled his lips against her hair. Then he said softly, "Ah, *querida, querida!*"

The regret in his tone was very evident to Penny, and she tensed. Why should Ramon be regretful about anything that involved her?

He settled her gently into a comfortable armchair, then went across to the sideboard bar. He flashed a smile at Elena as she came in with a bucket full of ice cubes. She said something in Spanish. Evidently she'd asked if there was anything else he wanted, because he said, "No, *gracias,*" and Elena left the room.

Phyliss, having finished her phone call, came in to say, "I think your foot should be propped up a bit, luv." She pulled a hassock over to Penny, who settled back comfortably, ashamed of herself for enjoying all of the attention, and yet finding it impossible not to. Ramon brought over gin and tonics and Phyliss said, "Let's have a look at the telly guide and see if we can find a good program." But before this could be accomplished, the telephone rang again.

"Shall I get it?" Ramon suggested.

"No," Phyliss said. "When the switchboard rings up here it's almost always for either Tony or me."

In this case, though, she was wrong. She reappeared after a moment to say, "Penny, the call is for you. It's your friend Jeff Eldredge. He said he expected that you'd be home last night."

Penny felt a flash of annoyance, because she'd not told Jeff when she was to be expected home, and there was no reason why he should have assumed that she'd come back on Saturday when there was no real need to return until Sunday. But as she started to struggle to her feet, prepared to go and take the call, Phyliss held up a detaining hand. "May I tell him what happened to you and give him a message, just for now?" she asked. "It's a fair distance from that chair to the phone, which is on my bedside table. It's ridiculous, really, that we don't have an extension phone in here, or at least one of those plug-in jobs. Anyway, may I act as your secretary, and you can call your friend back, once you're in your own room again?"

"Yes," Penny said and was vaguely surprised at the sense of relief she felt over being granted one more reprieve before having to talk to Jeff. "But why don't you tell him I'll call him tomorrow evening? I might have a better idea then of when Dr. Farrington thinks I'll be able to go home. Meantime, please explain what's happened to me, and ask him to phone the school and explain it all to them? They'll have to get a substitute for a couple of days."

"Will do," Phyliss assured her with a mock salute.

Ramon pulled up a chair fairly close to Penny's and looked at her with a discerning eye. "You do not seem anxious to speak to your friend," he observed.

He accented the word "friend" in a way that made her suspicious, and she said, "I'm not sure I like the way you say that."

"The way I say what?" he queried blandly.

"Friend. Jeff is my friend, to be sure, but you seem able to give the word a double meaning!"

"It is merely my English," Ramon told her loftily. "There are times when I do not express myself in the right idiom."

"Your English is excellent, and you know it," she retorted shortly. "Ramon . . ."

"Yes?"

"Have you found out anything more about the man who was in the garden last night?"

He shook his head. "Despite a great deal of questioning today, some of it rather covert, some of it direct to the

point of bluntness, I can find no man connected with the
embassy who will admit to having been in the garden last
night. I acknowledge that it might make a person feel a
fool to own up to it, but I think I conveyed the impression
that the matter was sufficiently serious so that most of
those I talked to would have been willing to appear a bit
foolish for the sake of truth." He drew a long breath.
"Had I not seen the note myself," he admitted, "I would
be tempted to think that you had imagined your man in the
garden, Penny."

"Thanks very much," she said frostily and added, her
tone laced with bitterness, "I appreciate your vote of
confidence."

To her consternation, she felt tears welling in her eyes,
and she clutched at the paper napkin Ramon had brought
her with the drink, averting her face from him. But she
was not quick enough.

"*Dios!*" he said, seeming honestly chagrined, "the last
thing in the world I want is to make you cry, Penny. What
I meant is that this man in the garden does seem
so . . . elusive. I would be the last in the world to deny
your charms, but it does seem a fool's errand to come and
stick a note under your door, like a smitten schoolboy, and
then to go and stand beneath your window, like a stricken
Romeo."

"I agree," she said testily. "But I don't think the man
in the garden was a stricken Romeo. Far from it! I think he
was deliberately trying to lure me not into the garden, but
into the elevator!"

"What are you saying?" Ramon demanded.

"I think this man, whoever he is, took advantage of the
fact that the elevator was old and slow and creaked a lot,
and tampered in some way with its mechanism. What I'm
saying is that I think he arranged my accident. Probably
he expected that I'd be killed!"

She looked directly at Ramon as she said this, and
she was appalled at his expression. He stared at her, his

eyes glittering, his face a mask of controlled fury. But before he had a chance to speak, an interruption came in the form of Mario. Normally, this was an interruption Penny would have welcomed, but just now she wished that Mario had stayed away until she'd managed to learn why her suspicion that the elevator had been tampered with had produced such a violent reaction in Ramon.

Mario exploded into the room, this seeming to be his custom, and when he saw Penny he exclaimed, "There you are! Up and about, when I was prepared to sit by your sickbed through the night, consoling you."

"Well," Penny suggested, "sit by my chair and console me, why don't you?"

"I don't know," Mario said darkly. "Here I find you in a deep conference with Martinez. What am I to think of that?"

Ramon said something in rapid Spanish, and Mario grinned. "My, but we are becoming touchy," he observed.

Phyliss came back into the room just then, preventing any further dialogue between Mario and Ramon, to Penny's relief. But she was frowning. "Your friend Jeff seems very much upset, Penny," she reported. "He appears to think that we've virtually kidnapped you. He says he's going to ask the school to find *two* substitutes, so that he can come down here himself, and I've the feeling he's about to don his Superman suit and rush to your rescue."

"Oh, God!" Penny protested weakly.

"Jeff?" Mario scowled. "Who is Jeff?"

"An old friend," Penny explained lamely. "Jeff Eldredge. We teach in the same school."

"Are you engaged to him?" Phyliss asked curiously. "He rather gave me the impression that you were."

"No," Penny said. She amended this to, "Not yet, at any rate."

"Not yet?" Mario demanded. "Do you mean that you intend to become engaged to him?"

Phyliss intervened smoothly, saying, "I rather think he intends to become engaged to Penny. But despite the fact that he was upset, he sounds quite nice."

"He is nice," Penny said. "He's very nice. But sometimes he tends to get . . . carried away."

Mario poured some gin into a glass, added ice and tonic, and then proclaimed, "A pox on him!"

"Oh, honestly!" Penny protested, but Mario's expression was so comical that she had to laugh aloud.

Ramon finished his drink and set his glass down on a table with a decided thud. Then he turned to Phyliss. "If you don't need me for anything, I would like to leave," he said flatly.

"If you must, Ray," Phyliss said.

Mario grinned. "Another Scandinavian alliance?" he questioned.

Ramon glowered at him even as Phyliss said lightly, "Mind your own business, child."

Ramon's goodnight to all of them was excessively formal, in Penny's opinion. Once he'd left the room and was definitely out of earshot, Mario asked, "What's happened to Ray?"

"Has anything?" Phyliss queried idly.

"I'd say so," her son assured her. "He's uptight, touchy; you can't say a word to him without his looking as if he'd like to put a knife at your throat! Ray's sense of humor is zilch at the moment, and if I didn't know better I'd suspect he never had one in the first place. But I do know better. Ray's always been serious, but he's still been able to laugh . . . even at himself." Mario shrugged, but there was nothing very Latin about his shrug. "I suppose," he admitted, "that you can trace some of his attitude back to his brother's death. He's never really been the same since Roberto shot himself. But he's gotten worse lately. Since Marita, I suppose," Mario concluded and added a dash more gin to his drink.

His mother was watching him with slightly narrowed eyes. "Ramon has had far more to cope with than most men twice his age," she reminded her son. "Since his father's death—and he was only in his early twenties when that happened—he's been the head of the family, responsible for the Martinez interests and holdings, and, as you very well know, they're extensive. Roberto was a trial to him, and as we all also know, he should never have become involved with Marita in the first place. Not, at least, to the point of deciding to marry her. I can become as dewy-eyed as any woman over the knight-in-shining-armor role, but Ramon carried it to extremes when he asked Marita to marry him. If she'd lived, she would have destroyed him."

"Destroyed him? Isn't that rather dramatic of you?" Mario suggested.

Phyliss laughed. "Possibly," she conceded. "But we all know that it wouldn't have been a marriage made in heaven, and it is Ramon who would have been sacrificed in the process."

Phyliss turned swiftly to Penny. "Luv, I'm sorry," she said. "You must think it dreadful of me to speak about Marita like this, especially when I know she was a close friend of yours. But she'd changed since those days when the two of you were in college. Especially since Roberto's death which, of course, was a tremendous shock to her. He shot himself, you know . . ."

"Yes," Penny nodded. Phyliss, at least, was not implying that Ramon had had anything to do with his brother's death, and she filed this fact away in her mind. Then she added slowly, "I begin to feel that I really didn't know Marita. The girl I've been hearing about seems so completely different from the girl I remember!"

"In life," Phyliss said soberly, "friends inevitably

reach a crossroads from time to time. Either we go along in the same general direction at this point, or we diverge. Sometimes our paths converge again; sometimes we never do get together again. We'll never know, of course, what ultimately would have happened with you and Marita, but I would say that when you came to your first crossroads you definitely took two different turnings. And you're right. The girl you knew in college was not the girl Marita became. Mary is blind to that, bless her, but . . ." Phyliss grimaced, "I'm talking too much," she said, "and we're all getting much too serious. Now, where's that telly program guide? Let's see if we can't find something that will cheer us up!"

Chapter 10

PENNY'S PHYSICAL PROBLEMS RESPONDED WELL TO treatment. By the middle of the week she was able to get around without a cane, although the going was still slow. Her aches were fading, but her emotional problems were more painful than ever. Since the night when Jeff Eldredge had again called the embassy and Phyliss had acted as intermediary, Ramon had seemed bent on avoiding her.

A new elevator had been installed the first thing Monday morning, the Ambassador having used considerable diplomatic clout to achieve this. It was a decided improvement over the old one, but it had taken a great deal of nerve on Penny's part to step into it for the first time, and she still didn't like doing so. Nevertheless, she didn't want to eat alone in her room, which meant that she had to use the elevator in order to get down to the second floor. It was at meals in the vast dining room that she mostly saw Ramon. And that was certainly not a setting that aided in reestablishing an intimate rapport. Anyway, he always had a reason for asking to be excused, usually before the dessert course was served.

On Monday, after Dr. Farrington had paid his daily visit to Mary de Villanueva and had paused to check the progress of Penny's ankle as well, she'd called both Jeff and her Uncle Fred. The doctor had been reluctant to give a definite departure date for her, and so she'd told both men that she'd be in touch again as soon as she knew for certain when she could leave Washington.

It had been a relief to be unable to be more precise than that. Penny had discovered that she didn't want to commit herself to anything definite. She was plagued by a growing restlessness and a sense that far too many threads had been unraveled in the tapestry of the late Marita Villanueva's life. She wanted to be able to tie them together so that she could make sense out of the total picture, a picture she'd felt very much involved in since that night when the elevator had crashed with her in it.

She and Ramon had not had any further conversation on that subject, and she'd not mentioned her suspicions to anyone else. But they hung like a heavy weight around her shoulders.

During the week after her accident, everyone—except Ramon—continued to be very kind to her. She and Phyliss discovered that they both liked to play cribbage and had some rousing contests. Mario stopped by the sitting room regularly, for Penny spent most of her waking hours convalescing there, and he introduced her to the intricacies of backgammon. One night she, Mario, the Ambassador, and Phyliss played bridge together, and she was astonished when she and Mario held their own, for she'd never thought much of her ability as a bridge player.

It would have been a pleasant life, something she could have looked back on fondly once she was home again, except for the nagging torment of having Ramon so near . . . and yet so disconcertingly far away.

Conchita visited her several times a day, and even

Carlos Smith stopped by to see her twice, as did two or three of the young men on the embassy staff whom she'd met the night of the reception. They were all charming, and she tried not to stare at them as she attempted to fathom whether or not there was anything about any of them reminiscent of the man in the garden. They had only one feature in common with her moonlight visitor: the dark hair. As Ramon had said, most of the men on the embassy staff had dark hair. Carlos Smith was a notable exception.

As the days passed, Penny had a number of conversations with Mary de Villanueva. It was impossible not to touch on the subject of Marita occasionally, but Penny did so with caution. There was too much about the Marita of the past three years that she didn't know.

What she did know, however, was that a cloud would hang over Mary de Villanueva's head for the rest of her life unless she could satisfy herself as to what had happened to her daughter. And, as she considered this, Penny found it more and more understandable, because she was similarly affected. Unless the truth could be learned about Marita's death, she'd never be able to fill in the tapestry, she'd never find out why she herself had evidently become a target . . . for someone.

But there were no further attempts to harm her. And she really could not blame Ramon for saying that if he hadn't seen the telltale note he'd have been tempted to think the man in the garden had been a figment of her imagination.

As her ankle grew stronger and she was able to get around more comfortably, Penny knew that the moment was at hand when she should go home. But she didn't want to leave. Not yet. There was something else to be done first.

The more she thought about it, the more Penny became convinced that there was only one place where there might be a chance of learning the truth about Marita's death. In Franconia. At the Snow Palast. She wondered if the Snow

Palast would be open at this time of the year, and she contemplated trying to telephone Eric Jenson, the young man who managed the lodge, to find out. But, with unaccustomed caution, she shied away from the idea of placing the call through the embassy switchboard.

Her greatest task, she knew, would be working out the logistics of getting from Washington to Franconia without anyone's finding out about it. And she felt that secrecy was imperative. The man in the garden, after all, had to have been connected with the embassy. Certainly he couldn't have been someone who'd simply dropped in off the street or even a casual guest at the reception. No . . . he'd been close to the embassy. She shuddered now every time she thought of the man in the garden. Whoever he was, she didn't want him to know that she was about to go back to the scene of Marita's death!

Finally, after breakfast on Friday morning, Penny confronted Phyliss and asked if she might use the telephone in order to call the airport and make a plane reservation to Boston.

Phyliss, after first protesting that she was not nearly well enough to leave them yet, sighed and said, ''I suppose you're anxious to get back to your Jeff. And to your job as well. I can't blame you, with Ray being such a thundercloud lately!''

Then, to Penny's consternation, Phyliss went on, ''It would actually be much easier to have your reservation made through the chancery.'' Before Penny could stop her, she buzzed Ramon on the intercom and asked him to take care of it.

This he did, with what appeared to Penny to be above-average efficiency. He could not have done a better job of demonstrating that he couldn't wait to get rid of her! Within half an hour he came up to the sitting room where she and Phyliss were chatting together to tell her that she had a confirmed place on a flight to Logan Airport the following morning!

He was so polite as he relayed this information that he couldn't be faulted. But Penny noticed Phyliss raising her eyebrows as she listened to him explain that everything was in order and that he would be pleased to drive the señorita to the airport!

To make sure I leave! Penny thought bitterly.

Phyliss laughed. "The señorita? Since when have you and Penny gotten back to such a formal basis?"

Ramon shrugged slightly. "I suppose it is a habit," he conceded. "Penny, then."

Despite Penny's best intentions, her heart lurched. And she was annoyed at herself as she said, "There's no reason for you to drive me to the airport, Ramon. I can perfectly well take a taxi."

"It would be my pleasure to take you," Ramon said smoothly, and for a moment she actually disliked him.

At lunch, Mario was thoroughly put out. He was disgusted both because Penny was leaving and because he had a previous commitment to go to a house party down on the Chesapeake, and so couldn't take her to the airport himself.

"But you will be seeing me sooner than you think!" he warned her.

She laughed. "You make it sound like a threat!"

"Perhaps it is," he said, chuckling.

Ramon had joined them for the midday meal, but he took no part in this byplay and, once again, he left before the dessert was served. Mario, watching him retreat from the dining hall, observed casually, "Martinez seems to be sagging from the weight he has on his mind these days. Perhaps the Scandinavian alliance is too heavy for him."

"She called him this morning," Conchita revealed. "I happened to answer the phone. One can't mistake that Swedish accent."

Penny felt a sharp little pang that had nothing to do with her recent injuries. She recognized it for what it was— jealousy, pure unadulterated jealousy! Damn it, she told

herself furiously, what's the point in being jealous of
Ramon? After tomorrow, I'll never see him again! And at
this thought a bleakness settled over her that made winter
seem tropical.

She tried to apply herself studiously to the delicious
fruit-and-sponge-cake concoction Elena had just served
her, but the food was like dust in her mouth. A foreshad-
owing, she thought dismally, of what her entire life was
going to be like from now on. Everything she touched was
going to turn to dust. She was going to be surrounded by
dust!

Mario asked, "What's the matter, *hija?* You look like
you've just lost your best friend!"

His mother chided, "You ask too many questions,
Mario."

"That," he told her imperturbably, "is how I learn so
many answers."

The conversation was sustained on this light note until
they'd finished their coffee. Then Penny went back up to
her room, supposedly to rest, but her napping period today
was a short one. Both Phyliss and Mary de Villanueva had
an engagement to play bridge, and Mario had left for the
Chesapeake directly after they'd finished lunch. In fact,
he'd kissed her goodbye lightly there in the dining room
and had again promised that he was going to turn up even
more often than the proverbial bad penny.

By three o'clock the top floor of the embassy was quiet,
and Penny smiled at her own timidity as she opened the
door of the Rose Room and started down the corridor. It
took all the nerve she could muster to summon the
elevator, then step inside and push the button that would
take her to the entrance foyer. As she waited for the
elevator to start to move downward, she suffered a bad
attack of nerves. The memory of that other terrible time
when she'd lurched helplessly to what could well have
been her death was much too recent and much too vivid.
But the new elevator moved along smoothly and slid

gently to a stop. She pushed the door open and stepped out on the first floor.

She moved slowly, limping slightly, because her ankle still hurt. And she also tried to move silently, because she wanted desperately to get out of the building without being observed. She'd already made up her mind that if she were interrupted by someone, she would say that she'd decided to go out for a walk as a sort of endurance test, since she'd have to be ready to navigate on her bad foot tomorrow, when she made the trip to Boston.

She was in luck, because the huge entrance foyer was deserted. Penny slipped across it and tugged at the massive entrance door, which opened more easily than she thought it would. Then she was out on the front step, standing under the porte cochere and trying to decide, as she faced Massachusetts Avenue, where she'd be likely to find the nearest phone booth.

She found a pay phone in a neighborhood grocery store and placed the call to the Snow Palast, after first getting the number from Information. After a few rings she heard Eric Jenson's voice. She found herself agreeing with Conchita that the Scandinavian accent was, indeed, unmistakable.

She'd wondered if the lodge manager would remember her and was relieved when he assured her that he remembered her very well. In answer to her question, he told her that while some of the facilities of the Snow Palast were closed, he would be able to accommodate her. This was their off-season, he explained, so the chalets were closed, as were some of the rooms in the lodge that needed painting or other redecorating. Further, he told her, he'd be happy to meet her bus in Franconia. He was familiar with the schedule, so was able to assure her that she'd have plenty of time to go from the airport to the bus terminal in downtown Boston and then to get a bus that would bring her into Franconia before dark.

As she hung up the phone, Penny was weak-kneed from

relief. This whole thing had been so much easier than she'd dared hope it might be—thus far, at least! She made one more call, this to Wareham, and once again was relieved when she learned her uncle was out so that she could simply leave a message for him with Mrs. Higgins. She suspected that her call had interrupted Mrs. Higgins's favorite afternoon soap opera on television, and that was fortunate too, because she was thus spared the necessity of answering a number of possible questions. On occasion, the housekeeper could be extremely inquisitive.

She concluded the conversation with, "Just tell Uncle Fred that I'll be back Sunday evening. And ask him to call Jeff, please, and to tell him to let the school know that they can expect me on Monday."

And so the deed was done; the die was cast.

As Penny started back toward the embassy, she realized that she'd overtaxed herself, because her ankle was throbbing and she was limping quite badly. But she'd gone barely a block when a shining black car pulled up alongside the curb and she saw Carlos Smith sitting at the wheel of it.

He leaned across to open the door and to ask pleasantly, "Going my way?"

"I'd love to go your way," Penny told him fervently, "if that means getting back to the embassy." She gazed down at her foot ruefully. "I wanted to see how much mileage I had in me," she told him, "but I'm afraid I've overdone it."

"I will be delighted to drop you off at the embassy," he assured her, and she promptly slid into the seat beside him, glancing down at her ankle to see that it definitely looked swollen.

Licenciado Smith said, "I am surprised to see you off the invalid list so soon. Should you be out walking around like this?"

"I thought I should try to," she told him. "I'm going

home tomorrow, so I felt a little outdoor exercise was in order.''

"A little," he teased, "but you did not stop at that, did you?" He flashed her a smile and then continued, "I am sorry to hear that you are leaving us, señorita. There has been a cloud hanging over the embassy ever since Marita Villanueva's death, and you have helped to dispel some of it. What a tragic waste it was, though, to have her die as she did. Do you ski, señorita?''

"Very poorly," she told him. "I haven't had much opportunity to get up to the mountains at the right time. You see, I live on the seacoast.''

"So you did not share Marita's passion for the slopes?''

"Frankly, no," she admitted.

"There is a beauty to skiing, I admit," he said, "but I myself am not much of an aficionado." He smiled. "Too much snow, too much cold," he said with a mock shiver. "I would prefer your part of New England, I think. Do you take part in many water sports?''

"Yes," she nodded. "I like to waterski, but lately I've done more windsurfing than anything else.''

"That I like," Carlos Smith agreed. "Whenever I have the chance I go down to the Caribbean, to an island I know where there is a usually deserted beach, and I take along my sailboard. Also, there is excellent scuba diving there. The water is crystal clear, and the undersea life is as fascinating as it is beautiful.''

"So far, I haven't done any scuba diving," Penny admitted. "That's something on my agenda for the future, though.''

She saw the embassy looming ahead of them. Carlos Smith skillfully swerved his car into the narrow little semicircular driveway and then leaned over to open the door, smiling as he did so. His smile was nearly as dazzling as Ramon's. Nearly, but not quite. No one's smile, Penny thought gloomily, could possibly be as dazzling as Ramon's!

He said, "If I don't see you again, have a good trip home. But please . . . come back again. We will welcome you."

"Thank you," she said, touched by this.

She climbed out of the car, carefully balancing herself before she started to walk. The *Licenciado* looked across at her anxiously and asked, "Are you sure you are all right? Would you like me to help you?"

"Thank you, no, I'm fine," she told him. "Just a bit awkward, that's all. It takes me a minute to get going!"

"Careful, then," he said, and waved in farewell as he started up the car and drove off.

It was not until the *Licenciado* had left her that Penny realized the embassy door would undoubtedly be locked. This meant that she'd have to ring the bell and face Juan again, just as she had the afternoon of her arrival.

Damn, she thought angrily, I should have asked Señor Smith to let me in with his key! Then even as she realized she was speaking out loud, and warned herself that this would be an extremely dangerous habit to fall into, the door swung open and Ramon confronted her.

He was furious. "Where did you go?" he demanded, his eyes searing her face.

She felt her own anger flare. "That's really none of your business, is it?" she asked coolly.

He drew her through the doorway with a roughness that was unlike him. The massive door thudded shut behind him. The vast entrance foyer stretched ahead, dimly lighted as it had been on the afternoon of her arrival. It was cavernous, gloomy, the far recesses full of shadows, and she shivered.

"At the moment, everything you do is my business!" he told her tightly. "While you are staying in this embassy you are under the protection of my country."

"I don't need the protection of your country, damn you!" she snapped.

"No?" She saw his mouth grow taut while the muscle at the side of his jaw began to twitch, and for a moment she thought he was going to hit her. Then he said again, ominously, "No? Miss American Independence, eh? Well, let's see how far that gets you!"

His arms came around her, and Penny struggled futilely to free herself from the vise in which he was gripping her. His nearness was overpowering to her. She could feel the abrasiveness of his tweed jacket against her cheek, she could smell the evocative aroma of the aftershave he used mingled with a tantalizing scent that was entirely Ramon's own.

Once more she tried to writhe away from him, and she gasped when he twisted her toward him with a roughness that spoke not only of his anger but of much more. Ramon, probably more civilized than any man she'd ever known, was in the grip of something extremely primitive.

Everything within Penny cried out to resist him, to escape. She remembered reading somewhere that it was the basic nature of a woman to be reluctant to commit herself to a man, that it was instinct for her to want to flee . . . especially when she was cornered. And Ramon was cornering Penny now. But even as she struggled to free herself from his embrace, she remembered the ecstasy they'd shared together, and inadvertently she moaned. A low moan, a small moan. She had just about enough breath for it. He heard it, and instinctively he released her, looking down at her, his blue eyes indigo. And at exactly that minute Juan emerged through the door that led into the chancery, stopping short when he saw them.

Penny would not have believed that she could be glad to have Juan come to her rescue, but now she welcomed him. And Juan, looking across at them, was startled, his mask of composure slipping for once. Quickly he said, "*Perdón!*"

Ramon nodded abruptly, then spoke to him in low-toned Spanish and, for once, did not apologize to Penny for using a language she did not understand. Then he said sharply, "We will go upstairs!"

"We" meant all three of them, she found, for Juan rode up in the elevator with them. The silence all the way to the top floor was a stony one. With Juan present, Penny took the opportunity to say quickly, "I'm going to my room," once they'd stepped out of the elevator, and although Ramon scowled he did nothing to try to stop her.

Out of the corner of her eye, she saw the two men continue down the corridor to the family sitting room. She could hear voices in the distance. Sometimes the Ambassador and Phyliss had a drink up there before going down to the Gold Room for a predinner cocktail, and she imagined that's what they were doing. Penny wondered if Ramon was going to report to them that she'd been out wandering through the city streets.

At dinner that evening the Villanuevas made a special effort to make everything pleasant for her, but Ramon did not come to the table at all, and Mario was in Maryland. Conchita was the only other person at the table beside the Ambassador and Phyliss, and the huge dining hall seemed vaster and more lonely than it ever had before.

Later in the evening Penny went to Mary de Villanueva's room to tell her that she felt she must return the rubies. Finally Mary yielded to her wishes, though reluctantly, and she did impose one condition.

"When you marry, you must accept these as a wedding present," she said, tapping the blue jewel box, which she was holding in her lap.

"I will," Penny promised, then added with an attempt at humor, which didn't quite come off, "But there's a good chance I'm going to wind up on old maid, Aunt Mary."

"There's more of a chance of the moon falling on the earth tomorrow," Mary scoffed.

Elena brought breakfast to Penny's room in the morning

without her ringing for it. "We knew you would try to come to the dining room," she explained, "and Madame thought you should conserve your strength. She said you were limping badly last night."

Later, while Penny was dressing, Phyliss and Mary de Villanueva came in together to see her, and, still later, they went down in the elevator with her and on to the chancery, where she was ushered into the Ambassador's private office. She couldn't help but reflect that this was quite a different reception than her first one, when she'd been led to Ramon's office via a back corridor!

Tony Villanueva gave her a warm and affectionate farewell embrace, and his insistence that she pay them a return visit was genuine. He walked to the chancery door with her, and it was only then that Ramon appeared. A moment later they were in his car, driving off down Massachusetts Avenue.

The ride to the airport seemed eternal. Ramon drove a green Porsche, and he was as competent a driver as Mario. He wove expertly through the maze of Saturday traffic as they left the city behind, trading the metropolitan area for the Virginia suburbs. It was a beautiful day, flowering trees and shrubs lent splashes of color everywhere, and normally Penny would have thoroughly appreciated the loveliness of the Washington area at that time of the year. But today everything seemed flat to her. Mentally she was seeing the world only in tones of black and gray, she thought dismally.

Ramon was studiously polite, asking her from time to time if she was comfortable, or if she was getting too much of a breeze from the open windows. She answered him in monosyllables. Beyond that, they were silent.

He dropped her off at the terminal building and told her that he would come back with her luggage as soon as he had found a parking space. Penny took a seat on a chair in a corner and tried to become absorbed in the glass-and-chrome world of the airport as she waited for him; she tried to imagine where people were going or where they had come from. But it was no use. This was no time for playing games. There was a tight knot in her throat. She knew that unless she could get better control of her emotions she was going to break down and weep when it came time to leave Ramon. And she was damned if she was going to give him the satisfaction of seeing her go to pieces before his scornful blue gaze!

Then she saw him coming toward her, and a love for him that she couldn't deny suffused her. There was pride in the way he walked, and he held his head high. But he looked tired, almost haggard. In fact, he looked quite as miserable as Penny felt!

He said, "There is still plenty of time for a cup of coffee. Would that interest you?"

"Yes," she said, nodding.

They walked toward the coffee shop slowly, Ramon gauging his stride to match hers. Their coffee came, but although Penny stirred some sugar into hers, Ramon didn't touch his.

Looking across the table at her, he said tensely, "Penny . . . I feel I must make an apology to you."

She could feel the knot in her throat tighten, and her voice sounded much too high as she asked, "Why?"

"From the moment you arrived at the embassy I seem to have made a series of mistakes. Unfortunately, I am not at liberty to explain to you why. I can only say that I have been involved in matters that involve my country and our internal politics. Matters that should not concern you."

She toyed with her spoon. Then she said carefully, "But they have concerned me, haven't they?"

He frowned. "Why do you say that?"

"Because I think that man in the garden the other night wanted me to be . . . killed."

She saw the wary expression in his eyes, but he said only, "You have a very vivid imagination."

She shook her head. "It wasn't my imagination." She

dared the question. "Someone did tamper with the elevator, didn't they, Ramon?"

He stared at her for a long moment before he answered. Then he said reluctantly, "Yes, they did. And that is one reason I have been so . . . frantic about you. The conclusion I was forced to reach is that someone thought you possessed information that might be . . . dangerous. But I think by now it has been realized that this was a wrong assumption. That you were—how shall I say this?—that you were only an innocent bystander. So there is no need for you to worry about your safety from now on, Penny. You can go away from here in peace. Nevertheless, I regret what happened the other night more deeply than you can imagine. In fact I regret everything unpleasant that has happened to you since the moment you met me."

Everything unpleasant? Didn't it even occur to this impossible man that everything unpleasant that had occurred was like a straw in the wind in comparison to the wonder, the miracle, of the precious time they'd spent together?

Penny said slowly, sadly, "I'm sorry you don't have more confidence in me."

He was taken aback by this. "It isn't a question of confidence, *querida*," he said, so hastily she knew that, for once, he was speaking without having thought out what he was going to say. "It is simply that I . . . "

She had to fight to control her voice, but there was a tremor in it anyway. "You don't need to make excuses to me," she told him.

"I was not trying to make excuses to you," he began. Then he stopped, listened, and said, "Oh God, they are calling your flight! We'll have to go."

He walked with her to the gate, Penny trying to hurry in order to keep up with him. The exertion was making her ankle throb, but her aches were by no means purely physical!

Ramon asked tautly, "Is someone meeting you in Boston?"

"Yes," she fibbed. "Jeff Eldredge."

The blue eyes were upon her, sharp, probing. "Then he is the one you telephoned yesterday?"

"No," she said before she stopped to think that it might be much better to say yes. "What makes you think I telephoned anyone yesterday?"

"Because it seemed logical to me that you might want to notify someone that you were coming home. And, though you placed no calls through the embassy switchboard, you took the trouble to go out for a supposed walk, even though your foot was hurting you."

"You checked the embassy switchboard for any calls I might have made?" she demanded.

"Yes," he admitted. "Yes, I checked."

Her cheeks flamed. "You should have been a spy!" she accused.

His smile was rueful. "Perhaps I am," he told her.

People were starting to shuffle through the gate. Penny took her ticket out of her handbag. She said, speaking with difficulty, "Good-bye, Ramon. And . . . thank you for driving me out to the airport."

She could no longer avoid meeting his eyes, and she saw in them an expression that was decidedly tender. Almost out of character, for Ramon. Then he leaned forward and kissed her, a light kiss that nevertheless managed to convey passion.

He said huskily, "*Hasta luego, querida.* And . . . take care."

She turned away from him quickly before the tears spilled over, and it was not until she was aboard the plane and fastening her seat belt that she thought back to those last words.

Hasta luego. In the past few days she'd learned enough Spanish to know that that meant, "Until later."

Hasta luego. Not *Adiós.*

Chapter 11

ERIC JENSON WAS WAITING AT THE BUS STOP IN FRANCO-
nia. Penny spied him from the bus window, standing near
a white station wagon with the words "Snow Palast"
emblazoned in gold on the side, but she didn't need this
extra identification. She would have known him anywhere.

He recognized her instantly too. "Miss Baldwin," he
said as he bent over her hand. He was considerably taller
than she was, and so he had to bend quite a long way, and
he did this with a manner that seemed very European to
her. For a moment she thought that he might go so far as to
kiss her hand, but he stopped short with a wide smile and
said, "It is good to see you again."

As she walked with him toward the station wagon, he
said, with a Scandinavian accent that was very different
from the soft Spanish accent she'd become accustomed to,
"I notice that you are limping. You have injured yourself?"

"I had a fall recently," Penny said quickly. "Nothing serious."

"That is good."

As they drove out of the parking lot, he said, "I am afraid you have not returned at our best season. As you will notice, spring is only beginning here."

That was true. Most of the trees were still bare, and as they went through the village and then along the road that led to the lodge Penny saw that there were still patches of snow lingering in some of the shaded culverts along the roadside. Nevertheless, it was a beautiful day, and the promise of spring was in the air.

The Snow Palast had been newly painted. It fairly blazed with brown and white freshness, and Crescent Mountain, towering in back of the lodge and the chalets, seemed more immense—and, somehow, considerably more terrifying—without the white mantle that had blanketed it the last time Penny had been there.

Crescent Mountain. The place where Marita had died.

Partly from the need to make conversation, partly because she couldn't keep her eyes away from the mountain that loomed over them, Penny said, "The snow's all gone from Crescent Mountain."

"Not quite," Eric said. "From this side you do not notice it particularly. But if you will look way up there—see?—there are still patches of snow. And in the ravines as well. Until two or three weeks ago there was even some spring skiing. But then the weather warmed."

His English was excellent, but the Scandinavian accent still fell strangely on her ears, and she had a sudden and irrepressible urge to hear a voice saying to her, "*Querida*, you must . . ." Ramon. She already missed him more than she would have believed possible.

Eric, pulling the station wagon up in front of the lodge's main entrance, said, "The Heilbruners—they are the owners, you know—are still in Florida. They will come back here at the end of the month." He frowned. "But then, you do not know them, do you?'' he asked her. ''I think when you came before, they had already left to go south.''

''They must have,'' she agreed. ''At least, I didn't meet them.''

''Well, I remain still in charge,'' Eric told her with a slight shrug. ''Right now, this is our slow season,'' he went on. ''We do not have our full complement of help, but there are enough to take care of the guests who are with us. I hope you will find that we offer enough activity for you.''

Penny smiled. ''All I want to do is sleep,'' she assured him.

Eric parked the car, and they walked up the front steps, Penny hobbling despite herself. Then he held the big front door open for her, and as she preceded him into the lobby she had the uncanny feeling that time had plunged backward and it was February again. She felt as if she were walking for the first time into the huge room with its vaulted, beamed ceilings, the whitewashed walls with their brown wood trim, the bright-colored rugs scattered across the polished floor, and the enormous stone fireplace with a fire crackling on the hearth and people in ski clothes sitting around it. This tall, blond young man now at her side was actually telling her very gently that she had come too late, that Marita was dead . . .

Eric's voice brought her back to the present. ''Miss Baldwin?'' he asked. ''Is there something the matter?''

Penny shook herself slightly. ''I'm sorry,'' she told him. ''No, there's nothing the matter.''

''Please, then,'' he said, completely the European innkeeper now, ''I will ask you to register.''

Penny nodded agreement and followed him across to the desk. She was faintly amused at the precise way in which Eric rapped the bell on the desk once she'd signed her name and address. Then she felt as if she'd stumbled into a book of European folk tales when she saw the little gnome of a man who appeared in answer to Eric's summons. He actually wore lederhosen, he was bald except for wisps of gray hair that circled the shiny pate atop his round head, and when he smiled he revealed a prominent gold tooth.

"This is Ludwig," Eric told her. "He will take your suitcase to your room."

Penny's room was charming. The curtains and bedspread were snowy white, and a thick old-fashioned quilt done in a bright floral print was folded back at the foot of the brass bed. Dark brown wainscoting came halfway up the walls, and the starkness of the whitewashed walls above it was broken by watercolors of the mountains.

The view from the window was incredible. She looked out across the slope on which the lodge was built to small picture-card chalets, each set far enough apart from the others to ensure privacy. Crescent Mountain rose just to the left, and she could see the chair lifts and the shed from which, she remembered, the red gondola started to the top. In February the area had been thronged with skiers; the lifts and the gondola had worked constantly. Today they were idle.

Beyond, to her right, the vista widened, so that she had a clear view through the valley of other, distant mountains, some of them still snowcapped. There was a majesty to them that was awesome. In their grandeur they seemed unassailable, and Penny, fascinated, turned away only because her ankle was reminding her rather forcibly that it really did need some care and rest.

She slipped off her shoes, noting that her right foot and ankle had swollen considerably. It was a relief to put on a comfortable robe and snuggle up on the bed, pulling the quilt over her.

She had not realized how tired she was. And though she had no intention of going to sleep—just of resting for a while—her eyelids soon grew heavy and finally her eyes closed.

She awoke to the sound of the phone ringing. She'd been dreaming about Ramon, and it took a moment for her to come back to reality. Then she groped for the receiver and heard Eric's voice at the other end of the line, even as she noticed that the sunlight was gone and dusk's mauve shadows were creeping across the room.

Eric said, "I have awakened you! I apologize."

"It's a good thing you did," Penny told him. "If I'd slept much longer I'd have stayed awake all night."

"Well," he said, "I called because I wished to ask you if you'd join me for a drink before dinner."

"I'd be delighted."

"Would half an hour be too soon?"

"Not at all," she told him. "I'll be there."

Penny showered quickly, then decided to wear a calf-length, button-front madras skirt that was belted at the waist. With it, she wore a ribbed turquoise turtleneck and topped the outfit with an oversized muted aqua suede shirt. Dining at the Snow Palast would not be formal, she knew, but she felt chic as she went downstairs.

A fire crackled on the hearth, and there were several people sitting around it, glasses in hand, chatting amiably. Eric avoided the hearthside, though, leading Penny to a corner where a small table, flanked by two chairs, offered more privacy.

Another tall, blond young man was on duty at the registration desk and, glancing toward him, Penny said, "He looks familiar."

"Otto Pedersen," Eric stated. "You probably saw him when you were here in February. He is one of the ski instructors in winter. Usually he leaves by now to go somewhere else until another snow season. But this year he decided to stay on with us. Ah, here is Ludwig. What is your drinking pleasure, Miss Baldwin?"

"I'd like a glass of Cinzano, please."

"Cinzano for Miss Baldwin, and Campari and soda for me, if you please," Eric told Ludwig.

As she sipped her drink, Penny chatted with Eric casually about the lodge and the various attractions this area had to offer. But all the time she was wondering just how much she could trust him. There were questions she needed to ask, and she had to start somewhere. Also, Eric was the only person she knew in Franconia. And not only had he known Marita well, he'd been there the day she died.

"You must have quite a variety of guests here over the course of a year," she began as a starter.

"Yes," Eric said quickly. "Yes, of course we do. We are building a good reputation. Our people come from everywhere, and more and more they return year after year."

"Like my friend Marita Villanueva?" Penny suggested.

"Yes, like your unfortunate friend, of course," Eric concurred, looking properly solemn at the mention of Marita's name. "She was such a . . . such an enthusiastic young woman," he continued after a brief search for a suitable adjective. "It was such an unfortunate occurrence."

Penny plunged. "I wish I knew more about . . . about exactly what happened to her," she confessed. "When I was here in February I spoke to a Dr. Lukens. But the shock was so recent I wasn't up to really hearing everything he said."

"And you believe you are now?"

"Yes, I think so."

Eric shook his head. "I do not see that it would do any good for you to talk to the doctor again," he said unexpectedly. "Marita de Villanueva is dead. What good can it do for you to look into something that may be very gruesome? The dead cannot be brought back."

"Yes, that's so. But . . . her death plagues me," Penny admitted. "I feel I must know more about it.

Whether or not Marita could have been saved, for instance.''

"Whether she could have been saved does not matter very much now," Eric said gloomily. He added, "I, myself, am a realist. I see no point in looking back when it can only bring suffering. That is past. My advice to you is to let it go.''

Penny was not anxious to pursue the matter further with him without giving it more thought, so she said, "Perhaps you're right.''

Eric was looking at her closely, and he smiled faintly. "You do not really agree with me, do you?" he asked her. "You do not feel that the past should be left alone.''

"Yes . . . when it's possible," she hedged.

"Marita Villanueva's death was an accident," Eric told her. "So I do not understand why you would wish to go into it again.''

"I suppose I think I'd be more at peace with myself if I knew more about it," Penny admitted.

He frowned. "I was not up on the slopes myself the day Marita died, Penny," he said. "I hope you do not mind if I call you by your first name?''

"Of course not. Please do." His courtliness was rather refreshing.

"Well, what I am saying is that I can only tell you what was told to me at the time.''

"Even that would help, Eric.''

"Well, it was a Friday. An unpleasant day. The weather was not so bad in the morning. As a matter of fact, the gondola and the chair lifts were running, and there were people going up on the mountain to ski. Down here, it began to rain. Up there," he pointed toward Crescent Mountain, "the rain quickly turned to ice. Later came the snow. By then it was afternoon, and the people started coming down. Several of the trails had been closed already, because of the ice. Do you ski?''

"Very little," she said. "And when I have tried to ski it's been strictly on novice slopes. I've never ventured out on anything remotely resembling your mountain."

"There are a variety of trails on Crescent Mountain," Eric told her. "Some of them are quite easy; some of them are very difficult. There are maps to clearly show this to people. We always urge that no one try anything beyond his skill. It is best to develop slowly, and the truth is that there are many who come here who never will become good enough skiers to be ready for the expert trails. Yet this is still a place of enjoyment; on the mountain we have something for everyone. Do you understand what I am saying?"

"Yes," she said quickly. "Yes, I do."

"Well, when the weather turns bad most people do not have to be told to come down off the mountain . . . if, indeed, they have gone up on the slopes at all. On a bad day they would rather be here in the lodge, talking with others in front of the fire. Then, also, the ski patrol is on duty at all times, and they keep a close watch on the weather and the condition of the trails as well. If a trail seems dangerous to them, it is they who close it, and there are few people who will defy such a closing. They will simply select another trail. But Marita Villanueva did not do this. She was found on a trail that had been closed by late morning. The ice there was very bad. I did speak, myself, to members of the ski patrol. They told me that she must have skidded and fallen in an area where there were rock outcroppings. She hit her head in this fall, and it was the blow to her head that killed her."

Penny fought back a sense of disappointment that Eric hadn't really told her anything she didn't already know. But she had one more question to ask that might bring results. "Who was with Marita?" she ventured.

"There was no one with her," Eric said. "And I admit that at the time, that seemed strange. It is, you see, almost a first rule of skiing never to ski alone, no matter how good you are. And, certainly, never to ski a closed trail. If the trail was not dangerous, it would not be closed. Also, if one is hurt upon such a trail, one is not apt to be found for a long time. The ski patrol, as a rule, works only on the trails that are open.''

"Yes, that's what I understood," Penny told him. "And I find it difficult to accept that Marita was up on that mountain alone, especially when the weather forecast wasn't good."

"I agree," he said, to her surprise. "Often I have wondered why Miss Villanueva would have gone up there alone. Certainly she knew better than to do something like that. She was a highly accomplished skier."

"I imagine you're an expert skier yourself."

"I have skied all my life," he said simply. "So it is natural to me. Yes, I would say that I am an expert."

"Did you ever ski with Marita?" Penny persisted.

"Yes, occasionally. But there was no chance for me to go skiing with her this last time she was here, and for this I have been sorry ever since. I only wish I had been with her that last day. Then, I tell myself, the accident might not have happened. But we were booked to capacity, and there was so much work to be done that I was not able to take any time off."

"If you were booked to capacity," Penny reasoned, "then this place must have been full of people."

"Yes, it was, of course."

"Then what makes everyone so sure that Marita went skiing alone?" she asked. "There must have been so many people around that you couldn't possibly have kept tabs on everyone. Certainly someone could have gone up with her without your noticing."

"Yes." Eric nodded. "Yes, that is so."

"Then," she said, triumphantly, "why are you so sure there wasn't anyone with her?"

"Because if there had been, certainly that person would have come down for help," Eric said reasonably. "Also, we asked questions of the other guests later. You must remember that Miss Villanueva was not found until the following day, after the snow had stopped. Not so very long before you yourself arrived here.''

She swallowed hard. She remembered only too well.

''There is another thing,'' Eric added. ''One of the couples staying at the lodge—people from New Jersey, if I remember correctly—recalled going up to the top with Miss Villanueva in the gondola car that morning. They did not like the conditions when they got there, and they came back down. But she was strapping on her skis when they left her.''

''And no one else went up in the gondola with them?''

''No one else,'' Eric Jenson said firmly.

Chapter 12

IT WAS A BAD MOMENT. PENNY'S EXPRESSIVE FACE betrayed her disappointment, and Eric, perplexed, said, "You seem unhappy with what I have told you, Penny. But can't you see that it makes sense? If there had been someone with Miss Villanueva, the accident would probably not have occurred."

Penny nodded, knowing that the expedient thing to do was to agree with him.

They were interrupted by Ludwig, who came to inform Eric that he was wanted on the phone. Penny watched him cross the room, pausing at the registration desk to say something to the young ski instructor who was manning it. Eric was an attractive man, she mused, yet she couldn't help comparing him with Ramon. Was she going to compare every man she met for the rest of her life with Ramon Martinez? Every time a man spoke to her, was she going to miss that soft Spanish accent, that sad-sweet smile that had such a devastating effect upon her?

Chances were, she told herself dismally, that she would

never see Ramon again. There was no real reason for their paths to cross. Yet even as she silently tried to convince herself of this, Penny's emotions went to war with her logic. To think of never seeing Ramon again was more than she could bear.

Eric came back and resumed his seat. "You look so thoughtful," he observed indulgently. "What is that saying you have? A penny for one's thoughts? Could one buy Penny's thoughts with a penny?"

"The price of thoughts has gone up along with everything else," she quipped, trying to lighten her mood as she did so. He laughed.

Some of the people who had been sitting near the fire were getting up and drifting toward the dining room. Nodding in their direction, Eric asked, "Will you join me for dinner?"

"Thank you, I'd love to, but I don't want to be a nuisance. I realize you have things to attend to and you probably should be circulating among your other guests."

"That can come later," he said, smiling. "Though we might wait a little longer, if you don't object. Then your friend can also join us."

"My friend?" she asked, startled.

"It was he who phoned just now," Eric nodded. "He was in the village, and he wished to be sure we had accommodations for him. We do, of course. He, too, has been a visitor here before."

Penny, wanting to scream, "Who are you talking about?" forced herself to remain silent as she fought for self-control. She was reaching the point where she might be able to voice the question casually when she was spared the need of having to ask it at all. The front door of the lodge opened and Ramon came in.

Her gasp was audible, and Eric heard it. He said swiftly, "Didn't you expect Mr. Martinez to meet you here?"

"No!" Penny exclaimed, trying frantically to get a grip

on her faltering composure. She felt as if she'd rubbed an invisible Aladdin's lamp only to have a genie appear in the form of the handsome, disconcerting man who was approaching them.

Eric said quickly, "I am sorry, Penny. You do not seem pleased. If I had known . . ."

"It's all right," she assured him quickly, knowing that there was no point in letting Eric become involved in anything between Ramon and herself. If Ramon had taken the trouble to make this trip to Franconia, nothing was going to dissuade him easily. She was certain of that!

"If you do not want him here, the situation could be uncomfortable," Eric suggested softly. "Perhaps I . . ."

If she did not want him here! It would be impossible to say that she did not want Ramon in Franconia no matter how much she might question his motives. There could never be a time in her life when she would not want Ramon.

"Eric, really," she said, "it's all right." She spoke quickly, urgently, because Ramon was nearing their table, walking with that Latin grace of his. In another second he'd be within earshot.

He was wearing corduroy slacks in a soft shade of rust and a matching turtleneck. His lightweight tweed jacket picked up rust and brown tones, and his leather moccasins were the perfect final touch to an outfit that was so unlike the meticulously tailored formal clothes he wore in the embassy. She could only stare at him. But he looked almost more handsome in this casual garb, Penny thought ruefully, then soon realized that the casualness was purely external. When his eyes met hers they blazed, the flames pure blue.

Eric gave Penny one last, uncertain glance, and then he rose, his training coming to the fore as he said courteously, "It is a pleasure to have you with us again, Mr. Martinez."

"Thank you," Ramon rejoined, equally polite. His nod

in her direction was stiffly formal as he said only, "Penny."

"May I offer you a drink?" Eric suggested.

"Yes. Scotch on the rocks, if you please," Ramon said, and without waiting to be asked pulled another chair up to the table and sat down.

Eric was glancing around for Ludwig, but the gnomelike little man was already hurrying to their table and, with apologies, whispered something in Eric's ear.

Eric frowned. "A small emergency has arisen in the kitchen," he explained. "If you will excuse me? I will send your Scotch on immediately, Mr. Martinez. Another Cinzano for you, Penny?"

"I don't think so, thank you," she told him.

To Penny, the coincidence seemed almost too pat. It was as if this incident had been prearranged, so that she would be left alone with Ramon. Still, she could hardly accuse Ramon of having created an emergency in Eric's kitchen.

After Eric left, they were silent. Penny didn't dare look at Ramon. Her feeling for him—she backed off from calling it love—warred with a deep resentment. Finally she couldn't stand the silence any longer and she blurted accusingly, "You followed me!"

"Yes," he agreed mildly. "Yes, I did."

She'd not expected such an easy acquiescence, and she looked across at him quickly to surprise a small smile lurking in the corner of his mouth.

"I had the thought, just a small thought but still it was there, that you might even be glad to see me, *querida*," he told her. "Not a thought, really. I should perhaps say a hope."

"Come, now," she protested immediately. "It was only this morning that we said good-bye to each other."

Her words trailed off. For he'd not really said good-bye to her, she remembered now. He'd said, *"hasta luego."*

Now he really did smile, and the effect was devastating. There was a light in his blue eyes that she didn't think she'd ever seen in them before. He looked younger, vital, so completely and tremendously alive. Penny wanted to bridge the small distance between them, to feel his arms around her. She wanted love from him and tenderness. . . and the kind of transcending togetherness they'd achieved that early morning in the Rose Room.

He said teasingly, "You are remembering my farewell to you. Your Spanish is improving."

She had to force back a fresh surge of resentment. Then, determined not to let him totally get the upper hand, she said, ignoring his comment, "You had no right to follow me, Ramon. My coming here is my own private business!"

His smile faded. "I must disagree with that," he told her.

"You've no right to disagree with it!"

"On the contrary, I believe I do," he said evenly. "You came here to see what you could find out about Marita's death, did you not?"

"Suppose I did?"

"Then it definitely is not your private business. I tried to tell you in Washington that you are getting into areas in which you have no business. But you would not listen to me . . ."

He broke off abruptly and, looking up, Penny saw that Ludwig was coming toward them, carrying a small tray. Ramon's Scotch was on it, and she noted that Eric had sent her along another glass of Cinzano anyway.

When Ludwig had left them, Ramon lifted his glance and toasted, *"Salud!"*

Penny ignored the toast, determined to get back to the matter at hand. But then she saw the strangely brooding expression in his eyes as he sipped his drink, and she stopped short.

From everything she'd heard at the embassy, Ramon's engagement to Marita had seemed what, she supposed, might be called an alliance of convenience. Marriages were still arranged between members of prominent families in other countries. Outward indications were that this would have been one of those arranged marriages.

But Marita had first been engaged to Ramon's brother. Penny remembered that, too. It was Roberto who'd been her sweetheart, virtually since childhood, Roberto whom she'd loved. After Roberto's death she'd gone on a wild, whirlwind tour of most of the globe, evidently trying to come to grips with her grief, to get over him.

Could Marita have transferred her love for Roberto to Ramon? It didn't seem likely, Penny conceded. Ramon himself was the one who'd brought up the subject of Marita having been involved with another man. He'd done so with a singular lack of emotion. Ramon, as she well knew, was a man who possessed a great deal of emotion. And he was proud. At the least, wouldn't his pride have been wounded by his fiancée's having become involved with someone else? And . . . if he had loved Marita . . .

Penny cast a sideways glance at him to see that he was staring toward the fireplace, where the logs still blazed, his expression abstracted. If he had loved Marita? Why wouldn't he have loved Marita? She'd been young, beautiful, very desirable.

If he had loved Marita, Penny went on to herself, then what must his feelings be now, here in this place where Marita had died less than three months ago? Was Ramon thinking about that now? Was he thinking about the fact that if it had not been for the tragic accident on the mountain beyond the windows he would, any day now, have been walking down the aisle with Marita in Washington's St. Matthew's Cathedral? Later, he would have stood by her side at a gala wedding reception in the embassy. Conchita, who was to have been one of the bridesmaids, had spoken about this when they were alone one afternoon. All of the plans had been made, in fact the invitations had been printed and the embassy staff had been about to begin addressing them when Marita had died.

Penny thought about that wedding that would never be, though it gave her a dull, aching pain to do so, and for the first time she wondered who the other bridesmaids might have been. Conchita had said there were to be eight of them. And who would Marita have chosen for her maid of honor?

It seemed strange that Marita had not included her in her wedding plans, Penny thought now. Could this possibly have been because she was not a Latin American? Knowing Marita as she had, she felt this unlikely. No . . . it seemed rather as if Marita had not really been taking her wedding plans seriously. It was almost as if she'd decided not to have the wedding.

The thought was like a thunderbolt; it struck with such force that Penny was totally taken aback by it.

Suppose Marita really hadn't intended to get married? Suppose she had never intended to show up for her wedding in May? Suppose she had planned another course of action entirely . . . as far back as that time in February when she had come to Franconia?

Overwhelmed by the mere idea of this, Penny nearly forgot about Ramon. But then she became aware that he was watching her closely, and he said softly, "Would it be too much to ask you to share some of your thoughts with me?"

"Yes," she hedged. How could she possibly tell him that she was thinking that Marita had been intending to jilt him!

He sighed. "Sometimes you are very much the Yankee maiden, Penny," he said. "Or you try to be. You try to be an austere New Englander, but that is not really you. The real you is warm and wonderful, giving, completely enchanting, *querida*. So why do you deny yourself? What are these secrets that you think you cannot share?"

Ramon was looking at her lovingly as he spoke, and it was difficult not to be completely swayed by him.

She said, "Regardless of what you may think, I am not denying myself. And I don't really have any secrets, Ramon. I came here because I wanted to. Yes, there are a few things I want to find out. But that's my affair, and I intend to handle it myself."

"*Dios*, but you can be trying!" he groaned, and then, his tone sharpening, he added, "I refuse to allow you to—what is that phrase you use?—to stick your neck out. And it seems to me that you are in danger of doing exactly that."

"It is my neck, Ramon," she reminded him.

"And it belongs to a very stubborn person," he said tightly. "I know that your motivations are good, Penny. I know that you are moved mainly by kindness, by a spirit of charity. You think that if you can find out more about what happened here in February you will be able to put together a puzzle, and you will ease Tía Mary's grief by doing that. But you are wrong. Entirely wrong. You do not know what you are getting into. Believe me, this is not an affair that concerns you!"

Stung, Penny was about to answer him hotly when he suddenly put his hand on top of hers, and she stopped short. At his touch, emotions that had nothing at all to do with anger flared, possessing her, and she closed her eyes. How could a man do this to a woman simply by laying his hand on hers?

"Careful!" Ramon warned tensely, his voice low. "Jenson is coming back here."

Emotionally, Penny sagged. She'd thought of his touch as a caress; now she saw that it had been nothing more than a warning. She opened her eyes to see Eric coming toward their table, smiling affably.

"Fortunately, it was a small emergency," he reported as he resumed his seat. "Our chef tends to be excitable. But then, most good chefs are."

Eric evidently was oblivious to the tension that, it seemed to Penny, must be sending sparks flying through the air.

"Would you care for another Scotch, Mr. Martinez?" he asked Ramon.

"No, thank you," Ramon said.

"Penny has agreed to have dinner with me. You will join us, I hope?"

Eric was close to being the perfect innkeeper, Penny conceded, and there was no denying the smoothness of his invitation. Yet anyone with even a dash of intuition would have known that he wanted to take her to dinner alone.

Ramon, who was very intuitive, evidently chose to ignore this. "I would be delighted," he murmured.

Eric pulled back Penny's chair for her. She stood and flexed her ankle slightly before trying to walk upon it. It stiffened when she sat for very long, and as a result her limp was a bit more pronounced when she started out with the two men toward the dining room.

Again she knew that Ramon was watching her closely, even though she refrained from glancing in his direction, and after a minute he said abruptly, "You are still having trouble with your ankle!"

"I expect to for a while longer," Penny told him, making light of this. "It takes time to heal a sprain. This wasn't much of a sprain, according to Dr. Farrington, but even so . . ."

"It was enough of a sprain," he said curtly. She saw that his face had darkened, and she knew why. He was remembering, just as she was, the night when she'd received the injury. When she'd regained consciousness, the first thing she'd been aware of was Ramon bending over her, speaking to her in soft, urgent Spanish. But she'd already been taken to the Ambassador's sitting room by then. Who'd found her, in the first place? She'd never thought about it until now.

She yearned to pose the question to Ramon, but this was certainly not the time for it. The more she thought about it, the more she concluded that the less Eric knew about her accident, the better. She was reasonably convinced that Eric had honestly told her all he knew about Marita. If he'd had any doubts originally about her death, the statement of the couple from New Jersey who'd gone up with her in the gondola car evidently had put them to rest. Eric had accepted the fact that three people had gone up in the gondola, two had come down, and one had stayed on the mountain. Eric obviously saw things in clear black and white. No gray tones. Penny almost envied him.

Ramon took her arm and, despite herself, she leaned on it. He said tautly, "You should be using your cane."

"I left the cane at the embassy," she snapped. "It wasn't mine; Phyliss borrowed it from somebody. Anyway, I don't need it."

"Stubborn!" he muttered under his breath, then once again added something in Spanish.

"I wish you wouldn't do that," she told him irritably.

"Do what, *querida?*"

"Speak Spanish!"

"But it is my language," he protested innocently.

"And you know I don't understand what you're saying!" she accused.

He laughed and pressed her arm, loving the feel of her softness beneath his fingers. He couldn't tell her he didn't want her to understand what he was saying. She'd cast a spell over him, he thought, part humorously, part morosely, as he guided her into the dining room, Eric leading the way for both of them. Though at moments she exasperated him completely. For one thing, she seemed to have no idea at all of the effect she had on men. Jenson, for example . . . he, too, was plainly mesmerized by her. And Mario had blatantly bemoaned her departure. Mario, lucky dog, had been able to moan aloud. He, Ramon, had been forced to keep his yearning for her a secret, clutched fast in the recesses of his own heart.

But then he'd known he'd be seeing her before long. Right after lunch he'd taken his car to the airport, caught a flight to Boston, and then rented a car at Logan and driven up here. There was something to be said for having diplomatic credentials when you wanted to do something in a hurry, he thought ironically.

But Penny, he thought with amusement, seldom made things easy for him. *Dios,* what a mind of her own this beautiful Yankee had! He was fair enough to admire her mind, while at the same time he wished fervently that for her own sake she would sometimes be more pliable.

How could he convince her that the danger to her was not a figment of his imagination but, rather, very real? Much too real, he thought bitterly.

The table to which Eric led them was situated in a corner of the room from which they could clearly see all the other diners. Not a bad place to be, Ramon admitted to himself as he pulled out Penny's chair for her. It might be wise to assume that he and Penny would be using this table for the duration of their stay. From here he could immediately see anyone entering the room. And, he hoped, he could spot any false moves made by anyone already in the room. Not that there is apt to be trouble tonight, Ramon told himself. No, they will wait until they find out how much she knows, and I know, and exactly what we're after!

The dinner was excellent. The first course was a tart cherry soup, which was served warm.

Penny, approving it, said, "I've never had fruit in a soup before."

"All sorts of fruit soups are popular in Scandinavia," Eric told her. "Sometimes they are served cold, sometimes hot like this. Fruit soups are popular in Germany too. This, unless I am mistaken, is a German recipe."

The soup was followed by Wiener schnitzel, with which they drank a dark beer. Dessert was an apfel strudel, and by the time she'd finished it Penny felt as if she'd made her way through two Thanksgiving dinners.

"I'll be wishing that the skiing season was on," she told her dinner companions. "If I'm going to eat like this I'll have to get some exercise, or I won't be able to fit into my clothes."

Both men laughed indulgently at this, but Ramon's eyes swept her body as they stood up to leave the table, and a telltale rush of color came to Penny's cheeks. Once again she felt that he was undressing her, just as she had during their first meeting at the embassy. Only now he was doing it with added expertise. He had undressed her, she remembered—and the memory was tantalizing. He knew her, all of her. . . .

Eric's pleasant but rather pedantic voice broke into her thoughts. "Shall we have coffee in front of the fireplace?" he suggested.

"Thank you, but I think not," Ramon said just as Penny was about to agree. "It is time for Penny to put that foot up. If you will excuse us, Mr. Jenson."

Eric excused them with professional politeness, every inch the perfect host. But Penny knew that his eyes were following them curiously as she and Ramon made their way back into the lobby and started up the stairs, and her cheeks were flaming.

"What do you suppose he's thinking?" she hissed.

Ramon chuckled. "Jenson? It does not really concern me, *querida*." He peered down at her. "You are embarrassed," he stated simply. "What is that supposed to mean? That you do care what our innkeeper is speculating about us?"

"Yes, of course I care," Penny told him hotly.

"Because of Yankee propriety, or because Eric Jenson is of interest to you?" Ramon asked, holding her arm as he steered her up the stairs.

"Both, I suppose," she retorted. "Eric is a nice person, and . . ."

"And he has an eye on you himself, is that it?" Ramon suggested.

"Don't be ridiculous," Penny snapped. "And don't try to play the part of the jealous Latin. It doesn't become you."

He laughed aloud. But then he said, "You think I could not be jealous of you, *querida?* Well, you are entirely wrong about that. Any man in his right senses could be jealous of you, Penny. I cannot blame Eric if he envies me at the moment. At that, he must have thought there was something between us. At least I would assume that is why he put me in the room right next to yours."

They had reached the top of the stairs. Penny released her arm from his grip abruptly and glared at him. "I don't want people th-thinking things about us," she stammered.

"Even if they happen to be true?" Ramon queried gently.

"Are you trying to tell me that you came up here because you . . ." The words stuck in her throat.

"Yes?" he prodded.

"Because you wanted to make love to me?" She looked up into his face, then laughed triumphantly when his expression, at first amused, almost indulgent, subtly altered.

"You see?" she said. "You give yourself away, Ramon."

"Do I?" he asked tonelessly. He glanced around as he spoke. Then he said, "Fortunately there is no one within hearing distance. We should not get into discussions like this when we are likely to be overheard. Do you have the key to your room?"

"Yes," she said shortly. "But I don't intend to let you come in with me."

His mouth tightened. "If you are saying that you don't want me to make love to you, I can assure you that I will not force my attentions on you," he told her coolly. "But I wish to talk to you in a place where we can have some privacy. In fact, I insist on talking to you, Penny, so please do not make an issue of it."

"Very well," she said, trying to match his coolness. But her heart was thudding as she opened the door to her room, and she was so acutely aware of him just behind her that her skin tingled.

It took all her self-control to limp across the room and sit down in the small armchair near the window. And Ramon, his eyes brooding, pulled out the dressing table bench, turning it so that he would be facing her.

"You should not have come here," he said, the words exploding from him. "I don't think you believed me downstairs when I told you this was a very dangerous thing for you to do. To make it worse, you refuse to tell me what you really have on your mind . . ."

"That's it, isn't it?" she pounced. "You're afraid that I may know something you don't know!"

"You could not be more wrong, Penny. What I am afraid of is that you are going to either fall into a trap or step straight into disaster. This is none of your affair, cannot I make you understand this?"

His English was not quite so fluid as it usually was, Penny noted, and his accent was more pronounced. Ramon was upset, and she eyed him narrowly.

"Before we go any further," she said, "there is something I must know."

"What is it you must know, Penny?" he asked wearily.

"That night I fell," she said slowly, wanting to be careful about the way she put this, "you were bending over me when I came to, in the Ambassador's sitting room. But . . . I've never known who found me."

He didn't answer her immediately, and she stole a glance at him. The bleakness on his face appalled her, and briefly she didn't care about hearing his answer. Her love for him set aside everything else, and she wanted to go to

him, to smooth away the lines of worry that were etching
his forehead, to run her hands through the satin of his hair.
But then he said slowly, plainly reluctant, "I found you."

"You?" Penny wished she could push his words away.
She didn't want to hear them.

"Does that surprise you so, Penny? And . . . why do
you look at me like that? Do you think I'm the one who
tampered with the elevator?"

"Ramon!"

"No. I've had the feeling all along that you think I was
the dark-haired man who beckoned you to come down to
the garden. Am I right about that?"

She flinched from the pain in his eyes. His voice was
low, but there was an agony in his eyes that tore at
everything in her, and all at once her doubts were resolved
and she knew the answer to his question, knew it without
reservation.

"No," she said, keeping her own voice low too. "No, I
know it wasn't you, Ramon."

He grimaced. "You do not sound entirely convinced,"
he told her. "I have the impression that you are telling me
what you think I want to hear . . . but that does not mean
that you believe it."

Penny shook her head. "You're wrong," she told him.
"I do believe you. I . . ."

"Because you want to believe me, Penny?" he asked
her. "Because your heart wants you to believe me? Or
because you really know that it was not I who tried to lure
you downstairs?" He sighed deeply, then went on without
waiting for her answer. "That night was hell for me," he
said simply. "I left the reception while there were still a
few people there and went to the chancery. There were a
couple of matters I had to attend to. They couldn't wait. I
had finished and was coming back into the foyer when I
heard the elevator bell ringing. The trouble bell, I guess
you might call it. I had a sudden, terrible feeling . . .
don't ask me why. I have never been a person to believe in

premonitions, but that night I could sense you were in danger. The elevator stopped at the first floor, you know. It did not go on down into the embassy basement. I had a hell of a time getting the door open, and then I saw you . . .''

"Oh, my dear," Penny said brokenly.

"I will never forget it," Ramon said solemnly. "If I become a thousand years old, I will never forget it . . .''

He met her eyes, and he said huskily, "I cannot bear the thought of anything happening to you, *querida*. That is why I am going to urge you to leave here in the morning. Go back to your town, to your job. If you do that, you will be safe."

She stared at him. "How can you suggest such a thing?" she demanded.

"Because it is necessary that you do so," he said after an instant's hesitation.

Penny had the strong feeling that he'd intended to say, "Because I love you." And, had he said that, she probably would have been unable to keep from promising him anything he asked of her.

As it was, she said, "All I really want to do is talk to the doctor who was called in when Marita was brought down from the mountain. Aside from that, there's really nothing else I can do."

"I presume you have already spoken to Jenson about Marita?"

"Yes," Penny confessed. "But the only thing he told me that I didn't know was that Marita went up in the gondola that day with two other people. Just two other people. They came back down because the weather was so bad. She stayed up there, alone. She was putting on her skis the last time they saw her."

"I see," Ramon said, his voice suspiciously calm.

"You knew that?" she asked him.

He shook his head slightly. "No," he said, still in that

calm, toneless voice. "As it happens, I didn't know it. Jenson never told me that."

Ramon stood slowly, his smile more sweet-sad than she'd ever seen it before. "You should be getting to bed, *querida*," he told her. Then he added, his voice low, "God knows that I wish I were going to share the same bed with you. But not tonight. It wouldn't be wise tonight."

Desire and remorse mingled to stab Penny with a pang of such intensity that she flinched from the pain of it. She, after all, had been the one who'd told him she wasn't even going to let him in her room tonight! But now . . .

"Ramon," she began, but he shook his head. Nevertheless, he came to her and gently enfolded her in his arms. For a long moment he held her close to him, his chin rubbing her hair, this gesture so poignant that it brought tears to her eyes. She could feel his warmth, smell the evocative scent of him, and she closed her eyes tightly, loving him unbearably much.

"It would not be right, just now," he told her, his voice husky. "You and I, we have been at odds, we are tired and upset for a variety of reasons. I do not want this kind of a beginning when I make love to you."

His lips moved from her hair to her forehead, gently trailing kisses down her cheek until they reached her mouth. Then he kissed her with a tenderness, a depth, that was more telling than anything else he could possibly have done. She clung to him, knowing that he'd confirmed their love in a very special way, and that it was a love that was going to go on forever.

Chapter 13

PENNY TOOK A LONG, HOT BATH, FRAGRANT WITH A scent of pine that reminded her of the air outside. Then she put on a deep yellow nightgown that had long sleeves and a frill of lace at the neck and climbed into a blissfully comfortable bed. Almost at once she sank into a deep and dreamless sleep, and when a loud, jangling noise intruded into this very private world she awoke with a jolt, feeling totally disoriented.

It took a moment to realize that it was the room telephone ringing. Ramon? Was it Ramon at the other end of the line? Sleepy though she was, she doubted it. Ramon wouldn't call her if he'd changed his mind about their being together tonight. He'd come to her.

She groped for the phone receiver, her voice still thick with sleep as she asked, "Yes?"

"I am sorry, Miss Baldwin." The voice was decidedly Scandinavian. "Otto Pedersen here. I am sorry to bother you. I was afraid you might already be asleep. But it is just a short time since the last guest went upstairs. I could not call you earlier.''

Otto Pedersen? It took a moment for Penny's thoughts to whirl into focus, and for her to remember that he was the ski instructor who'd been manning the registration desk today.

"What is it?" she asked him, suddenly alert.

"I do not like to disturb you, Miss Baldwin," he told her. "But I do not know when another chance will present itself. To contact you, that is." His English was very good, less accented than Eric's, actually. "If you would be inclined to come back downstairs for a few minutes," he went on, "I would very much like to talk to you."

She said, "It would take me at least a few minutes to get dressed."

"If you have a warm robe it will be sufficient," he suggested. "There is no one here; everyone has retired. Also, there is still some fire going, so you will be comfortable."

"All right," Penny agreed. "I'll be down directly."

The lights had been turned off except for a dim bulb over the registration desk and a single lamp in the corner. But flames still crackled in the fireplace, casting orange shadows out into the big room. Otto Pedersen led her toward the fireplace, motioning her to a low upholstered chair. She sank down into it and he pulled up a straight-backed chair, then leaned forward, the light from the fire touching his chiseled features and pale hair, making him look like a Viking god.

He lowered his voice so that Penny had to strain to hear it. "Eric says you are concerned about Marita Villanueva's death," he said without preamble.

"Yes, I am," Penny admitted.

"Eric says you were close friends, and I remember seeing you here last February," Otto told her. "Eric felt that perhaps I could reassure you."

"Oh?"

"Yes. I was, you see, one of the last people to see her alive. That morning—the morning of the day she died—I gave some ski lessons, but then the weather became too bad for them. Late in the morning I returned to the lodge. Soon afterward, Eric said he thought the ski patrol could use additional help, because of the bad weather. They had already closed some of the trails."

Otto paused, then went on, "I took the gondola back up the mountain. I understand I was the last to go up that day. It had, by then, started to snow. There were people at the top waiting to come down when I got there. I put on my skis and started out. My task was to verify that the trails that should be closed had been closed. And that is when I saw them."

"Them?" Penny queried.

"Yes. The visibility was still fairly good. But it was easy to recognize Marita anyway because the ski clothes she was wearing were of an unusual color. Purple, with a pink trim, I think you would call it. I could not see clearly the man who was with Marita. But he wore a blue ski suit. They moved away from me and I assumed they were going toward one of the trails still open and would ski back down the mountain directly. I went on about my own business, and then I skied back down the mountain myself. By then the going was getting difficult.

"I went into the lodge," Otto continued, "and I was taking off my cap and gloves when I looked out the window and saw the man in the blue ski suit walking across to a car. He was alone. But I did not think anything of that at the time."

"You're sure it was the same man?" Penny asked.

"Yes. His ski clothes were a very bright blue, with green bands. He had taken off his cap, and so I saw his hair. Black hair. But I still did not see his face. Then, before I had a chance to do so, one of the guests interrupted me. I did not think of the man in the blue suit again until the following morning, when Eric told me that Marita was missing. I remembered, then, that she had been with this man.''

"But you don't know who he was?'' Penny queried anxiously.

"On the contrary,'' Otto said, "although I did not see his face, I do know who he was. I had seen him on the slopes before, wearing those same ski clothes. Tonight,'' Otto added, "he returned here.''

"What?''

"Yes,'' Otto said. "Mr. Martinez.''

The shock was overpowering. Penny stared at the ski instructor, her eyes wide, aghast at what he'd told her. In little more than a whisper she demanded, "You're sure?''

"You are asking me if I am sure it was Martinez? Of course I am sure,'' Otto Pedersen told her, seeming perplexed by her question. "He was also our guest in the lodge at the time Marita Villanueva died. Eric said, I remember, that they were engaged.'' He shrugged. "To me they did not seem like an engaged couple,'' he admitted. "They did not seem to be in love with each other. I do not know why I say that . . . it was only my impression. But, no matter, he was there on the slopes with Marita that day. He must have been the last to see her.''

Penny's mind was in chaos, her emotions threatening to go out of control. "Why didn't you tell anyone about this?'' she demanded.

"I suspected that they had quarreled, and so he had come down alone,'' Otto said. "Later, it was established that Marita's death was an accident, which made me sure Martinez could not have played any part in it. I decided it was better not to say anything about what I had seen. Now . . . well, you may wonder why I am telling you about this. I admit,'' he said with an engaging smile, "that it is at Eric's request, but I sympathize with his wishing to set your mind at rest. Marita's death was an accident, a tragedy, of course. But there is no point in your looking back now. I thought perhaps if I told you this it would help you to forget it."

Forget it! Now Penny knew that she would never be able to forget what had happened up on Crescent Mountain that day in February, because Ramon had been there on the slopes with Marita!

Otto Pedersen said, "It could be said, I suppose, that Martinez should not have left Marita Villanueva when he did. But he knew she was an expert skier. If she had taken one of the other trails down, she would have made it. As it is . . . she chose to defy the posted warnings, and there is nothing any of us can do about that."

He was waiting for her answer, Penny saw, and she nodded. "You're right, of course," she said dully.

She rose and said, "Thank you, Mr. Pedersen. I appreciate your telling me this." But as she slowly climbed back up the stairs, her ankle throbbing, she wished dismally that Otto Pedersen had left her in ignorance!

It was very dim in the upstairs hall. There had been a ceiling light on when she went downstairs, Penny remembered, but evidently it had gone out.

Her door was the second from the end, and Penny had to grope her way for the last few feet. She'd left the door unlocked. Now she found the knob, turned it, and stepped into total darkness. Once over the threshold, she paused and frowned, because she was almost certain she'd left the bedside lamp on.

She groped her way toward the bed, stumbling over an end table in the process. Then, before she'd even had the chance to regain her balance, a deeper darkness descended. Suddenly, crashingly, everything was blotted out.

Once again Penny returned to consciousness to hear someone speaking Spanish to her. The words seemed to tumble over each other, and she could make out only one of them. *Querida*.

Slowly, painfully, she opened her eyes. Ramon had switched on the bedside lamp and he was on his knees beside her, holding a bath towel in one hand and a damp, cool washcloth in the other. Evidently he'd been pressing the washcloth against her forehead, because she discovered, upon feebly raising her hand to it, that it was quite wet.

She reached for the bath towel and wiped her head, protesting, "You're drowning me!"

Ramon scowled and said something in Spanish, and then stood up. "I'm going to call a doctor," he said. "You can't risk the possibility of a concussion so soon again."

Penny struggled to a sitting position, wincing as she did so. "I didn't have a concussion the last time," she said. "Anyway, I don't think this is anything like that. It's just a . . . just a lump, probably."

"Just a lump, eh?" he echoed tautly, his jawline tight.

"Yes." Cautiously, Penny tried to get to her feet, and he quickly bent over her, lifted her, and carried her over to the bed, where he deposited her gently against the pillows.

She stared up at him. "History seems to be repeating itself," she told him.

It was he who winced now, and he said, "I do not find it funny, Penny. Someone hits you over the head, and you try to make jokes about it. That is not my kind of humor."

She stared up at him. "No one hit me over the head," she contradicted.

"What do you think happened to you, *querida?*"

"I stumbled over something. A chair."

"And so you stumbled over a chair and wound up flat on the floor, with a lump as big as an egg on the back of your head? Does that make sense to you, Penny?" he asked with elaborate patience.

"It doesn't make sense to me to think that someone

would be waiting here in my room for me and hit me over
the head," she told him stubbornly. "Things like that
don't happen to people like me, Ramon!"

"Don't they?" he queried evenly. "Are you really so
naive, *querida?* Let me assure you that someone hit you
over the head. Where in hell had you gone, for that
matter, at such an hour of the night?"

"Downstairs," she evaded.

"Downstairs? In your robe and slippers. Where downstairs?"

"To the lobby."

"You are not making sense, Penny," Ramon said
sternly.

"Please, let's not get into what I was doing," Penny
pleaded. "Let's settle what happened to me first." She
frowned, trying to remember the sequence of events.
"The lightbulb was out at the end of the hall," she
recalled.

"It is still out," Ramon said tersely. "But when I went
to my room earlier it was on."

"It could have burned out."

"It did not burn out," he told her flatly. "I have a
flashlight; I have already investigated. There is no bulb in
the socket."

Penny leaned back against her pillows, her head aching
more than her ankle at this point, and reality brushed
her—a cold, frightening reality. "What do you think I
was . . . hit with?" she asked him.

He shrugged. "Something blunt. It could be one of a
hundred different objects. Whatever it was, your assailant
took it with him. There is nothing out of place; I found
nothing on the floor either here in your room or in the
corridor outside."

"How did you happen to come in here and find me?"
she asked, and saw his mouth tighten again.

"There is a suspicious note in your voice when you say

that," he said coldly. "If you are having thoughts that it is perhaps I who did this, forget them, Penny. I'll admit that it hurts me more than I can express to think you would be able to even imagine such a thing, but . . ."

His eyes darkened, and she flinched at the anguish stamped on his face. He shook his head hopelessly, and then in a swift movement came to sit on the side of her bed. She'd never seen a man look so stricken.

"Oh God," he said, "God! I don't think I can take it if anything more happens to you. You cannot know how much I wish you were out of this. All of it . . ."

"You haven't answered my question," she reminded him. "How did you know that I needed you?"

His mouth twisted. "Thank you for putting it that way," he said wryly. "I heard you fall, *querida*. Slender though you are, your body was dead weight as it fell and you made quite a thud. The walls are not that thick. I knew at once that something had happened, and I was prepared to break your door down, if necessary. But it was wide open."

"The door was open?"

"Yes."

"But I'd closed it behind me when I came in," she whispered, that cold reality coming to sweep over her once again. "I know I closed it!" Penny's mind was spinning, the need to get a grasp on things became overpoweringly urgent. "Ramon," she began again slowly, anxious not to provoke any more intense reactions in him until she'd found out some of the things she needed to know, "when you took me to the airport, were you already planning to come to Franconia yourself?"

He hesitated briefly. Then he said reluctantly, "Yes. I was."

"Did you suspect that I was coming here myself?"

He nodded. "Yes, I did, *querida*. There was something about your manner that made me wonder what you were up to. I felt certain you were not going back to your home in Wareham.''

''But you were planning to come here anyway?''

His mouth tightened. ''Yes,'' he said. ''At some point. I came sooner than I might have because of you.''

''Ramon . . .''

''Penny,'' he said impatiently, ''if you have something to say to me, say it! You do not need the velvet gloves when you speak to me!''

''Very well, then. You were here in February when Marita died, weren't you, Ramon? Or just before she died. Aunt Mary told me that . . .''

''Yes,'' he said very quietly. Too quietly. ''But if you already knew that, why are you asking me for confirmation?''

It was all she could do to phrase the words. ''Did you go up on the mountain with Marita that last day?'' The words were hoarse.

His head shot up, and his eyes were like coals. ''Good God, no!'' he exploded. ''Why would you even think such a thing?''

''Because . . .'' she said, this statement the hardest of all, ''because someone saw you.''

''Saw me, on that mountain?'' He shook his head vehemently. ''That is impossible!''

''Do you have a ski outfit that's deep blue, with green bands?''

His eyes burned her face; she cringed from the expression in them. ''Yes,'' he said. ''Yes, I do. What about it?''

''There was a man on the mountain with Marita,'' Penny said. ''He was wearing a blue ski suit with green bands. Later, someone remembered seeing you in this same suit.''

''Impossible!''

''A man with dark hair,'' she persisted.

He swore in rapid Spanish before he answered this.

Then he said, "Another man with dark hair, is that it?" His sarcasm was biting. "Like the man with dark hair who waved to you from the garden. How many men with dark hair are there, Penny?"

She said steadily, "I wouldn't imagine that there were too many here on that Friday last February who were wearing bright blue ski suits with green stripes."

He glared at her. "It is a fairly popular color combination," he pointed out. He was looking at her directly as he said this, and suddenly his gaze softened. "You look so tired," he said. "You look as if you have reached the end of your world, *querida*. This is hell for you, isn't it?"

"Yes. Yes, it is."

"Well, it is also hell for me," Ramon said bleakly. "the most important thing in *my* world is to make you believe me . . . no matter what you have been told. Otherwise there is no point to . . . anything at all."

He clasped his hands in his lap and drew a long breath. Then he said slowly, carefully, "I admit that I was here the day Marita died. But I left before anything had happened to her. That Friday morning the weather was getting worse. I had rented a car; I wanted to get back to Boston without running into a blizzard. I checked out of the lodge by ten A.M. I would think that Eric Jenson could verify this."

"If you tell me that's what you did, I don't need Eric to verify it," she said, looking him straight in the eye. "But if it wasn't you in that blue ski suit, who do you think was here that had one just like it?"

"I don't know," he admitted. "Further . . . you may be correct about one thing. This man with dark hair may, indeed, have been wearing my ski outfit, because it disappeared."

"It disappeared?"

"Yes. At the time, I did not think much about it. There were too many other things to think about once I learned that Marita was dead. But I have not seen that ski suit since that Friday in February. When I got back to Washington, my ski things were not in my suitcase.''

''And you never mentioned that to anyone?''

''To whom would I have mentioned it?'' he asked patiently. ''To the Ambassador? To your State Department? I thought very little of it, to tell you the truth. I assumed that I must have forgotten to pack the ski clothes, and ordinarily I would have called here and asked about them. As it happened, there soon were more important things to think about.''

''Do you think . . . do you think someone stole your ski suit, Ramon?''

He shrugged. ''I don't know. But it begins to appear so, doesn't it?''

He looked down at her anxiously. *''Querida,* you are so pale. I still think I should call a doctor.''

''I plan to see a doctor tomorrow,'' she said steadily. ''He can look at the bump on my head then.''

''Dr. Lukens?''

''Yes.''

''Dios, Penny, what can I do to convince you to stop now?'' Ramon demanded.

''Nothing,'' she said. ''I don't like to put it this way—but nothing, Ramon. I'd not be able to come to terms with myself unless I at least continued to the point of talking to Dr. Lukens.''

''When you have heard what he has to say, will you give up?'' Ramon persisted.

''Yes. Yes, I will,'' she told him. ''I wouldn't know where to go, beyond that.''

''Very well,'' he said. ''In the morning I will go with you to see Dr. Lukens.'' He sighed, a long, shuddering sigh that tore at her heartstrings. Then he said, staring directly ahead of him, his hands clenched together, ''I should leave you and hope that you will be able to get some rest. But first . . . there is something I must say to you, *querida*. The reason why I came to Franconia last February to see Marita was not a romantic one.''

"You don't need to explain your reason for coming here to me, Ramon," she said, trying to speak steadily and failing.

"I think I do," he contradicted her. "There are some things I can tell you, some things I must try to make you understand. You see, *querida*, there was never anything romantic between Marita and me. She was like a sister to me . . . the girl who had been in love with my brother." He went on steadily, his accent only slightly more pronounced than usual. "After my brother was killed, Marita came to depend upon me more and more. Perhaps I should not have let her lean on me so much. But I was sorry for her."

"Sorry . . . for Marita?" This was the last thing Penny had expected to hear.

"You find that difficult to believe?" he asked. And when she nodded, he added, "Well, you perhaps never saw the other side of Marita. She presented a sophisticated face to the world, but she was actually a very confused girl. Especially after my brother died. And then her own father, whom she loved deeply, was assassinated. And her politics—well, her politics were so mixed up! Marita's ideas were good at heart; that is to say, her intentions were good. But nothing can be changed in a day, especially by force."

"You think Marita believed in the use of force?"

"Yes . . . I do think so," Ramon said soberly. "I'd had reason to think so, even before Roberto's death. Then, when her own father was killed, I thought that she would surely change in her convictions. But I could not make her see the true picture. She completely blamed the wrong people for what happened to her father, and it became impossible to reason with her."

Ramon sighed deeply. "The people who killed Dr. Villanueva were terrorists of the purest sort," he said.

"They were brothers under the skin with terrorists who operate all over the world and who must be stopped, if we are ever going to begin to know the meaning of international peace.

"When Marita left Washington to come here in February, I knew it was more than just a ski vacation," he continued. "Then, at the embassy, I came across certain information that led me to believe she was playing a very dangerous game. I came here to tell her so and to take her back to Washington with me. There, at least, I could have kept an eye on her. And, yes, I would have gone through with our wedding, for her sake and the sake of our families."

Penny moistened her lips. "Did you talk to her?" she managed.

"Yes." Ramon nodded. "We had a long chat in her chalet Thursday afternoon, after I arrived here. At the end of it, I knew that Marita had gone way beyond me. She was committed to another man, both politically and emotionally. By mutual consent, we broke our engagement. I left her before dinnertime and returned to the lodge. That night I dined alone. I left the next morning without seeing her again. I was in Washington by midafternoon. I said nothing of my trip to the Villanuevas. And I thought I would give Marita the opportunity to tell her mother that the engagement was broken before I said anything about that.

"Then, the day after my return, we received word that they'd found Marita's body on the mountain. There seemed no point in adding to Tía Mary's agony by telling her of my last scene with her daughter. I had no wish to be the one to shatter her illusions."

"How terrible all this has been for you," Penny said simply. She looked at him with her heart in her eyes, wishing that she could make it up to him, that she could erase sorrow from his face forever. He smiled at her gently.

"How I need you right now, *querida*," he said huskily. "But now, even more so than earlier, it would be wrong for us. There has been too much between us tonight. Too much!"

"Ramon," she began, but he shook his head gently.

"There will be tomorrow, *querida*," he told her. "There will be many tomorrows."

Chapter 14

Tomorrow could not possibly come soon enough! Penny knew this as she lay awake in the small hours of the morning staring into nothingness, for there was no moon and even the stars had been blacked out.

Finally she could stand it no longer. Wishing she had a pocket flashlight, she left her room and carefully made her way to the one adjoining it. The corridor seemed stygian, and she was shivering as she rapped on Ramon's door. Short though it was, this hadn't been an easy pilgrimage after her recent experience.

She was about to knock a second time when the door opened. Ramon stood before her, his hair tousled, clad only in beige silk pajama bottoms. The table lamp behind him cast a golden glow around his silhouette, giving just enough light so that she could see the fine matting of dark hair on his chest and the powerful arm and shoulder muscles that gleamed as if they'd been cast in bronze.

She caught her breath, the onrush of desire she felt for him burning through her whole body.

"Querida! What is it?" Ramon demanded, obviously alarmed by her appearance.

"Please," Penny whispered, disconcerted by her own breathlessness. "Let me in!"

"But of course," he said, standing aside. It was she who pushed the door closed behind her.

She faced him, wearing only her sheer nightgown and met his eyes. "I couldn't stay away."

"I have been torturing myself trying to keep away," he admitted.

"There is no reason why you should keep away from me, my darling," she said steadily. "After what we've both been through tonight, we need each other more than ever!"

She felt his hands on her shoulders, and they were warm and strong. He said, "Do you know what you do to me, Penny? Touch me and you will know. Touch me, *querida.*"

Their eyes were still meshed in a glance that seared all the way to the soul. Penny touched first his chest, then his waist. Then her hands roamed slowly down the flatness of his stomach to his manhood. And she felt his arousal.

He shuddered as she touched him, and he said huskily, "You are making it impossible for me, Penny . . ."

She smiled, a secret smile as old as woman. "I want to make it impossible for you," she whispered.

"Dios!" He drew her so close as his lips fused with hers that she felt herself already a part of him. Then, with his mouth still on hers, he half carried her across to his bed and lay her on it. Slowly he drew his lips away, and his mouth began its own voyage of exploration while his hands roamed over the quivering contours of her body. And she, in turn, let her own hands roam, feeling the firmness of his hips, the hardness of his thighs, his skin satin smooth to her touch.

Then he cautioned, "I cannot wait forever."

There was triumph in her answering laugh. "Neither

can I," she told him, knowing that he was trying to be gentle, as gentle as possible, as he entered her. But Penny wanted him beyond all measure, so that nothing else mattered.

She had wanted him so much, and for so long. It seemed an eternity since that night in the Rose Room, and although she had thought that experience the ultimate in ecstasy she found out now that she was wrong. As their bodies merged, Penny felt herself joined in a pulsing rhythm with Ramon, their frenzy matching pace as they gave of themselves fully. And because she was so attuned to him, he was able to lead her into an even deeper dimension than they'd already known together. So, when their shattering climax came, Penny could feel tears on his cheeks and knew that they were his, even as she'd left her own tears on his beloved face, a testimony to her over-powering love for him.

They lay in each other's arms for a long time, holding, just holding. There was a sweetness to this nearness, to this touching, that brought its own kind of glory. Then Ramon let Penny sleep within the circle of his embrace, only awakening her as dawn filtered through his window to say, teasingly, "I must take you back to your own bed, *querida*, or there will be scandalous things said about you!"

She murmured sleepily, "I couldn't care less." But she let him lead her back into her own room, and suddenly she was aware of his wariness as he did so. Ramon was probing the very shadows in the hall with his eyes as they covered the short distance, and she could sense his alertness as they went into her room. Nor did he try to make a secret of it. Before he left her, insisting that she lock her door behind him, he had searched the adjoining bathroom and the closet, and she more than half expected him to look under the bed. It was disquieting, very disquieting. Even in the midst of love there was still fear, there was still terror. There was still danger.

She hated the thought of Ramon's leaving her. She held out an imploring hand, and he knew exactly what she meant by this gesture. But he said, "I cannot stay, *querida*. You might as well have stayed in my room, if that is what we were going to do. There is, however, one thing I ask of you. Do not open your door, unless you are sure it is me. Promise me that?"

"It sounds so . . . so melodramatic," she fumbled.

"It isn't, believe me! Do you promise?"

"Yes, yes. I promise," she told him.

He looked at her, his expression a mixture of tenderness and anxiety. "Is there anything you need before I go?" he asked her.

She wanted to answer in the affirmative; she wanted to tell him that she needed him. But instead she said, with a faint smile, "Yes. Say my name, will you please?"

"Penny?" he asked, surprised. "You just want me to say Penny?"

There it was again, that funny little lurch, and she laughed. "Yes," she said.

"Do I say it so differently?" he queried.

"You say it perfectly," she told him.

He bent and kissed her lightly on the forehead. "Sometimes I don't know about you," he told her. "I don't know what is in that mind of yours. Try to sleep, *querida*." And then he added, with a touch of mischievousness that was rare for Ramon, "Until later, Penny."

Penny would not have believed it possible that she could sleep. But she did. When she awakened, the sunlight was streaming through the windows and someone was knocking on her door.

Her breath caught in her throat, so it was a moment before she could call out, "Yes?"

"Ramon," he said, and there was no doubting that it was he.

She climbed out of bed to find that her ankle, though still stiff, felt considerably better. Then she opened the door to find Ramon looking down at her with an expression of such love and concern that it would have taken her breath away, if the mere sight of him had not done so already.

He was wearing a deep red sweater over a white turtleneck, and the color combination served to heighten his Latin good looks. Latin, that is, except for those surprisingly blue eyes. She stared at the physique that never failed to excite her. He seemed to her a storehouse of latent power and masculinity. She was so intent upon her appraisal of him that she was taken aback when he said teasingly, "Do I pass your inspection, señorita?"

"Oh!" she exclaimed, embarrassed. "Yes," she told him. "Yes, you do. You please me very much."

"In Spanish you would say, *'a mi me gustas tú,'*" he told her.

She repeated the words after him slowly, and he said, "Not bad! Of course, in Spanish that phrase can also have a deeper implication."

"I can imagine," she said dryly.

He laughed, then said, "I will wait while you dress, and then we can go down to breakfast together."

"You're not afraid that we'll start a whole grapevine of gossip going?" she asked provocatively.

"On the contrary. We can say merely that we met in the hall," he told her, quite seriously and without expression, and then he chuckled at the expression on her face. "You would make a terrible diplomat, *querida*," he said. "After one gets to know you, whatever you are thinking becomes so plain upon your face."

"I can't say the same for you," she retorted.

"Which is as it should be," he replied equably, "or I would be a traitor to my training. Now, put something on. Perhaps I should turn my back."

"What?" she asked, confused by this. My God . . . he knew every inch of her.

"Because if I watch you, they may not still be serving breakfast when we reach downstairs," he said, his intriguingly accented English enchanting to her.

She laughed, a rare happiness filling her, making her full, so full of love for this man who stood before her, sometimes closer to her than anyone had ever been, yet sometimes such a stranger. But right now there were no shadows, and she scooped clothes out of the dresser and out of the closet and then, still smiling, took them into the bathroom and closed the door.

She was still smiling as she slipped into narrow-legged blue jeans, which she topped first with a pale-rose ribbed turtleneck and then with an oversized blue workshirt. Barefoot, she pattered back into the bedroom, where, under Ramon's discerning gaze, she put on her low-cut, flat suede boots and then brushed her hair and touched a bit of gloss to her lips. No other makeup this morning.

Ramon said, "You should take something warm with you. It will be cool out." So Penny went back to the closet to pull out a pale-mauve mountain parka that had a heather plaid lining and hood. Then she was ready to go with him. Leaving the sanctuary of the room, she wondered just where their "going" would take them during the course of the day, and she was uneasy.

But downstairs, everything seemed very normal in the Snow Palast. Eric Jenson was at the registration desk, and he glanced up as he saw them. Penny thought she saw just a start of surprise when he realized they were indeed together, but he masked it quickly, instantly becoming the perfect European host as he insisted upon personally escorting them in to breakfast.

Penny had intended to settle for English muffins and coffee, but it took little persuasion on Ramon's part to make her decide on something heartier. To her surprise, she was hungry, and she did full justice to her bacon and eggs and toast, while Ramon demolished a stack of pancakes laden with maple syrup, plus a liberal side order of sausages. Her glamorous Latin, Penny decided, had a very down-to-earth appetite!

While Ramon went to bring his car around to the back of the lodge so that she would not have to walk down the front steps, Penny chatted with Eric about the weather and her surprise that it was so bright after last night's lack of both moon and stars.

Then Eric queried politely, "May we expect you and Mr. Martinez back for lunch today?"

There was no reason to feel her guard go up, but Penny stiffened, forcing herself to say, with no special emphasis, "I'm not sure, really. We're going to drive around and do some sightseeing, and it depends what we find of interest. Do you need to know? I mean, does lunch have to be preordered."

"At this time of the year, it is good to have an estimate," Eric told her. "But no, lunch does not have to be preordered, certainly we will be able to prepare something for you whenever you do come back. You may find it early in the season for very much sightseeing here, I should warn you. Winter is not that far behind us."

No, winter was not that far behind them, Penny thought with a slight chill. And she was glad when Eric, glancing through the window, said, "Ah, there is Mr. Martinez now," and then insisted on helping her out to the car and seeing that she was comfortably ensconced in it.

The car Ramon had rented was a blue compact, not nearly as exotic as his own Porsche, but he handled it with the same competency. As they sped down the road toward Franconia Village, Penny said, "Perhaps we can stop at a gas station and they can tell us where Dr. Lukens lives."

"I have already ascertained that," Ramon said complacently. "I thought since it was Sunday we should be sure he would be willing to see us." He smiled at her surprise. "We Latins can be efficient when we wish to, you know," he told her.

"Isn't that generalizing?" she asked him sweetly.

"Touché," he retorted smiling. "Ah, I shall have to watch what I say to you, *querida!*"

The doctor's home was nestled on a side street, a charming white frame house with a discreet black-and-gold sign in front of it. Dr. Lukens was waiting for them and led them into his private office, which was in an ell to one side of the house. It was clear that he remembered both of them and that he was curious about what had brought them back to Franconia, but Ramon was determined that Penny be examined by the doctor before they got into conversation about anything else.

If Dr. Lukens was curious about the way in which she'd gotten the bump on her head, he contained himself. He said only, "That's quite a lump you've got here, but I think it will take care of itself. A couple of aspirin, occasionally, should help. Just be sure you don't take them on an empty stomach."

"You might look at her ankle, too," Ramon suggested.

"Really," Penny protested, "that's not necessary. I had a fall while I was in Washington recently," she went on. "It's a slight sprain, that's all, and it's already very much better."

"Sprains take time to heal," the doctor said.

"Actually," Penny persisted, "the real reason why we've come to see you doesn't concern me at all." She didn't dare look at Ramon as she said this.

"I wondered," Dr. Lukens admitted. "Not that it wasn't a good idea to have your head looked at, you understand, but I suspected that wasn't what had really brought you here. Am I right to think that this has something to do with Miss Villanueva's unfortunate accident?"

Penny nodded, while Ramon said, "Doctor Lukens, Miss Baldwin was a close friend of Marita Villanueva, as you know, and Marita's death still troubles her. She thought that perhaps if she spoke to you again you might be able to clarify some of the details for her.''

The doctor was a big man, with iron-gray hair and a bluff yet assuring manner. His pale gray eyes were sharp behind their rimless glasses. ''I'd be glad to tell you anything I can,'' he said. ''But, frankly, I doubt if I can add much to what you already know, Miss Baldwin. Your friend was skiing on an icy slope that had been closed. She skidded and crashed in an area where there were protruding rocks. I see no point in going into the technical details which, of course, were a part of my report. Let's say, simply, that in falling her head struck a rock. The blow in itself might not have been enough to kill her, but it surely would have rendered her unconscious, and about that time it started to snow. If I remember correctly, it was a fairly long time before she was found. As I stated at the time, in my opinion death was due to a combination of the wound she received when she fell and exposure. It might console you to know that I feel certain she did not suffer. I doubt very much if she ever regained consciousness.''

''I see,'' Penny said slowly, aware of a mounting tension in Ramon. ''There is,'' she admitted then, speaking very slowly, ''something else that has been bothering me. What I've wondered is what might have happened if there'd been someone else skiing with Marita. If she'd had a companion, do you think her life could have been saved?''

Dr. Lukens considered this. Then he said carefully, ''That's a difficult question for me to answer, Miss Baldwin. In fact, it would be impossible for me to answer it accurately. But I think there would certainly have been a good chance of her life being saved had someone been with her. Yes, I'd think there would have been a very good chance.''

There was a thick silence between Penny and Ramon as they got in the car and drove away from the doctor's office. At first, Penny was too preoccupied with her own thoughts to think about where they were going. But then she noticed that he was driving away from Franconia Village, heading for the Notch, and she said sharply, "This isn't the way back to the Snow Palast."

"I know," he agreed. "But I personally would like to roam around for a while, if you have no objection."

"No, I have no objection."

His eyes on the road ahead, he said, "I suppose you hoped to learn more from Dr. Lukens?"

"Frankly, I did," she admitted. She sighed. "I am only beginning to appreciate Aunt Mary's frustration," she told him. "But what about you? Was I imagining it when I thought you wanted to see the doctor yourself?"

"No," Ramon said calmly. "No, I did want to see him."

"You didn't ask him anything."

"I didn't need to," he rejoined. "You did my questioning for me. I wanted to know, primarily, if there was a chance Marita would have been saved if she'd had a companion. Although he would not come out and say so directly, the doctor's answer convinced me that she would have been."

"And so you're thinking that if someone was with her and . . . and simply abandoned her, it would have been . . ." Penny paused, horrified at her conclusion.

"Would have been what, Penny?" Ramon asked her.

"Murder," she said weakly. "As you know, I'm sure, Aunt Mary thinks that Marita was murdered."

"Tía Mary has been through a great deal, and it is possible that her imagination has run away with her," he said gently. "And in any case, *querida,* it would be better for you to accept things as they are and to go on to other things . . . especially when you can do nothing at all about what has happened. It isn't wise to dwell so much upon the past," he added, to her surprise, for it seemed to her that he'd been as guilty of this as she was. Then he shook himself slightly and said, "Look there to your right. It is the famous Old Man of the Mountains."

Penny looked and saw the craggy rock profile high above the mirror-smooth lake that lay at the base of a great mountain, just now beginning to come to life under spring's tender green fingers.

"How absolutely beautiful it is here!" she exclaimed softly.

"Yes," he said. "The scenery is fantastic. I would some time like to come back here with you when we have nothing on our minds . . . except each other."

Would such a moment ever come? The wistful quality in Ramon's voice made Penny realize that he was as unsure of this as she was. And, underlying the wistfulness, she sensed his preoccupation with something else that precluded their forgetting about the rest of the world in their enjoyment of each other. As if to verify this, he said, "That night Marita called you, *querida*. Do you think you can remember exactly what she said to you?"

"Her exact words?" Penny frowned. "Not precisely, I suppose, but I certainly remember the gist of them. It was a Thursday night. My uncle and I had finished dinner. I'd brought home some English themes to correct, and I think it must have been nine or so when she called . . ."

"So," he mused, "she and I would have long since had our conversation. I would have been in the lodge by then, in my own room. I had a relatively early dinner, and I wanted to be alone. Marita, I suppose, was alone in her chalet?"

"I would think so, yes. At least I had no reason to suspect otherwise."

"Yes. So, then, what did she say to you?"

"Well, she told me she'd rented an adorable little chalet on the grounds of the Snow Palast complex. She said the skiing was fabulous and that she wanted me to come up and enjoy it with her. I reminded her that I'm an indifferent skier at best, but she brushed that aside. Marita had a way of brushing things aside when she didn't want to listen to them . . ."

"Yes, I know," Ramon said, his voice so expressionless that Penny glanced at him quickly, to see that telltale muscle twitching at his jawline once again.

"Marita could also be very persuasive," she said, determined to get through with this because he'd asked it of her, no matter how much it might bring back painful memories to him. "You know that too, of course. She told me that we'd seen so little of each other since college she was ashamed. She said she missed me. She urged me to come up and meet her at the Snow Palast." She paused. "Ramon, you already know all of this," she accused him.

"To an extent, yes," he agreed. "But go on. What did she say that convinced you to make the trip?"

"Well . . . maybe it was my imagination, but it seemed to be that, just briefly, her voice changed. She said to me, 'Penny, you must come. I am desperate.' But then a second later she was chatting again about what a good time we'd have."

"You are sure she was calling from her chalet?"

"That's what she told me."

"Then the call would have gone through the switchboard in the Snow Palast?"

"I don't know," Penny confessed, mystified. "But I would presume so."

"I'm sorry," he said. "I didn't mean to interrupt you. You said that Marita went on to chat about what a good time you both would have?"

"Yes. And I was sure that we would. We'd always had wonderful times together, and I'd missed her very much. It seemed to me we'd grown so far apart I'd had little hope of our ever really coming together again. Our lives followed such different paths. This seemed a real chance to be with her, to renew our friendship . . ."

"And so you made the decision to go?"

"I told her I couldn't come the next day," Penny remembered. "That would have been Friday, and it was the last day of school before the vacation period. But I promised I'd take the bus up on Saturday. We made our plans, and she told me she'd meet my bus."

"Penny . . . how did you really feel about making the trip?" he asked her.

"How did I feel about it? I was excited, of course, and looking forward to seeing Marita . . ."

"But you had doubts?" Ramon suggested.

"Some," she admitted. "I hate to say this to you, but I was sure that Marita's 'desperation' really did have something to do with a man. Normally I would have thought that when she murmured something about being desperate she was just being . . . Marita. But this time . . ."

"You suspected that she was involved with someone?"

"No . . . it wasn't exactly that. As I've told you, we hadn't really been in touch for a long time." She hesitated, miserable about this, and she said, "I shouldn't be telling you these things. Even though you've said that your relationship wasn't a romantic one, you were engaged. And . . ."

"Our relationship was definitely not a romantic one," he told her gently. "And you will not be wounding me by speaking of Marita's affairs with men, *querida*. I've known about Marita and men for a long, long time. Even with Roberto she could never be entirely faithful."

"I didn't know about Roberto," Penny confessed, "and I don't really know whether or not Marita was ever unfaithful to him. But . . . she could be quite a flirt. I knew that. Sometimes, when we were in college, she'd get herself involved with someone and then she'd find that it was going deeper than she'd intended. At that point, she'd inevitably suggest that we double-date, or that I arrange to walk in at a propitious moment. In other words, you might say that more than once she called upon me to bail her out. And I had an idea that this was what she might be trying to do this time. I mean . . ."

Ramon smiled faintly. "Despite my sometimes limited English, I think I know what you mean."

"Your 'sometimes limited English,' " she scoffed. "Your English is terrific!"

"Quite a compliment, coming from someone who teaches the language professionally," Ramon said succinctly, and as she glanced across at him she saw the hint of a smile at the corner of his mouth. But then the smile faded, and Penny sighed. Ramon's smiles never lingered long, and she sensed that he'd been forced into maturity much too early. His youth had been cut short by the necessity of his shouldering responsibility for his family after his father's death. And then, she suspected, all that had been left in him of fun and laughter must have come close to being finished off by his brother's tragic suicide. Yet, every now and then, he'd given her more than a glimpse of what he really could be like . . . aside from those ecstatic times that they'd shared with each other. And when he'd given her this glimpse, she'd had a tremendous yearning to bring back a smile to his lips, to his eyes, and to make him realize how young he was, how much alive he was, how much of life still remained ahead for him. She wanted, above all else, to bring him the fullest measures of hope and joy . . . and love.

He said softly, "You are staring at me, *querida*. Why?"

She shut her eyes, unable to answer this question, and when she opened them again she saw that Ramon was turning off the road into a parking lot in front of a green-and-white coffee shop.

He asked again, insistently, "Why?"

"Because . . ." she began, but she couldn't continue.

Bending close to her, Ramon said, "I think you are

blushing! Penny, why can you not tell me whatever it is you have on your mind? Am I so impossible to confide in?''

''No,'' she said quickly. ''No, it isn't like that at all!''

''But I am not to get my answer from you, am I?''

''Not right now,'' she hedged. ''Not right now. Please, Ramon . . .''

''This is not an inquisition,'' he told her gently. ''There is no need for you to react so strongly. Come, shall we get some coffee?''

''Yes,'' she agreed, fully conscious that she'd disappointed if not displeased him.

The coffee shop was upholstered in soft tones of gold and green. They succumbed to the smiling waitress's suggestion that they try the homemade apple muffins, and she also brought them fragrant, freshly made coffee in steaming carafes, and a pitcher of thick cream to go with it.

Ramon absently stirred sugar into his coffee and, as she looked at his face, Penny was dismayed to see that he once again had become a courteous stranger. It was almost as if they were back in the embassy again on that first afternoon when he had politely but firmly asked her to leave!

She wanted to plead with him not to draw away from her like this, but she couldn't find the right words. Then she heard a radio playing in the coffee shop's little reception area, and the music seemed to suffuse her, making her feel as if she were once again in the embassy ballroom, dancing in Ramon's arms.

''Spanish Eyes,'' she said suddenly.

He started. *''Perdón?''* he asked, in his astonishment reverting to Spanish. ''What was that you said?''

''Spanish Eyes,'' Penny repeated. ''They were playing it the night of the reception when you danced with me.''

''And you remember that?''

''Yes, I remember it,'' she said, her voice shaking slightly because everything seemed to be telescoping for her and her emotions were on edge. "It will always make me think of you," she continued unsteadily. "The lyrics speak about blue Spanish eyes, and you have such very blue eyes . . ."

Despite herself, the tears came to mist her vision, and she tried to blink them away. But even though she couldn't quite do this, she saw, as through a streaked windowpane, the expression on Ramon's face, and he'd never looked less like a stranger!

"Penny," he urged, *"querida,"* his velvet tones making her melt. *"Ay, te quiero tanto!"*

"If that means what I think it does," Penny told him, blinking furiously, "I feel the same way about you, Ramon!"

Chapter 15

IF PENNY HAD THOUGHT THAT A MUTUAL DECLARATION of love would smooth their path, she was much mistaken. Ramon was immersed in his own thoughts on their drive back to the Snow Palast. He let her off at the back door of the lodge so that, once again, she could avoid negotiating the flight of steps. And as Penny entered the big lobby where the fire was already crackling on the hearth, she felt despondent, which was all wrong, she told herself, when the man she loved had just confessed that he also loved her.

She saw Eric making his way toward her, and though she was not in the mood to talk to him right now—not in the mood to talk to anyone, for that matter—there was no way of avoiding him.

He was smiling, and he said cheerfully, "Your other friends have just arrived. Ludwig is showing them to their rooms."

"Other friends?" Penny echoed.

"Yes," Eric said, evidently not realizing that she didn't have the vaguest idea of what he was talking about. He glanced around, then asked, "Where is Mr. Martinez?"

"Parking the car," Penny said rather shortly.

"You will both require lunch, I would imagine. So will the others. I—"

"Thanks, Eric, but I'm not hungry," Penny interrupted him, ready to query him about these mysterious "others." She added, "I can't speak for Ramon, of course . . ."

"Well, I see that Mr. Martinez is coming in now," Eric told her. Then he added, like a benevolent uncle, "So we can permit him to speak for himself."

There were moments when Penny found Eric irritating, despite his perfect innkeeper facade, and this was one of them. She frowned as she turned to face Ramon, who was walking across the lobby toward them. Then the frown turned to an expression of pure astonishment as she looked toward the stairs and saw Mario and Conchita walking down them!

So they were the "others"!

Mario and Conchita were greeting Ramon as if it was the most natural thing in the world for them to be there, and then Conchita was scampering across to Penny, hugging her and smiling broadly as she teased, "You see! We caught up with you!"

Mario, following, first winked at Penny and then bent down and kissed her straight on the mouth. And suddenly she was glad Mario was there. Very glad.

"The troops have arrived," he told her. His tone was teasing, but that cold little chill of apprehension came to haunt her again. Yes, she was glad to have Mario there, and Conchita. But there was a reason for their coming, this she was sure of, and she only wished she knew what it was.

Eric, the faintest note of impatience coloring his voice,

said, "If you will excuse me, it will not be possible to get lunch much longer. Perhaps you would like to go to the dining room now?"

Ramon said, "Could we have some sandwiches and drinks served in front of the fireplace, instead?"

"But of course," Eric said, though he didn't sound exactly enchanted with the idea. Still, his training showed through and he personally took their orders for drinks and said he would arrange for the sandwiches.

As they moved toward the fireplace Mario said, accusingly, "You are still limping! That tells me you have been doing too much."

"No," Penny protested. "I'm a lot better. Really I am."

Still, once they'd arranged chairs in front of the fireplace and she'd sat down, she sighed with relief. The ankle, blast it, still did hurt. Ludwig appeared with drinks, and when they'd gone back to the kitchen, Conchita said, "What an adorable little elf of a man. And the tall blond who received us. *Que* Viking!"

"So ladies prefer blonds, eh?" Mario teased. "That puts you out of the running entirely, Ray. I, of course, have a somewhat better chance."

"You are impossible!" Conchita told him, making a face at him. But, watching Conchita, Penny had the suspicion that Conchita didn't find Mario impossible at all. This would have been an interesting thing to conjecture about under other circumstances. As it was, there were far more pressing matters on her mind.

Knowing that she was sounding testy about it, she demanded, "Would someone explain, please, how you two came to make this safari?"

"Because of you," Mario said, and there was nothing in the least flippant about the way he said it.

Penny couldn't remember ever seeing Mario this serious before, and she didn't like it. Mario, serious, was rather frightening.

Ramon, noting the expression on her face, began, "Look, *querida* . . ."

Mario broke in wryly. *"Querida,* yet!"

Ramon's lips tightened, and he began again. "Penny," he said, "You must take us on faith. That is a difficult thing to do, I know that. But it is what we must ask of you for a little while longer."

He'd lowered his voice as he spoke. Then he said, running an agitated hand through his velvet-smooth black hair, *"Dios,* I wish there were more guests around to make noise with their own conversation. This is like trying to talk in a damned goldfish bowl."

As if in answer to his wish, the front door opened and a party of men and women came in to be greeted jovially by Eric. They heard Eric say, "Yes, you are indeed in luck. In response to the many requests we have had, we decided to start again today."

Mario frowned. "Start what, I wonder?" he asked as they watched Eric shepherd the people back toward the entrance, pointing toward Mount Crescent as he stood with them in the doorway.

As if he had heard Mario, Eric turned and came across to them, smiling blandly. "Are the drinks satisfactory?" he asked and, when they nodded, added, "The new season has begun, in a sense. Those people are the first to go up in the gondola. We opened it today."

"Isn't it rather early?" Mario asked curiously.

"Somewhat," Eric shrugged. "But we have had many requests, and we go by the weather rather than the calendar. The weather has been good. In fact, the view from the top today should be sensational."

"Perhaps we should go up ourselves," Conchita mused.

"I think you would enjoy it," Eric agreed smoothly. "If, that is, you take with you a warm sweater or coat. It will be cool at the top. But there are very pleasant walks to be taken."

Conchita surveyed her shiny red slingbacks. "I didn't bring shoes suited for walking, I'm afraid," she said. "Even so, I would enjoy the view."

"So would I," Penny put in.

"Impossible!" Mario said quickly. "Not with that ankle. You would have another setback!"

"I agree," Ramon said with a speed she found suspicious.

But Eric shook his head. "I disagree. Penny could be driven to the shed right at the foot of the mountain. It is from there that the gondola departs. One can drive almost to the door. One sits down for the ride up, and there are benches in the hut at the top. I think that you too would enjoy it, Penny," he said, smiling at her.

"I think so too," she agreed.

She didn't dare look at Ramon as she said this. She could feel the cold wave of his displeasure. And when she did glance toward Mario, she saw that he was very tense. Even Conchita was quiet. But Eric, seemingly oblivious to the discord he had created, said agreeably, "Well, then, when you have finished your sandwiches you can go ahead. I will send word that you are coming."

As if on cue, Ludwig appeared with trays of open-faced Danish sandwiches, and Eric left them to enjoy their repast.

The food was delicious, but they couldn't enjoy it. They ate in silence, an uncomfortable silence, and once they were through Conchita said, "Why don't those of us with good ankles walk across to the hut? I could do with some exercise. And, Penny, why don't you put off going up in the gondola until another day. I thought when I first saw you that you look tired. A nap would do both you and your ankle some good."

Even Conchita was trying to get rid of her, Penny thought with astonishment. And that wave of apprehension returned, but this time it was stronger and colder than before.

"No," she said, knowing that she was being stubborn but also knowing that she had to go with them. Right now she had to be with Ramon! "No, I really want to see the view. But I can walk over to the hut with you."

"That is ridiculous," Mario told her abruptly. "Ray, go ahead with Conchita. I'll drive Penny over."

Mario, too, had a rental car, Penny discovered. And, when she asked, he said that he and Conchita had flown to Logan because they hadn't wanted to face up to the long drive all the way from Washington to Franconia.

But it hadn't been a matter of distance; it had been a matter of time! Penny was sure of that, but she knew it was no use to ask Mario any further questions. As he pulled the car up in front of the hut at the foot of the mountain, he turned to her, his face as taut as she'd seen Ramon's face much too often, and he said bluntly, "Look, let me take you back to the lodge so you can go take a nap like Conchita suggested."

She shook her head, but now she couldn't keep silent any longer. "Mario," she questioned him, "why don't you want me to go up in the gondola? What do you think is going to happen?"

"Nothing, I hope," he said. "But you shouldn't be here; you shouldn't be involved in any of this. You shouldn't have come back to Franconia, Penny."

"You sound like Ramon," she said bleakly.

"I have reason to sound the way I do . . . as does Ramon," he told her. "Look, short of carrying you bodily into the lodge and up the stairs to your room and locking you in, there's no way I can keep you from doing what you seem bent on doing. And to use that kind of force would be to play our hands at a time when we don't want to. So you're not helping, Penny!"

She stared at Mario, wide-eyed. Then she said, "I won't leave him, Mario."

"What are you talking about?"

"I won't leave Ramon. I don't know what this is all

about, but I do know that it has something to do with
Marita. And I deserve to learn what really happened to her
just as much as the rest of you do. If the answer lies up
there at the top of the mountain, then I'm going up to the
top of the mountain. If Ramon is going up there, I'm
definitely going up there!''

"So it is like that, is it?"

"Yes," she said. "Yes, yes, yes! It's like that, and
unless you really do want to take me back to the lodge by
force you're going to have to let me do this."

"Very well," Mario said. "But since you've insisted
on coming along I think I can fairly well assure you that
our trip up to the top of the mountain will be purely to see
the view."

He was as much as saying that she was interfering. He
was telling her that whatever had been planned to happen
at the top of the mountain would be called off because of
her presence. But she couldn't possibly be sorrowful
about that. If she could keep whatever was going to
happen from happening it would be a reprieve, at least.

As she hobbled into the shed with Mario, Penny knew
that she was thinking in circles. It was impossible to focus
on anything clearly, the tension was so great. Ramon and
Conchita were waiting inside, and Ramon, after a questioning glance at Mario, said, "The gondola's starting
down. It accommodates four, so we can go up together."

Penny saw that there was a tramway running out from
the center of the shed floor. Overhead cables stretched
through the open front, and Penny could see them disap-
pearing, high ahead, until they were invisible against the
green pines that studded the mountainside.

Then she saw the bright red gondola slanting downward, swinging out onto the cables, and she asked, "Does
it run by itself?"

"No," Ramon said. "There is a man in the control
room behind us. He operates it."

Penny turned and saw a dark-haired man in gray overalls bending over something. The machinery, she supposed. Strangely, even from this limited vantage point there was something oddly familiar about him.

She started to speak, but the gondola had reached the shed opening; it swung into place and slid along the tracks. The people who'd come into the lodge lobby earlier got out of it, and one of the women said brightly, "It's absolutely gorgeous up there. The view is unbelievable!"

Ramon stepped forward and took Penny by the elbow, and he said, close to her ear, "Steady, *querida*."

Conchita got in next, and Mario came last, closing the door behind him, and at once Penny could hear the machinery whirr and could feel the gondola sliding along the track and then lifting, lifting, heading skyward.

The ride was shorter than she'd expected it would be, though it was quite steep. The terminal at the top was a smaller replica of the shed at the bottom, and from it they went directly into the ski hut, which was pine-panelled and had benches all around the walls and a cheery fire blazing on the hearth.

Otto Pedersen was manning the hut, and he came forward to greet them, looking handsome and casual in jeans and a thick blue-and-white sweater.

Glass windows enclosed the hut on three sides, and the view was spectacular. Penny fought the faint feeling of dizziness that always came over her in high places—whether she was looking out from a mountaintop or through a skyscraper window—and she said, "It really is unbelievable!"

Otto, at her shoulder, answered enthusiastically, "*Ja. Such a day, too! The visibility is seldom better."

He started to point out some of the area peaks to her, but she began to feel giddy, and she asked weakly, "Do you mind if I sit down for a minute?" She always hated to own up to her fear of heights, so she added, "My ankle is throbbing."

"But of course," Otto replied, instantly solicitous.

Relieved, Penny sat down and let Otto show the others the local landmarks. Then Mario, with that serious note in his voice that was so unlike him, asked, "Do you really expect to have many visitors at this time of year?"

"Not many, but enough, especially on weekends," Otto replied easily. "People like those four who came up here before you are from the city. They drive out for a change, usually just for the day. Then there are a few at the lodge, too, who will want to come up and explore when there is no snow. But yes, it is early still. It is in the summer, and even more so in the fall when the foliage has changed color, that people wish to come to the top."

"So right now," Mario persisted, "there are just the four of us up here on the mountain. And you, of course."

"*Ja,* that is so," Otto agreed. "To me, anyway, it is in the winter that we are at our best. We have some excellent trails. There is a map of them," he said, indicating the wall opposite the fireplace. And Penny saw that it was almost covered with a map on which the ski trails were marked in varying colors, and there was a legend to be read that she could not make out from that distance.

"There are intermediate trails, advanced trails, and then there are one or two for the real experts only," Otto continued, this plainly one of his favorite subjects. "We are always here to advise, in the season. We prefer people to be sure of what they are doing before they attempt anything beyond their skills. We wish to avoid accidents."

Was there a hidden significance to that statement? Penny wondered.

"But you don't actually prevent people from going on any trail they wish to go on, do you?" Mario asked.

"How could we do that?" Otto retorted practically. "We must trust our patrons. They are not children. We cannot by the hand take them," he continued, his English a bit more convoluted than it usually was.

"Of course not," Ramon agreed. Then he asked, "Were you here the day Señorita Villanueva met with her unfortunate accident?"

"Ja," Otto said. "But, as you know, I could not stop her."

Ramon's face could have been carved out of ivory. "As I know?" he demanded.

Otto shrugged. "You were here," he said simply. "I saw you with her. I wondered later why you did not persuade her to give up trying that particular trail that day."

"You say you saw me?"

"Yes. Your back was to me, but Miss Villanueva must have seen me. It had started to snow, and I went down another trail. I expected you to follow me."

"So, you saw only my back?" Ramon persisted.

"Also your hair," Otto said. "Dark hair. Not then, of course, you had on your ski cap. But later, when you were walking back to your car."

"My car?"

"Yes. You had parked your car near the gondola hut. There was snow on the windshield, you must remember that. You brushed it off before you drove away."

"I did not enter the lodge. I did not go to a chalet. I simply drove off. Is that what I did?" Ramon asked.

Otto said irritably, "You must know yourself what you did, Mr. Martinez."

"No," Ramon said, "I do not know, because I was not there. You didn't see me. I checked out of the lodge that morning, as you can verify with Eric Jenson. By the time the person you saw got into a car and drove off, evidently wearing my ski clothes, I was flying from Boston to Washington."

They had not noticed the whirr of the gondola, but now

they heard the cab door close and heard the motor start again, and then, as if this had all been programmed, a gnome of a figure appeared in the doorway of the ski hut.

Ludwig was still smiling, he still looked as if he'd stepped out of Hansel and Gretel, and he was still wearing his lederhosen, but he had added a nylon quilted parka of the same gray-green color—and he was carrying a gun. A gun that he was now brandishing.

"Your reasoning is good," he complimented Ramon.

Mario interrupted, his voice tight. "Is it necessary to produce a weapon at this point?" he demanded.

"Not necessary, perhaps," Ludwig conceded. "But then, who knows? It may be needed."

The remark was made almost lightly, but his eyes— green, flat, and singularly impersonal—lingered on Penny. And she was convinced that he was quite capable of pulling the trigger effortlessly, emotionlessly.

Ramon, seeming remarkably calm, said, "Mr. Villanueva, Miss Lopez, and Miss Baldwin have all been disturbed by Marita Villanueva's death. I suppose you could say we have made a sad pilgrimage to see this place where it happened, so that we could perhaps better understand how such an accident could have taken place."

Ludwig smiled. "I am not a child, Mr. Martinez," he said reprovingly.

"I am not implying that you are, Mr. Heilbruner," Ramon rejoined, and Penny stiffened when she heard this name. The owner of the lodge was named Heilbruner, she remembered. Could Ludwig be the owner of the lodge?

As if guessing her thoughts, Ramon said, "Mr. Heilbruner is the brother of the Snow Palast's owner. Mr. Hans Heilbruner is still vacationing in Florida with his wife, as is their custom each season."

Ludwig's lip curled in a sneer. "The rich Mr. Heilbruner," he said. Then he added, "So . . . now you have all come here to see where the unfortunate accident that took the life of the young *Fräulein* Villanueva happened.

Well, I will show you . . . except for *Fraülein* Baldwin. With her bad leg, she cannot take such a walk, for the trail where the young lady fell is a steep one. You, too,'' he added to Conchita, ''had better stay behind. In those shoes, you would not get far. And you will stay with the ladies, Otto. Do not go back down the mountain until we return.''

There was a terrible moment of hesitation, and Penny's pulse began to thump wildly. She had caught the glance exchanged between Mario and Ramon, and she was terrified. Ludwig was a ludicrous little man, but he had a gun. If they attempted to overpower him . . .

They didn't attempt to overpower him. Ramon said tonelessly, ''Very well. We will go with you, Mr. Heilbruner.'' And he followed Mario out the door of the ski hut, with Ludwig bringing up the rear.

Penny heard the gnomelike little man say, ''To the right. We start that way.'' At the same time she heard the door to the gondola cab close once again, and footsteps echoed across the shed. But this time the footsteps continued straight ahead in the direction of the trails instead of turning toward the ski hut. She began to tremble as she realized who this must be. The man in gray, the dark-haired man who had bent over the machinery down in the base shed. The dark-haired man whom, she was sure now, she'd seen once before, hidden by the shadows in the little garden below her bedroom window in the embassy.

She felt sick. Somehow, she told herself, she had to warn Ramon! Somehow she had to find a way of getting to him! And she damned her injured ankle.

She turned toward Conchita, starting to speak, but Conchita's dark eyes flashed her an eloquent warning. Otto was posed in the doorway of the hut, effectively blocking it, and Conchita, who had been standing at a window, looked across at him and said, ''There's a phone to the lodge here, isn't there?''

He nodded. "Yes. But it is not yet connected."

"You could take the gondola down, despite what he said, and bring back help," Conchita told him.

"I could, Fraülein," he agreed, smiling slightly. "But I do not wish to be killed."

Conchita's eyes widened slightly, but her voice was still cool as she said, "You're not Scandinavian, are you? You're German."

"Half and half," he said. "Does it matter?"

"No," Conchita told him. Then she asked, "Is Ludwig German?"

"No, he is Swiss," Otto said.

"And, again, it doesn't matter," Conchita said bitterly. "In your group it isn't nationality that matters, is it?"

His voice was still casual, but his eyes were sharp. "I do not know what you talk about," he told her.

"Oh yes, you do!" She turned to Penny. "Marita was working for them, the poor little fool!" she said. "God knows how many of these wild, crazy terrorist groups there are in the world today, like the Crimson Brigade in my own country—they killed Marita's father—and the Red Brigade in Italy. I could go on and on.

"Marita always thought she was such a revolutionary, but this was because she wanted to fight poverty and oppression. She had no idea what these people really stood for. Also, she was in love, and love does strange things. But then she found that the man she loved was the greatest traitor of all! She found that he was planning total chaos for our country, which would result in power for himself. She found that he'd been responsible for both Roberto's suicide—Roberto was driven to suicide when he wanted to defect from the group—and for her own father's murder. She found that his followers were in our capital, waiting only for his signal to start a revolution. But I can tell you, Otto Pedersen, that signal will never be given! We have made certain of that. Your leader—our traitor—is at this very moment out on the mountain. This

is a trap we have set for him. And he will not survive it!''
Conchita finished passionately.

Otto Pedersen did not exactly laugh in her face. But he
said, indifferently, "You talk too much, Fraülein."

"Does it matter?" Conchita asked. "You see, Penny,
these terrorists planned to start action first in our embassy
by taking Don Antonio hostage. He is adored in our
country; he is also the Ambassador to your country. So
you can imagine what a great coup this would have been
for them."

"Will be for us, Fraülein," Otto corrected.

"No!" Conchita retorted furiously.

Then, incredibly, Penny saw a silhouette in the shed
beyond the hut. She could make out only a shadow at first,
but then she saw that it was Mario, and she closed her eyes
disbelievingly. He had one of his own heavy walking
shoes upraised in his right hand.

Her eyes flickered as he met her gaze, and he put his
fingers to his lips in a warning. And Otto, seeing the
direction of her glance, laughed aloud.

"That is the oldest trick in the world, Miss Baldwin,"
he said disparagingly. "You surprise me. I would expect
American ingenuity to offer something better. Do you
really think you can make me suspect I am being attacked
from the rear, so that I will turn around . . ."

He had no opportunity to complete the sentence.

As Penny watched, Otto slumped almost gracefully to
the floor. Conchita started to shake visibly and Mario
crossed the shed swiftly to encircle her in his arms while
she babbled in Spanish. Then, slowly, he disengaged
himself, retrieved his shoe, and put it back on.

Penny saw Mario, bending over Otto's prostrate form,
take something dark and lethal out of the fallen man's hip
pocket. Another gun! Then he started toward the door,
and Penny demanded quickly, apprehensively, "Where
are you going?"

"Back down. Ramon insisted that I do this, or I

wouldn't have come up here. Now he's alone on the trail with Ludwig . . ."

Even as he spoke, they heard one shot ring out and another one follow it.

Fear. Penny had never before known the true meaning of fear. First it turned her to wax, she felt like a figure in a museum. Then she came to life again. She jumped to her feet abruptly, her throbbing ankle forgotten, brushing past Mario as he tried to detain her.

She flew toward the direction from which the shots had come, only hoping that her ears hadn't deceived her. But a whole network of trails opened up before her, an entire spider's web of them, and she started to sob, the terror, the frustration overwhelming.

Then she felt a hand grip her shoulder, and she looked up into Mario's tortured face. "All right," he said. "All right, Penny. But let me go first. Let me lead the way."

Behind them, Conchita stumbled, calling, "Wait for me!" But Penny couldn't wait. She could only press on as fast as her physical limitations would allow her to go, swearing at her inadequacies. And when Mario came back to her, to offer her the support of his arm, she leaned on him, nearly falling anyway as the trail grew steeper, her progress further blocked by the tears that threatened to blind her.

As they were about to round a curve in the trail, the tone of Mario's voice arrested her, bringing her up short as he commanded, "Stay here, Penny!" And for the first time since she'd known him, Mario too said something in tense, urgent Spanish. She railed at not being able to understand the language.

But it was impossible to do as he asked. She didn't know how she managed it, but Penny forced herself past him. Then she stopped short, shock and horror claiming her with hideous, icy tentacles.

First she saw a man in gray overalls sprawled on the ground. Next to him sat Ludwig, his face in his hands, his gun no longer in evidence. Beyond, at the edge of the trail near the trees, Penny saw a dark head and an arm extended, the bright red sweater sleeve getting darker and darker and darker as she watched it. She forgot about the man in the gray overalls, she forgot about Ludwig, she forgot about Mario. She ran forward, her heart shredded, her breath coming in agonized gasps, and she dropped to her knees at Ramon's side.

Chapter 16

THERE WAS NO SKI PATROL ON DUTY AT THIS TIME OF year. Instead, men came from around the countryside to help, riding up in the gondola four by four because it was quicker that way.

First they made a stretcher for Ramon and carried him away on it. Otto and Ludwig were led back to the shed, under escort. Only then did the men go back for the man in the gray overalls, because it was too late for him anyway. And his beautiful white hair, now that his black wig had been removed, was like an echo of snow left over from winter.

They had insisted that Penny go back to the lodge before the rescue work began, and she knew that if she didn't go willingly Mario would pick her up and take her away bodily. So she had limped past Ludwig, then past the body of the man in the gray overalls. And when she glimpsed his face she knew a sharp moment of shock that she'd never forget.

Carlos Smith. The handsome, polished, charming

Licenciado. He had been Marita's lover! He had been the traitor!

Later—and Penny had no idea of how much time had passed—she sat by the blazing fireplace sipping the brandy Eric had brought her. But she was still shivering, every inch of her cold through, in the grip of a kind of iciness she had never felt before.

Mario came back from one of the frequent trips he had been making to the telephone and, before Penny could pose the question, he said briefly, "He's still in surgery."

Penny breathed hard, as if she'd been running a long race, before she could find the strength to ask, "What are they doing to him?"

She looked up into Mario's face as she asked this, and she saw him flinch. Then he said huskily, "Carlos had a forty-five. It tore up Ray's upper arm and shoulder quite badly. I gather there has been considerable nerve and arterial damage. It's his right arm too, worse luck. I don't want to alarm you needlessly, Penny, but they . . . they may have to amputate."

"Oh God!" she murmured, swaying. Then she told herself sharply it would be much too easy to faint right now. Much too easy! She forced herself to get control of her swimming senses, and she said, her voice very small, "The only thing that matters is that he makes it. Oh, Mario . . ."

Mario said, "Ray is tougher than he looks, *hija*. He'll make it. He *has* to make it."

"When can you call the hospital again?"

"They said to call back in an hour."

Conchita said, "Would it help if we went over there?"

"To the hospital? No," Mario said flatly. "We'd only be in the way. Penny, do you remember the Chief of Police? He says he met you in February."

She nodded. "Yes. Yes, I remember him."

"He wants to talk to all of us later. He wants to get our statements. Meantime, he is holding both Otto and Ludwig. Eventually, he will also have to talk to Ray. But Ludwig has already given a statement. He is anxious to cooperate now to save his own skin,'' Mario said caustically.

This was also a rough question, but she had to ask it. "Did . . . did Ramon shoot Carlos Smith?''

"Yes,'' Mario said, the torment on his face giving lie to the coolness of his voice. "And you cannot possibly know what that means, *hija*. Ray hates guns. He's refused to have a gun around ever since Roberto killed himself. I think he would never have taken a gun to another man to save his own life. But he knew Carlos would be coming up to the mountaintop. And once he had taken care of Ray and me, he would go back for you.''

"Ramon killed a man because of me?''

"To save your life, *hija*,'' Mario said solemnly. "And yours as well, Conchita. Though maybe you could have made a run for it. Otto Pedersen was too much out of things to have rallied enough to hold you back.''

"But if Ramon hates guns so much, how does it happen that he had one?'' Penny asked.

"Once they started down the trail, he had little trouble in taking Ludwig by surprise and getting his gun away from him,'' Mario said. "That's when he sent me back to take care of Otto. He wanted me to stay with the two of you, but I knew he was going to need help. Only . . . I wasn't quick enough. Carlos has skied this mountain time and again with Marita. He knew the trails by heart. He was able to take shortcuts so that he came out just below where we were. He and Ray fired at each other at the same time.''

"Did Ramon know that Carlos Smith was . . . the dark-haired man?'' This question, too, came with difficulty.

"Ray had been accumulating evidence that all seemed to point to the *Licenciado*,'' Mario admitted. "He was confused only by one thing. The dark hair. When he discovered that the elevator had been tampered with, he was convinced that you were in real danger because Marita's murderer thought you knew much more than you actually did. But he was thrown off course when you told him the man who had beckoned you to come down to the garden had dark hair.''

Mario added, ''Then Pedersen said that the man he'd seen with Marita had dark hair, and that only clouded the issue further. The odd thing is that Pedersen was speaking the truth. He did see a man with dark hair on the mountain with Marita that day, and later he saw the same man get into a car and drive off. The man was wearing Ray's ski clothes, and Pedersen really believed it was Ray. Although he was one of Carlos's men, Carlos did not confide in him to that extent.''

''So Carlos Smith really was on the mountain with Marita?''

''Yes. He had been meeting her here for a long time, though even the management—Eric Jenson, in this instance—was not aware of the affair that was going on right under their noses. Carlos was very discreet. It was Marita who would rent a chalet, and then he would join her in it . . . always after dark. Meantime, he had his own accommodations in the lodge. According to Eric, when he saw Carlos and Marita together it seemed a casual thing. Eric said that in public he treated her like a daughter.

''It seems clear that when they skied together, daytimes, Carlos always wore the dark wig. When they had their final rendezvous on the mountain he also 'borrowed' Ray's ski suit, an easy enough thing to do when Ray was out of his room. I think Marita must have called that last rendezvous. It couldn't wait until night, because she'd invited you to come here, Penny. She may—in fact I think she must—have told Carlos that she was going to confide in you. It is likely that he assumed she had already, to a certain extent.'' Mario sighed. ''It seems incredibly stupid that we didn't think of a wig,'' he admitted.

"When I saw him today, bending over the machinery in the base house, there was something so . . . familiar about him. I started to say something to Ramon, but then we were all distracted," Penny confessed unhappily.

"Penny, you have nothing to blame yourself for," Mario interposed. "You could not possibly have known. It was a clever ploy. Carlos's own hair was distinctive, since it had turned white prematurely. All he had to do was change the color of it, and he had an instant disguise."

"Carlos Smith was a very handsome man," she said slowly. "He was rich, successful. Why would he have ever become involved in a terrorist scheme?"

"He was handsome, yes," Mario agreed. "But it is his ugly wife who has the money. Carlos had never been that successful. He was clever, yes, highly intelligent. First he went into engineering; he had an aptitude for mechanics. That's why it was easier for him than it would have been for most people to tamper with the elevator. And, to go back for a minute to your 'accident,' we have learned that Dolores, one of the maids in the Embassy—you may remember her—is also one of Carlos's people. It was she who put that note in front of your door for him. I think at that time he did believe Marita had said too much to you, and he wanted to get you out of the way, at least temporarily, Penny. Later, I think he was on the verge of deciding that you didn't know as much as he'd feared. But then you came to Franconia, and his suspicions were aroused all over again.

"We had planned to make this trip to Franconia ourselves," Mario went on.

"Yourselves?" Penny queried.

"Yes." He slanted a questioning gaze at her and said, "I am sure Ray would tell you this himself. Conchita and I work with him . . . quasi-officially, shall we say. We felt sure that if we came up here Carlos would follow, wondering what we were up to. But then . . . you beat us to it, *hija*, and that posed all sorts of other problems. Ray was paranoid in his fear for your safety."

Mario sighed. "To go back to Marita. Carlos had a weakness for gambling, that's where most of his money went, and he had a weakness for women. Marita was only one of them. I am sure he promised her he'd divorce his wife, just as he had a number of others before her.

"Meeting her here at the Snow Palast, in the privacy of her chalet, served a dual purpose. He made his contacts with Ludwig in that chalet. Ludwig was his principal ally, because Ludwig was power hungry himself and he'd always been under the thumb of a rich older brother. We can only think that Marita must have begun to have serious doubts about Carlos's feelings for her, and that is why she called you, Penny. You were evidently one of the few people she trusted."

"If only I could have gotten here sooner," Penny moaned.

"I doubt if the outcome would have been any different," Mario told her. "Though we may never learn the exact details, it seems to me likely that she and Carlos had a quarrel up there on the mountain and she took off in anger on a slope that had been closed. We all know what happened after that. Probably if Carlos had gotten help for her immediately she would have lived. But . . . he chose not to.

"Ray has been convinced for quite a while that this lodge had something to do with the whole scheme," Mario continued. "For a time he thought Eric Jenson was involved. Ray had been making inquiries through one of the Scandinavian embassies—through the blond young lady you worried about, Penny," Mario paused to say with a slight grin. "But he found that Eric was quite an exemplary citizen. The supposedly Danish Mr. Pedersen was not in this country on a Danish passport, though, and after that one thing led to another. When you came to the embassy, things were mounting to a crisis, and Ray

wanted to keep you out of it once he realized that you'd
been a bona fide friend of Marita's. After you left
Washington he had the strong suspicion that you'd come
here, because he knew you were still disturbed about
Marita's death. He was frantic when he called here and
verified your reservation. He couldn't get out of Washington fast enough!''

She said thoughtfully, ''Ramon seems to have been the
one most involved in . . . in trying to put all of this
together, Mario. Why? Doesn't this sort of thing go
beyond an attaché's, usual function?''

Mario glanced around, as if fearing eavesdroppers, and
even when he was satisfied that he had nothing to fear, he
lowered his voice. He said, ''Ray is not the usual attaché,
Penny. He has a law degree, among other things. And,
since his brother's death, he has been playing a dual role.
He is a counterespionage agent for our government, as
well as an official member of our Diplomatic Corps.''

''Too many secrets,'' Penny said softly.

''What?''

''Ramon has had too many secrets to keep,'' she
brooded. ''There has been too much tragedy in his life,
too many shadows. Mario . . .''

''Yes?''

''Hasn't it been an hour yet?''

''Close enough,'' Mario told her. ''Come with me,
hija, and we'll phone the hospital about Ray.''

The hospital room was painted pale yellow and had
floral-printed curtains at the windows. The sunlight
streaming under partially drawn shades seemed to be
reflected in the bowl of forsythia someone had placed on
the dresser.

Ramon was propped up against a mass of pillows, his
right arm enveloped in what appeared to Penny to be a
mountain of bandages. She had slipped in very quietly,
for the nurse had told her he was dozing and she'd

promised not to wake him. But she'd come to the end of her emotional rope, managing to convince everyone involved that she couldn't go on for another hour without seeing the man she loved.

As she came near the bed she saw his long, jet lashes flutter, and then he opened his eyes and saw her. At once he shut them tightly and then opened them again to ask, "Penny?"

"Yes, dearest," she said, and as she moved close to him felt herself beginning to tremble.

He was alarmingly pale, and this, plus the whiteness of his pillow covers, made his hair look black as ebony. But he'd never seemed more handsome to her, despite the pallor. His face was thinner, too, she thought, studying every line of it. And he looked as though he'd been through hell.

As she watched, he closed his eyes again and his lashes brushed the edges of his high cheekbones. Watching him, Penny felt frightened and completely powerless. The tears that had been threatening could no longer be held back. They started to stream down her face, and she groped in her handbag for a handkerchief, angrily daubing at them, only to become conscious of two intensely blue eyes fixed upon her face.

Ramon said, his voice low, "This morning the doctor told me that very definitely I am going to live."

Startled, she exploded, "My God! I should hope so!"

"Then why are you weeping as if this were my funeral?" he demanded. "You are acting more like a Latin girl than a young American career woman."

"Damn it, Ramon," she began, and then saw the faint edge of a smile curve his lips.

"Ah, *querida,*" he said, "that is more like you!"

The tears surfaced again, and she said brokenly, "This isn't very funny, you know."

Something surprisingly intense flared in his eyes, and he tried to move toward her, then gave up as he admitted bleakly, "I can do nothing at all with all of this cement, or whatever it is they have on me, holding me down!"

"Don't try to," she advised quickly. "And . . . forgive me for crying like this. I . . . I don't seem to be able to help it." She sniffed. "I've waited so long to see you."

To her surprise he asked, "What day is this?"

"Wednesday," she told him.

"Por Dios! Do you mean that since last Sunday . . ."

"Most of the time since last Sunday you've been pretty much out of it," she answered.

"So it is Wednesday?" His eyebrows rose. "Shouldn't you be in school?"

"I called them and told them I couldn't come back for a while," she said, averting her eyes as she spoke.

"You called the school and said you couldn't come back for a while?" he echoed. "Is that giving full consideration to your career, Penny? And what about that young man you are planning to marry?"

"If you're speaking of Jeff," she said, "I never said I was going to marry him. But just to be sure he understood that I wasn't, I called him and . . . and made it very clear."

"Can I believe what I am hearing?" he asked her, and she saw a surprising gleam in his eyes. "Now, what about Mario and Conchita? Where are they?"

"They went back to Washington this morning, when we were all sure you were going to be all right. You know, Ramon, I believe they're in love with each other, but they just don't seem to realize it! Conchita isn't too close a cousin for them to become serious, is she?"

His lips twisted, and he actually laughed. "No," he said. "I would not say that she is too close a cousin, *querida.*"

"They're both wonderful; they've been marvelous to me. But . . . that's not what I want to talk about," she told him. "I'm afraid they're not going to let me stay in here with you very long. As a matter of fact, you're supposed to be asleep. And so I have to know how . . . how you are . . ."

He smiled wryly. "It could be worse," he admitted. "Much worse. They have saved the arm. But they tell me it will be a long time before it will be of much use to me again. I understand that tomorrow I am to be transferred to Boston for special treatment."

She hesitated, hating to get into this. But then she said, "Mario said to tell you that there are . . . no charges. About . . . about Carlos Smith, I mean. The Chief of Police concluded that it was definitely a case of self-defense."

His smile faded. "A death is still a death," he told her soberly.

"But," she said. "But . . . you saved my life. And probably Mario and Conchita's lives too . . ."

He nodded. "That is why I can live with it, *querida*," he told her. "Don't look so stricken. I can live with it. But I just pray to God that I will never have to touch a gun again!"

"There . . . there's something else," she began, and this was almost the hardest subject of all to get into. "I also called my Uncle Fred, and I've told him all about you. By the time I talked to him I . . . well I knew they were going to send you to Boston for further treatment. As I understand it, after a time you'll be able to go to the hospital for therapy on an outpatient basis. When I told my Uncle Fred that, he said to tell you we have a large house in Wareham and an excellent housekeeper. So, he wants you to know that you will be more than welcome as a guest in our home for as long as you need to go to Boston for treatment. It's only about an hour's drive."

"That is very kind of your uncle," Ramon said, all at once being scrupulously formal. "But, much as I regret it, I will have to decline his offer."

"Why?" Penny blurted.

"One reason is that I will not be able to drive a car during the course of this time, Penny."

"Transportation will be arranged for you."

"No, no, that would be too great an imposition," he protested.

"We don't think so. Soon it will be summer, and we're right next to Cape Cod. For that matter, there's a beautiful private beach we have access to, and you can watch the ships coming in and going out of the Cape Cod Canal. By the time the water gets warm enough for swimming, the doctors will probably be prescribing that type of exercise for you . . ."

"Look," Ramon said, and his accent was definitely more pronounced, this giving Penny a subtle key to his feelings. "I am sure there would be no more wonderful place to convalesce in than your uncle's house, *querida*. But . . . it is out of the question."

Exasperated, Penny said, "You know, I may very well throttle you, bad arm and all. I didn't tell the school I needed a few more days off, Ramon, I told them I wouldn't be back till next fall, if then. Because I planned to spend my time acting as your chauffeur, señor," she went on, her anger fading as she saw the disbelief on his face. She added, almost mischievously, "I planned to spend my time on the beach with you watching those ships and, later, going swimming. Also, I think I'd be great at giving you therapy. They'd just have to give me a few lessons . . ."

His smile was beautiful, but incredibly sad. He said, "You make it almost irresistible, *querida*, but I still must say no. And . . . please," he said as she was about to speak, "don't make this even harder for me. The doctors are hopeful about my arm, but they do not know how much use I will have of it. In fact, it will be a long time before we definitely know about that. And there are other things that must be faced . . ."

"And you must face all of them by yourself, is that it?" she asked. "You've always been a loner, haven't you Ramon? I admit it's going to be difficult for you to change the pattern. But don't you think this is the time to begin?"

He averted his face from her, and she was shocked to see tears glisten on those long eyelashes. But she was not about to stop now. She said, with a firmness she was far from feeling, "I refuse to let you shut me out, Ramon. I love you entirely too much. Which reminds me—Conchita has been teaching me a little Spanish . . ." She began slowly, carefully, *"Te quiero, mi corazón. Te quiero con toda me vida, toda mi alma, todo mi ser . . ."*

His voice was shaky. "Do you know what you are saying, *querida?"*

"Yes," she told him. "I'm saying that I love you with all my heart, my life, my soul, and myself." She paused. "Frankly, I think it sounds better in Spanish than it does in English."

He turned toward her, his blue eyes glistening, torn between laughter and tears. He said, "Ah, Penny . . . Penny, there are so many differences between us. I think I am far more aware of them than you are. Marriage can be difficult enough between two people who have been born and brought up in the same environment . . ."

"Like Jeff and me?" she suggested.

"I suppose so," he said reluctantly. "Though I did not intend to be that specific. What I am saying is that I am afraid you are not thinking clearly, *querida*. I would have to ask you to come with me wherever my government ordered me to go . . . and that could be anywhere in the world. And when we were in my country you would find everything so different. God knows I would do everything in my power to make you happy, but I am not sure it would be possible to succeed. And I know that once you were mine I could not bear the thought of losing you . . ."

"I *am* yours," Penny said, a catch in her voice. "You know when I became yours. So do I. And I will never change, Ramon."

"Penny . . ."

"And if you ever felt you were about to lose me," she went on, "there's only one thing you'd need to do."

"What, in God's name?" he demanded.

"Just say my name," Penny told him, then laughed delightedly at the expression on his face.

Then he said, despairingly, "*Ay, querida! Mi corazón, mi vida, mi alma, mi ser.* What am I going to do with you?"

"You have one free arm," she pointed out. "And as far as I can see, your lips are completely unencumbered. So . . ."

Ramon stretched out that free arm to pull her toward him, and as she edged carefully down on the bed beside him his mouth claimed hers with consummate tenderness. She ran her fingers through his dark, thick hair, her love for him overpowering. Nor, even now, was passion absent. But, Penny told herself, passion could wait. They had all the time in the world for passion.

Again he drew her to him, and he muttered, "You know what you are doing to me, do you not? When I am powerless to do anything about it? I shall have to make you pay for this, *querida!*"

She smiled down at him. "Please do," she whispered before his kiss came to stifle out her words. "Make me pay, Ramon, again and again and again . . ."

The nurse, who had been about to come in to announce that the visitor's time was up, peeked and then carefully withdrew, closing the door behind her. Wisely, she decided that there were moments when other things were far more beneficial to a patient than mere rest.

READERS' COMMENTS ON SILHOUETTE INTIMATE MOMENTS:

"About a month ago a friend loaned me my first Silhouette. I was thoroughly surprised as well as totally addicted. Last week I read a Silhouette Intimate Moments and I was even more pleased. They are the best romance series novels I have ever read. They give much more depth to the plot, characters, and the story is fundamentally realistic. They incorporate tasteful sex scenes, which is a must, especially in the 1980's. I only hope you can publish them fast enough."

S.B.*, Lees Summit, MO

"After noticing the attractive covers on the new line of Silhouette Intimate Moments, I decided to read the inside and discovered that this new line was more in the line of books that I like to read. I do want to say I enjoyed the books because they are so realistic and a lot more truthful than so many romance books today."

J.C., Onekama, MI

"I would like to compliment you on your books. I will continue to purchase all of the Silhouette Intimate Moments. They are your best line of books that I have had the pleasure of reading."

S.M., Billings, MT

*names available on request

If you enjoyed this book...

Thrill to 4 more Silhouette Intimate Moments novels (a $9.00 value)— ABSOLUTELY FREE!

If you want more passionate sensual romance, then Silhouette Intimate Moments novels are for you!

In every 256-page book, you'll find romance that's electrifying...involving... and intense. And now, these larger-than-life romances can come into your home every month!

4 FREE books as your introduction.

Act now and we'll send you four thrilling Silhouette Intimate Moments novels. They're our gift to introduce you to our convenient home subscription service. Every month, we'll send you four new Silhouette Intimate Moments books. Look them over for 15 days. If you keep them, pay just $9.00 for all four. Or return them at no charge.

We'll mail your books to you *as soon as they are published.* Plus, with every shipment, you'll receive the Silhouette Books Newsletter absolutely free. *And Silhouette Intimate Moments is delivered free.*

Mail the coupon today and start receiving Silhouette Intimate Moments. Romance novels for women...not girls.

Silhouette Intimate Moments

MAIL THIS COUPON
and get 4 thrilling
Silhouette Desire®
novels __FREE__ (a $7.80 value)

Silhouette Desire books may not be for everyone. They *are* for readers who want a sensual, provocative romance. These are modern love stories that are charged with emotion from the first page to the thrilling happy ending—about women who discover the extremes of fiery passion. Confident women who face the challenge of today's world and overcome all obstacles to attain their dreams—*and their desires.*

We believe you'll be so delighted with Silhouette Desire romance novels that you'll want to receive them regularly through our home subscription service. Your books will be *shipped to you two months before they're available anywhere else*—so you'll never miss a new title. Each month we'll send you 6 new books to look over for 15 days, without obligation. If not delighted, simply return them and owe nothing. Or keep them and pay only $1.95 each. There's no charge for postage or handling. And there's no obligation to buy anything at any time. You'll also receive a subscription to the Silhouette Books Newsletter *absolutely free!*

So don't wait. To receive your four FREE books, fill out and mail the coupon below *today!*

Silhouette Desire®
120 Brighton Road, P.O. Box 5084, Clifton, NJ 07015-5084

Yes, please send me FREE and without obligation, 4 exciting Silhouette Desire books. Unless you hear from me after I receive them, send me 6 new Silhouette Desire books to preview each month before they're available anywhere else. I understand that you will bill me just $1.95 each for a total of $11.70—with no additional shipping, handling or other hidden charges. **There is no minimum number of books that I must buy, and I can cancel anytime I wish.** The first 4 books are mine to keep, even if I never take a single additional book.

☐ Mrs. ☐ Miss ☐ Ms. ☐ Mr.   BDM3R5

Name	*(please print)*
Address	Apt. #
City	State Zip
( )	
Area Code	Telephone Number

Signature (If under 18, parent or guardian must sign.)

This offer limited to one per customer. Terms and prices subject to change. Your enrollment is subject to acceptance by Silhouette Books.

D-OP-A